Traders

On The Galactic Tunnel Network

Also by the author:

Independent Living

Assisted Living

Date Night on Union Station

Alien Night on Union Station

High Priest on Union Station

Spy Night on Union Station

Carnival on Union Station

Wanderers on Union Station

Vacation on Union Station

Guest Night on Union Station

Word Night on Union Station

Party Night on Union Station

Review Night on Union Station

Family Night on Union Station

Book Night on Union Station

LARP Night on Union Station

Career Night on Union Station

Last Night on Union Station

Soup Night on Union Station

Meghan's Dragon

Turing Test

Human Test

Magic Test

Traders
On The Galactic Tunnel Network

Book Two of EarthCent Auxiliaries

Foner Books

ISBN 978-1-948691-30-7

Northampton, Massachusetts

One

"Why is everybody dressed so funny?" Ellen asked her escort, a local journalist who covered the crime scene in New York for Earth's new press syndicate. "Did they all get their clothes at old thrift stores?"

"The suit that guy is wearing cost more than I earn in a year, or at least it did back when they made them," Gerald replied. "Didn't I tell you that the theft was from a Grenouthian reenactment preserve? The bunnies are furious because they use an image of the building's facade in their promotional material. Somebody stole all of the statues from the top section, up above the Greek columns."

"That facade?" Ellen asked, squinting up at the front of the stock exchange building. "Are you sure the Grenouthians weren't talking about somebody stealing the clothes off of the statues? Some of those guys up there are naked, but the women look pretty overdressed."

"You're seeing a hologram the bunnies slapped up from their stock footage when they noticed the theft. They've hushed the whole thing up so far, and the police went along with it because they're supposed to provide security for this section of Wall Street, even though it's part of the Grenouthian preserve. I have a good source in the department who let me in on it because she was pissed off that nobody is going after the thieves."

"Are you sure that's a hologram? It looks awfully real to me."

"Here," Gerald said, producing from his rucksack a bulky set of goggles that might have been from an old virtual reality game. "I bought these from a hacker."

"What do they—oh!" Ellen said, staring through the goggles at the empty space that had been occupied by statues a moment earlier. "I'll buy the story, but I suspect my publisher is going to want to warn the Grenouthians before we run it to give them the opportunity to come clean first. Have you gotten anywhere with your investigation, or are these missing statues and the hologram the whole thing?"

"I've been walking around Manhattan with the goggles for a couple of days now, and the statues from the New York Stock Exchange façade aren't the only ones missing," Gerald said. "The thieves took a page from the Grenouthian playbook and started substituting holographic projectors themselves—the single-use Horten things you can buy anywhere. But I'm told the battery on those hologram cubes is only good for a few months of continual use. When they start running down, building owners all over town are going to notice a lot of missing gargoyles."

"Gargoyles?"

"They're pretty common on cornices, the decorative ledges around the roofs of old buildings. Whoever is stealing all the statues has been smart enough to avoid the ones at ground level that kids can climb on, but I've seen some pigeons get the surprise of their lives when they try landing on a hologram."

"Did you inform your police contact of the other thefts?" Ellen asked.

"Yeah, and she told me it would be better if I just published the story to force the department to take action. She doesn't have a lot of faith in her superiors. I spent the last few days documenting everything, and I have a special camera that captures images through the goggles. If you hadn't arrived today, I would have put the story out on our syndication feed, but I knew you were coming so I decided to wait."

A row of floater buses pulled up and began discharging hundreds of alien tourists, most of them Drazens and Frunge, but also a few slow-moving Verlocks. Umbrella toting guides rounded up their assigned groups as efficiently as sheepdogs and herded them into the restored stock exchange building.

"Is it a museum now?" Ellen asked. "I've visited a couple of the Grenouthian preserves where they feature pre-industrial-age reenactments, but what is there on Wall Street to attract tourists? When EarthCent's head of public relations showed me around town, she said that the whole financial industry has moved into the sky."

"Into the cloud," Gerald corrected her. "Everybody calls it that because it's easier to think about all the details of our lives being up there in fluffy white clouds than stored on computer hardware that belongs to some private company or another. Most people I know keep part of their savings on a programmable Stryx cred as a hedge for in case the cloud turns out to be nothing more than water vapor."

"Makes sense, I guess. After all the Grenouthian documentaries about Earth's financial history that I've seen, I'd be hesitant to keep any money on this planet. So is that what they've got in there?" she asked, pointing towards the stock exchange. "A lot of Earth-built computer equipment for the aliens to make fun of?"

"Since you've never been, it would be a shame not to take a look while you're here. Let's trail along with the group that just arrived. Show your press credentials and say you're working on a story if they ask."

Ellen fished her Galactic Free Press badge out of her purse and hung it around her neck. "When I visited the European preserves, the guides made me put on period clothes and hide my press badge. They said it ruins the experience for the aliens if there are humans wandering around who aren't part of the show."

"I've never been to a preserve other than Wall Street. Are the rest of them all from the Middle Ages, or do they include a range of time periods?"

"They basically match them up with the Grenouthian documentaries that had the highest ratings, and then promote the preserves as package tour vacations during rebroadcasts," Ellen explained. "The aliens are fascinated with our industrial revolution, especially child labor and the rudimentary sanitation. The guides make jokes about chamber pots and outhouses. You haven't lived until you've seen a line of tourists from advanced species waiting for their turn in a little wooden shack with a moon carved in the door."

"Seems a bit childish," Gerald said, flashing his ID to the guard inside, who passed the reporters through.

"It is, but you have to consider that most of the aliens on these tours are retirees, which makes them at least a few hundred years old. A lot of them were born before the time period the reenactors are portraying, so it's not ancient history to them the way it is to—what's that noise?"

"Open outcry, and they're just warming up. The reenactors playing stock traders give the aliens a few minutes to figure out the system and the hand signals, and then they stage a crash."

"A crash?" Ellen asked.

"You know, a collapse in stock prices, where everybody wants to sell and nobody wants to buy? You'll know when the noise level picks up."

"When what?"

"When it gets noisy," Gerald shouted, his mouth just a few inches from her ear. "Watch the aliens."

Ellen kept her eye on a group of Frunge tourists because she had traded quite a bit in their space and was familiar with their facial expressions. As the noise level rose and the reenactors frantically tried to sell stock at any price, the hair vines of the aliens began trembling with repressed laughter. They took turns moving to the front of their group, so that their friends and family members could capture video of them with the trading floor chaos in the background.

"It's too loud for me," Ellen told the journalist. "Let's go out."

"What?" Gerald asked.

"OUT," she shouted, and led the way back to the street. "That was wild in there. Is it an exaggeration, or is that how the financial markets really used to operate?"

"It's supposed to be accurate, though somebody told me that the reenactors sometimes do futures trading that actually took place at a different exchange in Chicago. And the trading floor is only one of the attractions here. Upstairs they have a replica of the conference room at the New York Federal Reserve Bank where the governors would decide how much money to create. Then there's a boiler room and all sorts of brokerage ephemera. It's pretty interesting if you have a morning to kill, but once you take the elevator to the next floor, you can't get out of the building without going through the gift shop."

"I thought the boiler room would be in the basement," Ellen said.

"I'm not talking about the heating plant, it's what they used to call a room full of high-pressure salesmen making phone calls and working various pump-and-dump stock swindles," Gerald explained.

"So rather than hauling the tourists to different buildings around the city, they brought all of the interesting stuff here to make it easier to run the gift shop trap?"

"That, and all of those old bank towers got converted to condominiums when I was just a kid. My sister has a two-bedroom in the Federal Reserve building. When she moved in, her bathroom was papered with old hundred dollar bills. It was funny for a few weeks, and then she covered it over with a floral pattern."

"So why are there so many reenactors on the street if all the action is in the stock exchange building?" Ellen asked.

"If you eavesdrop on the reenactors outside, you'll find that most of them are engaged in insider trading or price-fixing. Plus, I heard that the Grenouthians had to guarantee employment for at least a thousand union actors to make the deal with the city, and if they put them all to work inside, there wouldn't be any room for the tourists. Sometimes when they do the crash of 1929, they get stuntmen to jump from the upper story windows," Gerald added, pointing up at the front of the building.

"Who would want to watch something like that?"

"I don't believe what I'm seeing right now!" Gerald dug in his rucksack again and put the goggles back on. His whole body went rigid, and he whispered hoarsely to

Ellen. "Don't move, I think it's looking at us. I'm going to count to three, and then we'll make a run for the door."

"What are you talking about?"

"There's something up there where the statues used to be and it's worse than a gargoyle. I thought it was an addition to the hologram, but it's like some sort of monster with a body like a lion and wings that—"

"Semmi?" Ellen interrupted, looking up and clapping her hands. "Don't worry, she's with me."

The gryphon launched herself from the ledge and glided down to street level in a lazy corkscrew. Gerald clenched his teeth but stood his ground as Semmi came in for a landing.

"You have an alien pet?"

The gryphon turned her attention to the man and let out a screech.

"Don't call her a pet," Ellen said. "She's a Tyrellian gryphon, and they have a highly advanced society. The young ones travel as companions to various aliens to gain experience of the galaxy before returning home."

"You're saying she's not fully grown?"

"She's just a kid, so, yes."

Semmi clicked her beak twice, and Ellen produced a treat from her pocket and tossed it to the gryphon.

"Has she been flying around above our heads ever since I picked you up at the subway station?" Gerald asked.

"No, it's a game we play. John, my partner, has our ship, his ship really, parked at the long-term lot for the space elevator. He was supposed to wait an hour after I took the train for the city before sending her to find me."

"Did you have your cell phone homing signal turned on?"

The gryphon gave a snort of disgust and turned away to watch the action in the street.

"You really do know how to get on her bad side," Ellen said. "No, Semmi doesn't need a cell phone to find me. I know that she has phenomenal eyesight, but John jokes that she can smell my thoughts or something."

Semmi clicked her beak again and Ellen tossed another treat. The gryphon turned her head just enough to catch it, and then went back to watching the Wall Street reenactors as they grabbed each other on the sidewalks and engaged in whispered conversations.

"Will she follow instructions if you ask her to do something?" Gerald asked cautiously.

"If she feels like it. What do you have in mind?"

"I've been documenting the stolen statues by first capturing images of the replacement holograms, and then using the special camera and the goggles to get a picture showing that there's nothing there. But the roofs are all restricted access, and I only got a single picture of a Horten hologram cube with a drone."

"Too windy?" Ellen asked, looking up again.

"The wind makes it tough, but it was more a question of getting lucky once when the cube wasn't inside the projection," Gerald explained. "I couldn't send up a drone with my hologram-piercing gear because of the weight, and then a drone-killer took it out for peeping."

"A drone-killer?"

"All of the big buildings enforce strict anti-peeping laws. The city has allowed delivery drones for over a century, but they have to fly at prescribed heights, and hovering is prohibited unless they are making a delivery. Every building maintains at least one drone-killer to protect the privacy of its inhabitants."

"So you want to send Semmi up there with your goggles and camera to get a picture of a holocube?" Ellen asked.

"Not for the stock exchange, for more recent thefts," Gerald said, glancing again at the gryphon. "But I don't know where we could mount the gear unless you have a saddle."

"She can handle playing cards with her front paws, so carrying the goggles and camera won't be a problem if she's willing. Where's the closest building?"

"There's an apartment building missing a gargoyle just one block away," he said, pointing up Wall Street.

"Semmi?" Ellen asked.

The gryphon spun around, sat back on her haunches, and held out her front paws with the claws retracted.

"I just give it to her?" Gerald asked, having second thoughts about his idea.

"Does the camera attach to the goggles?"

"The hacker added a mount so it fits right inside one of the eyepieces." He fished in his shoulder bag, drew out a cylindrical device that was barely recognizable as a camera, and snapped it into the right eyepiece of the goggles from the back. "I'm setting it on continual capture."

Semmi grew impatient with Gerald's hesitation at handing over the goggles, and with a lightning-fast swipe, snatched them away. The gryphon experimented with various holds using both paws, and then inserted her head through the strap and pulled the goggles down to her neck.

"Oh, that's a good idea," Ellen said approvingly, and cinched up the band. "Can you monitor the video, Gerald?"

"On my tab," he said, pulling his standard reporter's tab from its belt pouch. "Are you going to be able to communicate with her when she's flying?"

"She's probably better at interpreting hand signals than those reenactors inside," Ellen said confidently. "I'm not as good at them as John, but I know enough to get the job done. Go ahead, Semmi. We'll catch up."

The gryphon leapt into the air and quickly gained altitude, flying lazy circles above the two journalists as they walked up the block.

"So you've been teaching her sign language?" Gerald asked. "That must have taken an incredible amount of patience."

Ellen gave him a wry smile. "She's been teaching us, and John is better at it because he has more patience than I do. He thinks it's Huktra battle language, so she probably learned it from the alien she was accompanying before she came to us."

"You must know a lot more about alien technology than I do, being from up there," he said, waving vaguely at the sky. "I've been trying to figure out how the thieves are stealing statues in the middle of a city that never sleeps. I know that industrial floaters can go as high as necessary because I see them all the time on construction jobs, but even if they're working at night, you'd think somebody would spot them with all the lights."

"The Cherts have a form of invisibility that works by projecting false images," Ellen mused. "But it's also possible to work inside of a hologram, and if the projection is strong enough, that will hide what's really going on within that space."

"I'll bet that's what they're doing," Gerald said. "I've been assuming that the holograms were to make it look like the statues hadn't been taken. If you can get your gryphon to fly up close to where the gargoyle used to be and she disappears from view, we'll know the hologram actually extends out further, maybe far enough to have hidden a floater."

"You don't think they would have dialed it back when the job was done just to save on battery life?"

"Oh, you're probably right." They came to a stop in front of an upscale apartment building that must have been two centuries old if it was a day. "See that gargoyle on the corner?" he asked, pointing up.

"That's a nasty-looking one," Ellen said. "Why did people want monsters like that on their buildings?"

"I did a little research and they were probably copied from churches where they were supposed to scare away evil spirits," Gerald said. "That one is a hologram and the original was stolen at least a week ago."

"Maybe the same crew that did the stock exchange job saw it when they were leaving and returned for it another night." She clapped above her head and then began making hand signs mixed with arm motions, which seemed to puzzle the circling gryphon. Then Ellen pointed directly at the gargoyle hologram, and Semmi immediately wheeled around to go in for a closer look.

"This is perfect," Gerald said excitedly, staring down at his tab. "It seems like she knows exactly what I'm looking for because she's going directly for the holocube. Did you tell her to get a close-up? She's a natural."

"Uh-oh," Ellen said, as a large drone closed in on the gryphon from above. "Do those drone killers have onboard cameras too?"

"I'm pretty sure they do," Gerald said, studying the tab intently. "I think she's headed right for it. Hey, it's retreating."

"Smart drone."

"I think she's catching up with it."

"Let's get out of here before somebody figures out the three of us are together and wants us to pay for a replacement," Ellen said. "Semmi can find us later."

Two

"—and then Larry paid my bail, which was only a hundred creds, and we left the planet," Georgia concluded. "So the next time you're looking for a freelancer to do a story about a Vergallian queen's ban on human reporters, please ask somebody else."

"Did you get a receipt for the bail?" Roland asked.

Georgia pulled a slip of parchment out of her purse and handed it to the editor in charge of Galactic Free Press freelance operations, who ran it through a scanner on his desk and returned it to the former food reporter.

"That's it? You'll reimburse me?"

"I thought it was your partner's hundred creds, but, yes. It will show up on your programmable cred by Friday at the latest."

Georgia broke into a wide smile. "Thanks. I wish we could have spent more time in the Empire of a Hundred Worlds. Those tech-ban planets are beautiful, and you've never seen so many horses, or whatever they call the local equivalent."

"I've been keeping track of your itinerary and it makes me wonder if your, uh, Larry is trying to set a record for most planets visited in a year."

"Larry's my partner, which is like being married for traders, and since he got stuck as the acting Minister of

Trade for the Human Empire, he's been trying to visit all of the sovereign human communities that rely on exports."

"I know he won the chair for the Department of Trade working group at the auction here last year, but I didn't realize they had started assigning ministers," Roland said. "Is the empire paying him a salary?"

"Are you kidding?" Georgia asked. "He doesn't even get expenses. And the last thing he wanted was to get stuck with the job after they agreed to go ahead with the Human Empire on the Thousand Cycle plan. But every one of the working groups voted their chair into the position of acting department head and then disbanded. It was a classic bait and switch."

"At least all of the traveling around gives you plenty of opportunities to write about the local cuisine and get a good feel for the galaxy. I remember a young food reporter sitting in that chair one year ago and lamenting about how the only place she'd ever been off Earth was Union Station."

"Touché. But what's good for me isn't necessarily good for Larry."

"Trust me on this. I've been married for longer than you've been alive, and a happy wife is always good for a husband."

"Anyway," Georgia continued, "now that the Human Empire's mentor finally showed up, either they'll work something out or I'm going to get Larry to resign. He already does enough uncompensated work organizing Rendezvous as the head of the Traders Guild council."

"Will you be working with Ellen at Rendezvous again this year?"

"I hope so. I'm really looking forward to it, though I'm not so crazy about the idea of returning to Earth. I mean,

Rendezvous is actually going to take place in orbit on Flower, but Larry wants to meet my parents."

"That seems like a reasonable request for a life partner," Roland observed.

"My mother is an alien denier, even though you can see the space elevator stalk from their kitchen window on a clear day. It's embarrassing. Can we talk about something else? I thought this was supposed to be my official one-year evaluation as a freelancer."

"Did you think I was going to critique your work as a journalist? I've bought over ninety percent of the stories you've submitted, and that's probably a record for a first-year freelancer."

"But you rejected both of the interview pieces I did, and it wasn't easy getting those," Georgia said. "That Verlock trader who specialized in antiquities talked so slowly that it took me a whole day just to get five hundred words out of him. According to the interview template on my tab, that's the minimum the Galactic Free Press accepts for the *Interviews with Aliens* section."

"The word count was fine, but I couldn't buy that piece because of the content," Roland explained. "Other than the bit about his sealing wax collection, it was all monosyllabic answers to your leading questions."

"Leading questions? I was just trying to get him to speak!"

"You were putting words in his mouth." The editor waved his hands over his display desk, did some scrolling and poking, and bringing up the text of Georgia's interview, he began to read out loud. "When you lay out your blanket at a fair and arrange the oil lamps by size and species, do you always separate the tunnel network antiquities from the rest of the galaxy?"

"What's wrong with that?" Georgia asked.

"He answered 'No,' and you went on to your next paragraph-long question," Roland said. "Making statements and asking the interviewee to agree is what political reporters do, not real journalists."

"But I did ask a question at the end."

"You're missing the point. The goal for feature interviews is to get your subjects to describe their work in their own words. As the interviewer, you have to develop a rapport with your subjects and get them talking freely about motivations. I don't want to discourage you, but the two interviews you submitted gave me the impression that you believed you knew the answers when you sat down and you were merely seeking confirmation from the subjects."

"Am I really that bad?"

"It's not you, it's your technique. Here, watch this." Roland gestured over his display desk again, and grabbing a holographic thumbnail from the resulting menu, pulled it to the active section. A frozen hologram appeared of a girl in her late teens in the act of sitting down in a café across from a scruffy-looking man in his mid-twenties with multiple face piercings.

"Wait," Georgia said before the editor could start the hologram playing. "Isn't that the girl from the Children's News Network whose interview with a Swiss banker the Grenouthians featured in a documentary about Earth's pre-Stryx monetary policy?"

"Lena. She's a natural at interviews, and now she's freelancing for us. In this one, she's talking to Cringe, the lead singer of a popular Apologist band, the latest big thing on Earth. This is the raw footage, so just watch how she works." He made a small gesture and the hologram went live.

"Is this your regular hangout?" Lena asked the singer as she settled in. "The décor is a bit weird."

"All of those black discs are vinyl records from the twentieth century," Cringe told her in a cultured voice that didn't match his appearance. "The plastic ribbons supporting the records are old seventy-millimeter film that was once projected in theatres. All of the performers who live in town do their interviews here."

"Have you ever been to Zurich?"

"The club?"

"The city. There's a cool café there with hundreds of lamps and light fixtures, like a showroom," Lena said. "I go there for tea with my friends."

"Nice," the singer said, taking a sip from his coffee.

"When you wrote the lyrics for, *I'm Sorry, but I'm only Human,* did you know right away it would launch a new subgenre of music?"

"I felt that the song had potential, but I didn't really commit to it emotionally, if you know what I mean, until I sat down with Blush, our keyboardist, and she did the arrangement. I actually wrote it after my then-girlfriend gave me a whole list of the qualities she felt I was lacking, but a big-name DJ assumed that I was talking about being human versus alien, and it sort of took off from there. The truth is, I do feel like we could all learn a lot from the aliens, especially when it comes to the basics, like not littering."

"Did you have the jacket back then?"

"This?" Cringe brushed the sleeve of his leather jacket. "I've had it since high school when I got an electric dirt bike. My dad bought me this expensive jacket because he said it would be more cost-effective than a skin graft if I dumped on pavement."

"Was he being serious?" Lena asked.

"I think so. It's hard to tell with parents sometimes."

"And then you took the album on tour and your concerts kept getting interrupted by bomb threats from the Human Pride movement. Did that have any effect on your art?"

"If anything, the threats pushed us to be even more honest," Cringe said. "People who don't understand the lyrics branded us as apologists because we try to acknowledge our shortcomings as a species, but taking a hard look in the mirror has always been a big part of what songwriting is about. I mainly listen to twentieth-century music myself, and there were lots of songs about waking up with a hangover and finding a goodbye message written on the mirror in lipstick, or being on the road and not staying faithful. Those singers weren't bragging, at least, most of the time they weren't. They were giving voice to failings we all have as human beings. It's an interesting fact—"

Roland banished the hologram mid-sentence with a wave. "See how Lena works? She's guiding the direction of the interview by establishing context for each question, but the questions themselves are invitations for the interviewee to speak, and then she stays out of the way."

"But what was all of that about cafés and jackets?" Georgia asked. "I was beginning to wonder if she'd ask him about his favorite dog breed, or what kind of tree he'd be if he was Frunge."

"An ability to make small talk is the key to establishing connections quickly," Roland said. "If you approach interviewees like you're testing their knowledge, they're likely to freeze up or just give you safe answers. I'm going to send the raw hologram to your tab and you can watch it at your convenience. The run time is almost two hours for what turned into a twenty-minute interview after editing, about three thousand words in the print version."

"If you think it will help," Georgia said, trying to keep the skepticism from her voice. "I'd like to see her do that with a Verlock though. They're tough."

"So why did you choose to interview one?"

"His ship was parked next to ours at the fairgrounds on the Drazen world we were visiting, and the antiques he laid out on his blanket for trade were really interesting. Larry stayed up half the night bartering with him."

"Why didn't you interview Larry instead?"

"Would that be ethical?"

"We'd include a disclaimer about your relationship, but it would be in italics, and nobody reads those. At the last planning meeting, Walter Dunkirk, our managing editor, asked for ideas to increase our coverage of the Human Empire before everybody forgets that it exists. An interview with the acting Minister of Trade would fill a need."

"I thought the paper's reporter on Flower was covering the Human Empire."

"Dianne, and she is, but there's not much happening." The display desk chimed and Roland grimaced. "Late again," he said. "I've got to run, but keep the food stories coming and don't give up on interviews. Being able to connect with people and getting them to open up is a big part of being an investigative journalist as well."

Georgia navigated her way through the maze of desks and cubicles that filled the main office of the Galactic Free Press and entered the first available lift tube capsule.

"Mac's Bones," she told it, and added, "Are you there, Libby?"

"I'm always here," the Stryx station librarian replied.

"I was wondering about that deal we made to put all of my stuff in storage with an option to get my apartment back. I've been with Larry for a year now, and I don't know when I'll be returning."

"What were you wondering?"

"I remember something about you charging ten percent of my previous rent per cycle for the service. It seemed like a great deal at the time, but now I'm wondering if I'm just throwing my money away."

"I can deliver all of your furnishings to Mac's Bones and you can take them with you," Libby offered.

"No, we don't have room on Larry's ship. I just wondered if there was, like, a discount possible? For longer-term storage?"

"If you're willing to forgo the option of having your furnishings restored to a new apartment on twenty-four hours notice, I can lower the fee by half."

"To fifteen creds a cycle?" Georgia asked.

"Sixteen. I've been taking thirty-two creds a cycle out of your security deposit, which is half exhausted."

"Could we, uh, make the new deal retroactive, since I never actually moved into a new apartment? I'm trying to save up enough to buy my own trading stock so I'm not just the supercargo who does some journalism on the side."

"You've certainly learned something about driving a hard bargain," the Stryx librarian replied. "Very well, but if I'm still holding your things in storage three years from now when your security deposit runs out, I'll be disappointed."

"I'm good for it," Georgia promised. "You can just take it out of the programmable cred the paper pays me on."

"If we reach that point, I'll be disappointed because it will mean that you're camping your way through life. If you don't plan on setting up a permanent household, you should sell what you don't want. I have a liquidation service."

"I'll think about it," the reporter promised as the doors slid open. "And thank you for the discount."

The man who was waiting in the corridor as she stepped out frowned. "Do the lift tubes on this station charge, like on a private orbital?" he asked.

"No," she reassured him. "I was talking to the station librarian about something else. She's very nice."

Georgia practically skipped the rest of the way to Mac's Bones, and she waved to the Horten girl at the Tunnel Trips rental kiosk as she passed. She cut through the EarthCent Intelligence training camp where she'd taken the mandatory kidnap avoidance course for Galactic Free Press reporters and made a beeline for Larry's ship. The cargo hatch that formed a ramp when lowered was still down, so she entered and called up the ladder to the bridge, "Anybody home?"

A few seconds later, Larry's face appeared at the top of the ladder. "We're still working on the controller swap, but it's almost finished. Why don't you stock up for us at the chandlery?"

"You'll trust me to choose meals for you?"

"Tell Kevin I'll take the usual set. I have no doubt you'll get one of everything new for yourself just to show off that you've got a strong stomach."

"Hey, I get paid for adventure eating," Georgia responded. "And Libby cut my storage fee by half and made it retroactive so I can stop saving for when my security deposit runs out and start buying some trade stock on my own account."

"Great, it will give us something new to argue about," Larry said, and ducked back out of sight. Georgia stuck her tongue out at the empty space, and then walked over to the chandlery, where a giant Cayl hound accompanied by a toddler waylaid her for attention.

"No scaring away the customers until after they buy," the owner of the chandlery said, scooping up the little girl and attempting to push away the hound without success. "Welcome back, Georgia. I'm going to have to start paying you commission if you keep writing favorable reviews about Zero-G squeeze tube meals. People who live on the station and wouldn't set foot on a small ship to save their lives have been coming down here and buying out my stock just to have some ready-to-eat meals in the cabinet at home."

"I'm sorry," the freelancer said reflexively. "I shouldn't have mentioned your chandlery without asking you first."

"Don't apologize, I love running out of stock. The manufacturer is right here on one of the industrial decks and I can get a resupply in under an hour. The president of the company asked to meet you, by the way, but I told her that you were the incorruptible type."

"Thank you, it would have been awkward," Georgia said. "I mean, I'm used to meeting the owners when I review restaurants, but the squeeze tube reviews are as much about my trying to figure out how to enjoy the meal in Zero-G as about the food, and I've said some pretty harsh things about some of them."

"Like the liver-and-onions." Kevin laughed and pointed at a piece of paper taped up over the counter. "I paid the print-on-demand place to print the food section from that edition for me just to get a copy of it. The funny thing is that sales of liver-and-onions went up."

"But it stunk out the whole ship! Larry claimed that the smell even got into some coffee beans we were carrying and he had to trade them at a loss."

"Some people like stinky food. So what will it be this trip?"

"Larry wants the standard trader's set, and I'll take whatever's new since the last time we stopped in, which must have been—"

"Yesterday," the little girl in Kevin's arms said.

"That's her new word," the chandler said proudly. "Margie doesn't quite have the usage down yet, but she has the direction right."

"The direction?"

"Yesterday is for everything in the past and tomorrow is for everything in the future. Joe says she has the makings of a poet."

"Oh, I get it. And I think we were last here two cycles ago. Has the manufacturer released any new squeeze tubes since then?"

"At least a dozen, that's probably what the president wanted to talk to you about," Kevin said. "I don't know what the free publicity is worth to them, but I imagine it's a lot. I bet they'd start putting your face on the squeeze tubes if the Galactic Free Press would go along with it. I'll put together the trader's set of meals and fill a box with all the new options. Do you want the usual number of coffee and water boxes?"

"Just the coffee," Georgia said.

"So you've finally started drinking the recycled water. Looks like Larry is going to make a real trader of you yet."

"Eel trader," Margie echoed.

"Actually, if you have any suggestions for trade stock, I want to give it a try this trip," Georgia said.

"What's your passion?" Kevin asked.

"Well, my job freelancing for the Galactic Free Press. And Larry, but I'm not trading him."

"No hobbies? Have you ever had a collection?"

"I was a weird kid. I just studied all the time I wasn't doing chores in the commune."

"People with kids living on open worlds and outposts always need educational supplies, but there aren't that many traders who stock a real variety," Kevin told her. "The teacher bots work great for all the book stuff, but I grew up on a family trade ship, and my favorite part of homeschooling was all of the educational toys, especially puzzles and science kits."

Georgia stared at the chandler like she was really seeing him for the first time. "That's brilliant! I walk around every market where Larry lays out the blanket, and I had the feeling that something was missing, but I couldn't put my finger on it. Do you have any idea where I could find stock?"

"You could visit some of the retail shops in the Little Apple for ideas, but I don't know if there are any wholesalers of human-appropriate educational toys on Union Station. Are you stopping at any Verlock open worlds? They tend to have lots of puzzles and science kits."

"Fyndal is our next stop. Oh, I'm so excited now I can hardly wait. Do you sell anything that I could bring there to barter for educational supplies?"

Kevin broke into a wide grin, set the little girl on the deck, and pulled a large heavy crate out from below the counter. "It's salt cod," he said, pulling a small wooden box out of the crate. "My mother-in-law likes to keep a couple of boxes in the house and at the embassy for the Verlock ambassador. I asked a trader who does the Earth route to pick up a few boxes for me, but he misunderstood and brought back three cases. I'll let you take two on consignment."

"Do I have to worry about it spoiling?"

"It's all protein and salt. If you store salt cod somewhere dry it will last for centuries. It will go like hotcakes on a Verlock world as long as you can find merchandise you want to accept in barter. It's heavy, though, so I'll put your order together and bring everything by."

"Bye," Margie echoed her father, and added an enthusiastic wave.

"Bye-bye," Georgia responded.

Three

John hauled the standard-issue EarthCent Intelligence extravehicular spacesuit out of the emergency locker and stepped into the legs one at a time. Then he worked his arms into the gauntleted sleeves and kept shrugging to get the suit up over his shoulders. Next, John reached back and pulled up the flexible helmet that hung like a hood down his back and made sure the transparent faceplate wasn't pushing on his nose. Lastly, he thumbed closed the magnetic seal around his neck and down his chest.

"Suit integrity confirmed," the ship's controller announced over his implant. "You have twenty minutes of air supply remaining in the integrated storage cells. EarthCent Intelligence guidelines recommend not exiting the ship without the standard backpack tanks containing a four hour supply."

"They're too bulky, and I'm coming right back if there isn't an atmosphere retention field over that crater," John replied, even though the ship's controller wasn't sentient, just an expert system capable of natural language processing. "Let me see the other ship again, and show me the prow this time."

The main viewscreen activated with an image of a much larger ship that was parked nearby. Because the Sharf two-man trader that John captained wasn't half the height of the Huktra vessel, the view of the prow was foreshortened, and he couldn't quite make out the nose art.

"It's probably just my imagination," he muttered to himself, and then dropped through the hatch to the cargo deck with one hand sliding along the outside of the ladder. He bent his knees slightly before impact, and then gripped the ladder hard to prevent a rebound.

"Your weight is one-sixth of Earth standard on the Moon and I advise moving with caution," the ship's controller said.

"I know how to handle myself in low-gravity environments," John replied reflexively. "Seal the bridge hatch, activate the atmosphere retention field over the cargo hatch, and lower the ramp."

"Playing stored message from your co-owner," the controller said as the ramp descended.

"You be careful out there," Ellen's voice sounded in his head, "and remember that you can't hold your breath in a vacuum for hours like some aliens I won't mention by name. And stop handing out open-ended favors or you'll find yourself diving in sewage for somebody's lost wedding ring."

John sighed, lost control of his momentum while trying to shuffle down the ramp, and then overcompensated and bounded high above the lunar surface. Then he realized he was headed right for the opening of the crater the ships were parked alongside, and hoped that the faint crackle of energy he saw was indeed an atmosphere retention field. As he passed through the barrier, he felt the air pressure altering his trajectory, and saw a number of work lights illuminating an array of alien equipment on the crater's floor.

"Stop fooling around and get down here," the Huktra called in rough English without looking up. "We've got a two-hour window to get this done before the next patrol comes by."

John grabbed the cargo netting on the side of the crater before slamming into the wall and took a moment to unseal his suit. Breaking the seal cut off the emergency air supply, conserving it for later use.

"I can't believe I let you talk me into helping you pack up a bunch of old equipment somebody dumped in a crater," John said as he scrabbled his way down the net. "What is this stuff anyway?"

"This," Myort said, stretching out his wings and gesturing to encompass all of the gear, "is the finest multi-frequency recording hardware you could buy on the open market a few hundred years ago when it was installed."

"So why was it abandoned here?"

"The mission was aborted when the Stryx opened Earth and made the planet a protectorate. The equipment was still working just fine until I disconnected the fuel pack around two hours ago."

"Wait," John said, finally reaching the floor of the crater. "Are you telling me this is part of a Huktra listening post that was spying on Earth?"

"We were here keeping an eye on the Vergallians, who once had plans to absorb Earth into their empire, but they waited too long," Myort said. "Their planners didn't expect your people to attempt species suicide via monetary policy, which triggered the Stryx intervention."

"And Huktra Intelligence is finally retrieving the hardware a century later?"

"One of my first assignments was to come here and put up active camouflage netting when your species showed signs of developing rockets capable of carrying probes as far as lunar orbit. I used my vacation time and hung around for a few weeks to read and enjoy the music."

"You listened to old rock-and-roll?" John asked.

"This was earlier, big bands and folk. There were a few half-million-watt radio stations that came through clear as a bell—you could probably pick them up on Jupiter's moons with a decent antenna. I imagine that people living on nearby farms could run their toaster without plugging it in, given all that power in the air."

"There's a legend in my family that some ancestor back then built his own crystal set and used his bedsprings for an antenna," John said, and then he looked at the quarter-ton dragon-like alien suspiciously. "Why didn't Huktra Intelligence come and collect the equipment when the Stryx opened Earth?"

"What do you know about EarthCent Intelligence's budgeting process?"

"Nothing. I've always been a field agent. But you know as well as I that EarthCent Intelligence was set up to run at a profit by selling commercial-grade information to business subscribers, so I imagine they try to keep things in balance."

Myort shook his reptilian head, gently placed an expensive-looking bit of gear in a custom travel box, and latched it closed. "Humans really do go out of their way to be different. In the real galaxy, the annual budgets of intelligence agencies are based on the prior budget, plus or minus some percentage depending on how enthusiastic the current government is about spying. Therefore, whatever allocation we receive, it's imperative to spend the full amount."

"You're telling me that your agency abandons perfectly good equipment and buys replacements for the sake of using up your budget?"

"That's a simplistic interpretation," Myort said as he began stripping dipoles off an antenna array. "For starters, it would have cost Huktra Intelligence a pretty sum to send an agent here to retrieve the equipment. Then it has to get logged back into inventory, tested, and stored until it's needed, by which time there may be a superior technology available. Besides, the fuel pack is the most expensive part of this setup, and it's over eighty percent depleted."

"Alright," John said, accepting a dipole and slotting it into a pocket of the fabric holder that the alien had rolled out for that very purpose, "but why is Huktra Intelligence reclaiming all the stuff now?"

"They're not," Myort grunted, and telescoped that array's central mast down to a cylinder a fraction of the original size.

"What do you mean—you got me out here to steal this stuff with you?"

"As I said, it was abandoned in place. But now that so many Humans are taking over lunar craters for private vacation homes, it's only a matter of time before somebody stumbles on the equipment. I wouldn't want them thinking that Huktra Intelligence was using the place as a dump."

"Why don't I believe you?"

"Because you aren't an idiot, John. I don't do business with idiots."

"So what's this business you're dragging me into?"

"The Grenouthians will go crazy for the recordings of early Human radio traffic. I have a deal all set up with one of their reenactment preserves, and they'll put all this equipment on display to show the provenance of the recordings."

"If everything is all set up, what do you need me for?"

"Delivery," Myort said, rolling up the fabric holder with the disassembled array. "It's not like I can show up at a Grenouthian preserve and sell them this stuff in person. A certain amount of discretion is expected of intelligence agents."

John pinched the bridge of his nose and squinted his eyes shut. "I know I owe you, Myort, but I'm going to have to run this past my boss. EarthCent Intelligence may not approve of my acting as a go-between for—whatever you call this."

"I doubt they'll have any problem with it, but suit yourself," Myort said. "Ten percent."

"Ten percent what?"

"I think that's a fair commission for carrying a partial cargo from the Moon to Earth when you were returning there to pick up Ellen in any case. How is Semmi doing?"

"Let's stay on subject if you don't mind. You're offering me ten percent of some unknown amount to deliver all this stuff to a Grenouthian preserve that's just five light-seconds away?"

"Less than two," Myort corrected him. "If you're going to try to talk technical, at least be precise. Fifteen percent."

"I wasn't bargaining, I was just trying to wrap my head around a senior officer in Huktra Intelligence asking a senior officer in EarthCent Intelligence to deliver a cargo of listening post equipment and data to an alien business on Earth that's no doubt a front for Grenouthian Intelligence."

"Good, then we're back to ten percent. The Grenouthians are paying a premium because they want a story to drown out the news about statues stolen from their preserve."

"What do you know about that?" John demanded. "I just read the story that Ellen bought for the Galactic Free Press on my way here. She sent me a pre-publication copy as a courtesy to EarthCent Intelligence since we're the closest thing to an extraterrestrial police agency for humanity."

"Leaking each other confidential information sounds like a solid basis for a relationship," Myort observed dryly. "I may have seen something about a Free Republic fence selling authentic Earth statuary at a collector's fair at the Phileist Orbital on the Horten/Sharf frontier. Help me finish this up and I'll check the agency feed on my ship to refresh my memory. Now, you start throwing this stuff up and I'll catch it."

The Huktra drove himself into the air with powerful wing beats. John decided on the spot that his alien friend's cooperation on the thefts from Earth outweighed any considerations about the legal status of the abandoned listening post, and grabbing the nearest travel box, heaved it upwards with all his strength. The weight of the box on the Moon was only seventeen percent of what it would have been on Earth, but it wouldn't have made it out of the deep crater if Myort hadn't reached back and snagged it with his tail.

"Sorry," John said, feeling like a kid who had made a throw that hit the dirt in a game of catch. "That one was awkward." He waited for the Huktra to place the box to the side, and then picked up a piece of equipment that felt warm through his gauntlets and prepared to heave it upwards.

"Do you have a death wish?" the Huktra roared at him. "Put that down! It's the atmosphere retention field generator."

"I thought the portable ones had the warning stencils showing a pin popping a bubble," he shouted back in protest after setting the unit down again.

"It's on the other side. Throw me the antenna roll next."

This time the EarthCent Intelligence agent overdid it, and the fabric roll containing all of the hollow aluminum dipole elements sailed past the Huktra, who immediately launched into flight after them.

"If you just wait a few seconds, gravity will bring it back down," John cried after Myort, who of course couldn't hear because there was no atmosphere outside of the retention field to carry the sound waves.

The Huktra caught up with the antenna package before it reached the apogee of the throw, and returning to the lunar surface, set it down and leaned into the crater for the next package.

"What is it now?" Myort asked when John failed to throw the box he was holding. "You have that 'I need to ask you something or I'll explode' look that you get at least twice every time we meet."

"I get that you can hold your breath in a vacuum, but how can you fly when there's no air?"

"Magnetic fields," the Huktra replied. "They're mainly a crust effect here on the Moon, but it's strong in this area. I'm equally at home in atmospheres and magnetospheres, but we're both going to be swimming in hot water if we don't get this crater emptied out before the next patrol."

With that encouragement, John worked up a sweat tossing all of the packaged equipment up to Myort, and finally, the only thing left was the atmosphere retention field generator.

"Now this could be tricky," the Huktra cautioned. "The generator is set to produce a hemispherical field, so if it maintains its orientation during the throw, I should be able to set it down out here without dumping the remaining air. But you better put your hood up just to be safe. How much air do you have left?"

"Maybe nineteen minutes. Plenty of time to climb the cargo netting and get out of here."

"You can't just jump?"

"Maybe halfway," John said, flipping the flimsy helmet back over his head and thumbing the seals.

"Give me a second to do the math," Myort said, and then slapped one hand into the other, producing a sound not unlike a catcher pounding a fist in his mitt. "Alright, toss it up here. As soon as I set it aside, you jump as high as you can and I'll let you grab my tail."

John grimaced, but it wasn't the first time he'd accepted aid from the nethermost part of the alien's anatomy, and there was nobody around to see. He got his hands under the last piece of equipment in the crater and attempted to channel the spirit of his caber-tossing ancestors, which may have been why the generator performed a slow rotation. There was an explosive whoosh from the air emptying out of the crater, and as John was just bringing his arms down, they acted like wings and he was almost thrown free.

Myort reached with his tail and snagged the EarthCent Intelligence agent, who hadn't gained quite enough momentum from the sudden decompression to clear the crater's edge. Rather than setting John down again, the tail continued in a broad arc and deposited its passenger a few steps from the ramp of the Sharf two-man trader. The EarthCent Intelligence agent took the hint and carefully shuffled up into his cargo bay. Once he was inside his ship's atmosphere retention field, he turned to check on the Huktra's progress moving the equipment. A bundle of dipoles was already on the way.

"Hey, don't throw the heavy stuff," John shouted. "Just because those travel boxes don't weigh much doesn't mean the mass is gone. I'll get knocked off my feet if I try to catch one."

"He can't hear you," the ship's controller informed John. "He can, however, hear me, and I've relayed your message to his comm."

The fabric roll of antenna parts arrived, and the EarthCent Intelligence agent had just enough time to click his heels to activate the magnetic cleats before the light bundle could knock him off his feet. He made the catch and slid the package under a cargo net in the empty section of his hold before turning back again. To his relief, Myort was clomping up the ramp, a large box pressed against his body under each arm.

"You don't have to tell me about your physical limitations," the Huktra said as soon as he was inside the ship's atmosphere retention field. "I wrote the book on Humans."

"Is that an expression, or are you being literal?" John asked, taking a box and stowing it away.

"I mean that after my time on Earth recruiting intelligence sources to our mutual benefit, I got tapped to update the manual on your species with my first-hand experience. But we can talk about that another time." Myort put the second box on the deck and trudged back out onto the lunar surface for another load.

"How do Huktras survive in the vacuum?" John asked out loud.

"Their bodies include cavities for air storage that can be put under compression using their flight muscles," the ship's enhanced controller replied. "They also have the ability to supercharge the oxygen in their bloodstream, allowing for extended periods without breathing."

"With all that pressure inside, what keeps them from rupturing in the vacuum?"

"Thick skin," Myort replied as he returned with another load. "And before you ask, I mean that both literally and figuratively, so you don't have to beg my forgiveness."

"It just doesn't seem like the sort of capability that would evolve naturally, even if the Huktra have had space travel for millions of years."

"Now you really are lucky that I have thick skin," Myort said, snorting a short flame and dropping two more boxes on the deck. "It's considered very insulting in some circles to bring up genetic engineering. Try to keep that in mind when you're dealing with the advanced species on the Phileist Orbital."

"Your information better be solid if I'm dragging Ellen all the way to the Horten frontier," John called after the alien's back. He moved the boxes under the cargo netting and tried to remember how many more there were to fit in. To his surprise, the Huktra only carried one box on his next trip.

"That's it for the museum stuff, I'll get rid of the rest myself," Myort said, setting down the final box and using it as a seat. "Those other boxes and the antenna are for show, but this one contains all of the data. It's encrypted, but the Grenouthians should be able to crack it without a problem, and it speaks to the authenticity."

"How much can there be in that one box?"

"Compressed audio? There's around forty years worth, though the first ten aren't that interesting because there weren't that many powerful radio stations on Earth, and the last ten are bloated with military traffic, but the Roaring Twenties and the Depression years make for interesting listening."

"I didn't realize you were such an expert on Earth," John said.

"I told you, I've been here a few times and I like the music, or at least, I used to. Now let's go over a few things quickly and then I've got to get the rest of that stuff loaded in my ship and scram. I set up a code-phrase with the Grenouthians, so you just go right up to their receptionist and say, "I'm Beethoven and I'm here about the music."

"You're making this up, aren't you?"

"It's either that or you can tell them that you're John from EarthCent Intelligence and you're there to sell them some hot espionage."

"Beethoven it is."

Four

"It looks like some kind of medieval torture device," Georgia observed as Larry strapped himself into the framework of carbon fiber tubes using rubber tethers attached to reels. "They used to rack people in the Spanish Inquisition, you know."

"Could you help me with my right wrist? The instruction holo showed the demonstrator pulling the band tight with his teeth, but I must have gotten the starting slack wrong."

"And what if you were alone and you couldn't get out of bondage when it's all over?" she asked, pushing off her chair and floating gracefully over to the latest piece of exercise equipment Larry had installed while they were visiting Union Station. "Just because Flower Shipyards keeps sending you prototypes doesn't mean you have to try them all."

"You know how important exercise equipment is in Zero-G, and give them credit for not settling for a straight copy of a standard two-man trader. Even though they're buying all the major propulsion systems from the Sharf and building the hulls using the original assembly line, they're showing a lot of creativity about customizing the interiors. I may even bring our ship in for a retrofit."

"It will be 'our ship' when I pay you for half, and I'm a long way from that kind of creds," Georgia said, pulling the strap tight around his right wrist. "I'm not going to waltz in here and overturn three generations of trader customs just because you find me irresistible."

Larry stretched against the tethers, gave a grunt of frustration, and then made a convulsive effort to reach the control box, which had floated away from his left hand while he wasn't paying attention. Georgia casually pulled herself around the collapsible framework and snagged the little device. "Looking for this?" she asked sweetly.

"They should have tethered it to the frame with everything else," he said. "I'll put that in my user feedback. Can you turn it on for me? Try the medium setting."

"I'll try the slow setting," she said, and twisted the dial all the way to the left. Then she hit the red button.

The powered reels made remarkably little sound, and for a moment, it looked like all of the tethers were pulling tight simultaneously, as if it really were a torture device intended to pull the victim's limbs out of their sockets. Then the pattern of winding and unwinding became apparent, and Larry began moving his arms and kicking his legs in a fair imitation of swimming the Australian crawl.

"Turn the speed up," he begged her. "It's hard going this slow. I'm just letting the reels pull me through the motions."

Georgia inched the dial to the right and watched him carefully. "Why do you keep turning your head to the right?"

"Because the headband tether keeps pulling it that way," he replied, his breath coming easily.

"I can see that, but what's the point?"

"So I don't drown. Haven't you ever gone swimming?"

"There's no water."

"There's no gravity either, Georgia. The whole point of the Zero-G exercises is to simulate the real thing as closely as possible. It's been a while since I've been swimming, but the arm motion feels about right when I make an effort. Putting reels on both ends of the tether and making the body attachments at the midpoint lets the machine control the resistance pretty accurately, but if you don't put any muscle into it, the reels will just drag you through the motion. I think the leg tethers need adjusting because my thighs are already burning."

"That's probably because when you swim in real water you don't kick as much as you should. Most people don't. Do you want me to turn it up higher?"

"No, I'm good," Larry replied a little louder than he intended. "You should give this a try when I'm done. Maybe you could get a story out of it."

"It looks incredibly uncomfortable," Georgia said. "You've got tethers on your ankles, knees, waist, elbows, wrists, and head. That makes twenty powered reels pulling your body parts back and forth, and you look like you're trapped in a giant's game of cat's cradle. When I lived on Union Station, I used to go on the Physics Ride in Libbyland. They rented out coveralls with magnetic monopoles sewn into the fabric and you could swim in the air on magnetic fields."

"There's a Stryx doing a zillion computations a second and constantly adjusting the magnetic field to make it work," Larry told her. "That's why it's unique to Union Station."

"What are these colored buttons on the side for?"

"I think different strokes. Don't—"

"Oops," Georgia said, as Larry's arms and legs were jerked back at the same time in a rough transition to the breaststroke. "I'll put it back."

"No, this is better," Larry said. "They really have to add voice actuation to the controller."

"There's a little button on the bottom that looks like an old-fashioned microphone."

"I missed that," he said, then took a deep breath. "So I didn't have a chance to ask how your annual review at the paper went before we headed out."

"Great, sort of. Roland told me he accepted a higher percentage of my stories than any other first-year freelancer he could remember, though he also told me I need to work on my interviewing skills. I got some footage of that annoying girl from the Children's News Network to study for homework."

"Who do you mean?"

"Lena, the one the Grenouthians made famous. She just turned eighteen."

"And that annoys you?"

"She's a kid!"

"Maybe she's been doing interviews since she learned how to talk. See if they have a sidestroke icon on there."

Georgia squinted at the tiny icons on the dial. "I think my eyes are starting to go," she said. "Either that or this artwork isn't that good."

"Just pick one. The worst thing that can happen is it will be—" Larry's feet were pulled together and his arms swept outwards at the same time as the tether around his waist jerked his body upwards, "—the Butterfly," he grunted. "Pick something else."

"Sorry." Georgia pressed the microphone button and said, "Sidestroke."

Larry's orientation in the framework of carbon fiber tubes and reels shifted, and suddenly he was doing a leisurely sidestroke, though his scissors kicks were coming dangerously close to hitting the frame.

"Speed level thirty percent," Larry requested, and the spooling of the reels picked up slightly. "Now this is living. Why don't you interview me for practice?"

"We've been living together for a year. I know everything about you."

"What was my favorite toy growing up?"

"I meant I know everything about you that matters," Georgia said. "Speaking of toys, the chandlery guy gave me a great idea. I'm going to trade salt cod for educational toys on Fyndal and make that my specialty."

"Plenty of traders take Kevin as a sort of guru even though he's not even thirty yet," Larry said. "He grew up in a trading family and his sister became a sort of priestess for an alien religion because she has the second sight or something. I think Kevin has a touch of it himself because he's good at drawing people out with just a few words."

"So now you're saying that everybody is better at interviewing than I am."

"I didn't say that and you know it. Go ahead and ask me anything."

"Why did your ex break your nose?"

"Anything not related to Thistle," Larry qualified his offer.

"You'll feel better if you tell somebody."

"I don't need therapy, Georgia. It's just a sad memory for me."

"Fine," she said with a scowl. "What was your first trade?"

"That's an easy one," Larry said. "We were on a Frunge world at a Seedling Day festival, and I insisted on staying behind to watch the blanket while the rest of the family went to see the procession. My parents weren't too worried because the bulk of our stock that trip had been alloys they picked up at a Sharf recycling facility, and they sold all of that for cash the first day."

"How come you're breathing so easily?" Georgia asked.

"You know how many hours a day I spend on the machines. I'm in excellent aerobic condition."

"I was just asking an off-topic question to gain your trust."

"Huh?"

"It's an inside joke at the Galactic Free Press. Tell on."

"So the only inventory set out on the blanket that morning amounted to a dozen pairs of children's shoes and some pewter steins that were made to look like antiques."

"You mean fakes?"

"I'm getting to that part, but no," Larry said, letting the tethers do the work of pulling his limbs through the leisurely sidestroke while he talked. "My folks were big into turned-wood products in those days because my mom had back-to-nature cousins on Earth who made wooden bowls using hydro-powered lathes driven by their water wheel. That salad bowl you found in the back of the picnic locker was made by them."

"I think you mentioned that once," Georgia said. "I can see why they wouldn't put any of that stuff out on a Frunge world, much less on Seedling Day."

"Exactly. So there I was, alone on the blanket for the first time and trying to look like a real trader—"

"How old were you?"

"Eight. I remember because it was my birthday the day before and my Dad gave me a gag gift of oversized boots with dirt in them. He always thought it was funny to pretend to go native wherever we were stopped."

"Is putting dirt in shoes really a Frunge thing?"

"For the kids. They have vestigial roots on their feet when they're little and it's how they get their essential minerals. Anyway, a Grenouthian trader who could have cared less about Seedling Day processions stopped and took an interest in the steins."

"Wait. This was before you had an implant?"

"Right, but the bunny had one of those external translation boxes hanging around his neck and he was carrying a backpack that was about four times bigger than I was. I said he was a trader, but he might have as easily been a tinker, because when he started pulling things out of the backpack to offer in trade, they were mainly alien tools and odd pieces of mechanical assemblies, like gears and pulleys. And I could tell he was old because the fur on his knees and elbows was all worn away."

"I don't think I've ever seen an old Grenouthian, or a poor one," Georgia said. "Your description makes him sound a bit like the hobos who used to stop by the commune where I grew up, except they were humans, of course."

"The bunnies are all members of extended clans that take care of their own, but they have their misfits just like the other species. I've met dozens of bunnies running solo trade ships over the years. Some of them are pretty talkative.

"So you traded him a stein for old machine parts."

"Are you asking or telling?"

"Sorry," Georgia said. "I'm supposed to be working on my tendency of making statements rather than asking questions. So did you make your first trade with the Grenouthian?"

"Yes, I did," Larry said. "But I didn't really know anything about the steins, and when he asked me if they were antiques, I said I thought so."

"Did you know what antiques were?"

"I thought anything older than eight years was ancient, but the Grenouthian was no fool. He asked me whether they were silver, and I thought it was a color rather than a metal, so I said they were. He took his time studying all of the steins, and then he pulled all this random stuff out of his pack and asked me what I wanted in trade."

"That doesn't seem like a fair thing to do to a little kid," Georgia said.

"I was alone on the blanket with the goods," Larry reminded her. "He might have thought that it was an important rite of passage for eight-year-old humans, and now that I look back on it, maybe that's why my parents let me stay by myself. Anyway, we went back and forth, with me choosing some random bit of hardware from his collection and him choosing a stein to take against it, and in the end, we probably broke even in terms of weight. The bunny left with our whole collection of pewter steins, and I was left with a pile of unidentifiable repair parts for obsolete alien equipment."

"So what did your parents say when they got back?"

"You know what my folks are like. My mom said it sounded like the Grenouthian was down on his luck so trading with him was a good deed, and my dad told me that I could have those random bits of equipment as my personal trade stock and he expected great things of me. Talk about pressure."

"Based on that lazy sidestroke you're doing, maybe it takes a little pressure to get you moving," Georgia said. "When we first partnered up, you warned me that you were addicted to trading for ancient alien artifacts. But the biggest trade I've seen you make since we've been together was for a hold full of children's clothes."

"You have to match your inventory to your customer base," Larry said. "But Fyndal is the last world with a sovereign human community I plan on visiting before Rendezvous. I was too busy with the election last year to even think about entering something in the artifacts competition, but I can't miss it twice in a row."

"I guess someday you'll trust me enough to show me this alleged treasure trove of yours, but until then, seeing is believing."

"I'm a treasure hunter, not a collector. Everything I own is on this ship."

"Are you serious? I always assumed you had all of your furniture and stuff in storage somewhere, like my things on Union Station."

"Stop swimming," Larry instructed the voice-activated box, and then twisted around in the tethers to look directly at Georgia. "Why would I have furniture? You know I lived with my folks on their trade ship until I went out on my own. Not getting attached to stuff is one of the most important skills you can have as a trader. No matter how good you are at bartering, if you aren't willing to let go of your merchandise, you end up becoming a collector."

"I always assumed that your parents had a house somewhere they go back to for part of the year," Georgia admitted.

"What made you think that? I probably told you that my grandparents got a place on Void Station when my grandmother got tired of camping all the time and spending a quarter of her life in Zero-G. But my grandfather kept the ship and he does delivery runs to keep his hand in."

"So where are you going to get an artifact to show at Rendezvous?"

"We're shifting to the collectors circuit after Fyndal," Larry said. "You should be happy with the story opportunities because you meet all sorts at those places."

"Collectors circuit?" Georgia asked.

"It's like anything else on the tunnel network," he explained, and took advantage of the fact that the sidestroke had ended with his hands together to undo the wrist straps. "People, I mean, sentients with similar interests end up gravitating to places where they can be around other like-minded sentients. After a while, you end up with fixed places that specialize in different aspects of trade."

"Like all the artificial people working in the garment industry on the Chintoo orbital."

"That's a different phenomenon because the whole place is really a giant cooperative factory. The collectors circuit is more like the music circuit or the art show circuit, with regular festivals, and certain worlds and space habitats where the full-timers stay in the offseason. My grandfather tells a story about how he wanted to run away with the circus back on Earth when he was a kid because the town where he lived was a regular wintering spot for a number of traveling shows. It's the only thing I miss about not having a ship with a jump drive."

"If you had a jump drive you'd run away to join the circus?"

"You really do ask the weirdest questions," Larry said, bending double to free up his ankles. "I can only visit the collectors circuit stops on the tunnel network without a jump drive."

"None of the other collector hangouts are reachable by passenger liner?"

"Have you ever heard of a trader traveling on a commercial service?"

"I guess not," Georgia said. "I didn't realize it was a thing. But while you're visiting alien antique shows, where am I going to find customers for my educational games?"

"Get some that are cross-species," Larry advised, folding up the carbon fiber framework of the swimming machine to save room. "Around half of the children's clothes I stock will sell to Vergallians, Drazens, and Hortens, at least if they're desperate. The Verlocks sell educational toys to all of the species. You'll just have to be careful not to stock up on ones that are too complicated for us."

"That was the shortest exercise session I've ever seen you do. The machine wasn't any good?"

"It's going to take a while to get accustomed to, and it kept pulling my limbs in directions they didn't want to go," Larry said. "I'm used to having more degrees of freedom when I'm exercising, and I ended up letting the machine do all the work. It would probably be really good for rehab."

"So, do you want anything to eat?"

"I think I'm just going to see if I can catch a nap because it's going to be morning at the academy on Fyndal when we arrive. You should try to get some sleep too if you don't want to be too tunnel-lagged."

"I sleep better in the tunnel after I have a meal," Georgia said. "Is there something wrong with your shoulder?"

"It's fine, just strained a little," Larry said. "I guess what I used to think of as sidestroke was really doing the dog-paddle with my head turned to the side."

"Pick the apple, pass it to the other hand, put it in the basket. That's how I was taught."

"Then you're the one who should test the machine. I'm looking forward to visiting the factory on Flower and seeing a two-man trader under construction. We'll stop after Fyndal, I'll get the Human Empire meeting out of the way, and then we're free until Rendezvous."

Five

"I still can't believe you let Myort talk you into fencing stolen Huktra Intelligence equipment," Ellen said to John as the elevator began to rise. "Those Grenouthians who came for the stuff this morning were the shadiest looking pair of bunnies I've ever seen. I swear that the big one would have murdered me if you hadn't been there."

"That's because he knows you're the Earth Syndication Coordinator for the Galactic Free Press. Did you think the Grenouthians would thank you for buying that story about the missing stock exchange statues the paper published?"

"We gave them a chance to make a statement. Besides, after some of the other syndicated journalists from around the globe kicked in with stories about thefts of statues on their beats, the Wall Street preserve story had plenty of company. I still think the bunnies had a lot of nerve bribing the police not to investigate."

"I suspect they were trying to keep it quiet long enough to bring in replicas or buy back the originals," John said. "As far as the Grenouthians are concerned, the loss was nobody's business but their own."

"But it's a historical site," Ellen protested. "I thought the bunnies just leased it from the city."

"They bought the block outright and got extraterritorial status from EarthCent."

"I didn't know that. I'm sorry if I got us in trouble with EarthCent. I'll take the blame, and if they want us to pay a fine, remind me to get a receipt."

"Is that why you think we've been invited to the president's office?" John asked.

"Hildy didn't say when she called, but I figured she was being circumspect because these cell phones aren't secure."

"I suppose she was being cautious, but not for the reason you think." The car stopped with a grinding noise, and as the doors opened, the elevator announced, "QuickU Incorporated."

"Why are we getting off?" Ellen asked.

"The president's office sublets from QuickU," John explained. "EarthCent doesn't have a big operation here, you know. The president's main job is meeting and greeting alien businessmen and running interference for them if the local governments make problems."

"Oh. Do we have to go through QuickU to get there?"

"EarthCent has its own entrance a little further down the hall, though QuickU has expanded to take all the rest of the space on the floor, plus half the floor above us. They hit a gold vein when they expanded into providing recreational personality upgrades to non-human-derived artificial people. It's funny how sometimes a business creates a product for a specific purpose and it ends up being used for something else."

"Hold up," Ellen hissed, grabbing her companion's elbow. "If that pair in trench coats aren't Horten pirates I'll eat my umbrella."

"Start chewing," John said, and strode forward to greet the aliens. "Kusha, Farillo. What are the two of you doing standing in the hall?"

"We just stepped out for a smoke," the female Horten said, displaying the pipe that was hidden in her palm. "Humans treat you like a criminal if you light up in an office."

"I told her it's banned inside everywhere on Earth but she refuses to believe me," Kusha said, shaking hands with John. "It's a good thing we registered at the hotel under false identities or we'd probably get hit with a special room-cleaning fee after we leave. One of your agents?" he added, glancing at Ellen.

"My trader-law wife," John replied. "Watch what you say around her because she works for the Galactic Free Press."

"I thought they had to identify themselves at all times," Farillo said.

Ellen sighed and pulled out the lanyard with her press badge from inside her turtleneck. "I didn't know it was cold out and I didn't think when I went back to change clothes. I take it the two of you aren't pirates?"

Kusha snorted, knocked his own pipe out on the heel of his shoe, and said, "We're cops."

"It's like an inter-species police convention in there," Farillo added. "I didn't see a Chert or a Fillinduck, but you'll recognize the Drazens from that thing we did two cycles ago, and there's the Frunge detective who got the big headlines for cracking the stolen orbital case."

"Somebody stole an orbital?" Ellen asked. "I never heard about that. How could it not have been the biggest news story in the galaxy?"

"It was, about a hundred and fifty years ago. Humans weren't part of the galaxy back then."

"Shall we go in?" John asked, holding open the door. The female Horten took a last draw from her pipe, knocked the ashes out against the sole of her shoe, and followed the others into EarthCent's headquarters.

"Ellen!" a woman cried and hurried over. "I'm so glad you could make it. Do you want to sit through the ISPOA briefing, or would you rather just come into my office for a summary and then let me beg a favor?"

"I guess John can fill me in later if it's not classified," Ellen said. She turned to get his reaction, but he had already been dragged off into a group of alien policemen who were pressing him for EarthCent Intelligence's position on some legal issue. "Is this all about the stolen statues?"

"That was just the tip of the iceberg," Hildy said, and ushered the journalist into her office. "At least we'll be able to hear ourselves think in here," she added, closing the door behind them. "I've got my own coffee machine if you'd like a cup."

"John and I had lunch at a deli on the corner and I had two cups," Ellen said. She noted the expression of alarm that fled across the face of EarthCent's public relations director. "What is it?"

"The deli with the sidewalk hologram of cows grazing in a mountain pasture?"

"Yes. That's what convinced us to try the place."

"Did you have the sausage?"

"Both of us had pastrami sandwiches. Why?"

"It's okay then," Hildy said with a sigh of relief, then waved her hand to dismiss the matter. "Now what I'm about to tell you has to be off the record until you hear about it from another source. Do you accept my condition?"

Ellen held up her hand in the station scouts pledge. "Freelancer's honor."

"I guess that will have to do. Those alien cops are all here as guests of EarthCent to get around the jurisdictional issues over operating on this planet. Without going into ancient history, Earth has a centuries-old international agency for police cooperation, INTERPOL, but it had been underfunded for so long that it was basically nonfunctional. A while back, EarthCent Intelligence applied to ISPOA, the Inter-Species Police Operations Agency, for a grant to update Earth's law enforcement infrastructure. Since so much of the new criminal activity on the tunnel network originates here, the aliens agreed."

"Wasn't that three or four years ago?" Ellen asked. "Some of the crime reporters in the news syndicate I helped set up for the Galactic Free Press have written about the national or city-state police agencies in their areas getting equipment upgrades, but they were all local interest stories."

"The main challenge to getting INTERPOL up and running again was that Earth's remaining law enforcement agencies had all been using their own information technology, most of it purchased from fly-by-night alien vendors, and none of the systems could talk to each other. Rather than throwing money at us, ISPOA obtained donations of certified-interoperable second-hand equipment from its member species. The real work was transferring all of the old data to the new systems, and since the local police all insisted on using favored vendors, it's taken years to get the job done. The worldwide system just went live last month."

"So is that why all those alien cops are here? For a photo op with their donated equipment?"

"I wish that were the case," Hildy said. "The way it was explained to me, the value of the information technology upgrade is that the aliens have developed all sorts of data mining techniques that can connect the dots between seemingly unrelated police reports from all over the galaxy, or in this case, from all over Earth. To make a long story short, it turns out that somebody has been systematically looting our planet for decades now, maybe ever since the Stryx opening, but nobody put it all together."

"Can you give me an example?" Ellen asked.

"I can tell you about one I stumbled across, though at the time, I had no clue it was part of a planet-wide crime spree. When Flower was being outfitted for her mission, I convinced the Norwegian government to split the contents of the old Svalbard Global Seed Vault with her, so she could distribute appropriate seeds to our sovereign communities on alien worlds. But when the time came to make the pickup, it turned out that somebody had already withdrawn half of the seeds from the vault."

"Who?"

"There wasn't any record of the withdrawal, the seeds were just gone," Hildy said. "The Norwegians accepted my argument that it only proved the value of diversifying the holdings, so they went ahead and split the remainder with Flower. But the Svalbard Global Seed Vault showed up on a list of hundreds of thefts from all around the world that, according to the first run of the ISPOA data mining algorithms, are related."

"Do they think that the statue thefts and the missing seeds are connected?" Ellen asked.

"Possibly, but the statue thefts are a recent phenomena, and some of the other data points go back seventy years or more. The consultants are hoping to integrate old newspaper archives with the police reports for a broader picture, but that will take years and run into copyright issues. The initial analysis suggests two distinct criminal gangs at work, one of which is focused on gathering organic samples of our flora and fauna, and the other which is stealing what I can only call trophy pieces."

"Like that theft of a Gutenberg Bible from the university?"

"Exactly," Hildy said. "But we aren't just talking about museum pieces. One example the data mining turned up was something called a Big Boy locomotive that disappeared over sixty years ago."

"Somebody stole a toy train set?"

"The name was descriptive of the biggest steam locomotive ever built, it weighed over five hundred tons. The historians tell us that only twenty-five were ever built, and now there are just six left."

"Isn't that nineteen of them missing?" Ellen asked.

"We believe the others were sold for scrap, which is what the police assumed happened to the missing one when they closed the case. But the ISPOA system matched it with a locomotive sold at TrainCon the same year."

"TrainCon?"

"A convention for train enthusiasts from around the galaxy that takes place in a different empire roughly once a century. The last TrainCon was held on a Dollnick orbital, so they had a record of the transaction, including holo-imaging."

"What's the statute of limitations for receiving stolen goods in Dollnick space? Is the owner trying to get it back?"

"The owner was an outdoor train museum that's long since gone out of business, and the seller at TrainCon had a receipt showing the locomotive had been purchased," Hildy said. "And that turns out to be a pattern for some of the thefts."

"If there are receipts, why do you call them thefts?"

"Because the receipts were given by entities that didn't have legal title to the objects sold."

"In the case of the locomotive, maybe there could be insurance fraud involved," Ellen speculated. "Was the theft covered?"

The public relations director shrugged. "We don't know, and it's unlikely those records still exist."

"So are all of those alien police here because of the old crimes or the new crimes?" Ellen asked, gesturing at the closed door.

"They're here to represent their interests. Did you know that the Frunge collect change from schoolchildren to protect the petrified forests on Earth?"

"I don't know what a petrified forest is, but it sounds like the sort of thing that should be in a nature preserve."

"A lot of the land on this continent is in the old national park system, but the funding for rangers dried up as the population left Earth, and in some cases, the parks now depend on alien charity," Hildy said. "But as the ISPOA data mining showed, that hasn't stopped the removal of protected objects, like petrified logs, fossils, and the poaching of wildlife. Up until now, law enforcement agencies had all been working under the assumption they were dealing with local problems."

"So the species that donate to Earth charities are upset because we aren't doing enough to protect their investment?" Ellen asked.

"That's pretty much it in a nutshell. To some extent, it's the fault of the Stryx, because when they opened Earth, they forbade local governments from interfering with spacecraft coming and going. That was necessary to give Earth's citizens a choice of whether to stay or leave, and as you know, the majority voted with their feet. But it also means that most local authorities don't bother tracking the arrival and departure of spaceships."

"But Earth doesn't have customs control and the Stryx don't search the ships coming and going through the tunnel."

"Exactly," Hildy said. "That's been a boon for legitimate trade, but it presents a real problem for law enforcement. Stephen and I hosted the Vergallian representative from ISPOA last night, and she suggested contacting the artificial intelligence who manages our tunnel exit and requesting the data from all of the transits since it opened."

"If you include the independent traders, there must be thousands of ships arriving or departing through the tunnel every day," Ellen objected. "If you add them all up since the Stryx opened Earth, that would give us tens of millions of suspects."

"As the Vergallian pointed out, how many of those ships are capable of landing on Earth and leaving with a five hundred ton locomotive, or a submerged wreck?"

"The aliens have been stealing sunken ships?"

"Some gun turrets have gone missing from wrecks of old battleships. While an alien spaceship large enough to raise and abscond with a whole sunken vessel might go unnoticed in a remote area of the ocean, the mass would probably raise questions with the AI running the tunnel exit. That locomotive was the heaviest single item in the data set to be smuggled off Earth to date, but of course, we don't know what we don't know."

"So off the record, you've given me a scoop I can't publish, and now you want to ask a favor?"

"We're hoping that your news syndicate can help get to the bottom of this, but somebody has to point them in the right direction," Hildy said. "Anything they can uncover independently is fair game for publication, and we're hoping that some publicity will bring out eyewitness accounts that will help with the investigation."

"That sounds fair," Ellen said. "The stolen statues give me cover to ask for follow-up stories about thefts of cultural heritage. But I'm leaving Earth with John tonight, and I won't get a chance to meet in person with any of the syndicated reporters until I'm back here next month. I can post the request to our open-interest board, but I've been looking forward to this vacation for a year. We've both agreed to go off the grid for two weeks, and if our employers don't like it, they can complain to the Stryx."

Hildy grimaced. "I hate to be the one to tell you this, but there was a sealed envelope for John in the last diplomatic bag from Union Station. I'm afraid you might have to put those vacation plans on hold."

"It's not fair! John hasn't had a week off since the Farling doctor brought him back from the dead after he was poisoned. Now I'm beginning to know how Georgia feels."

"Georgia?"

"You met her at the last Rendezvous. She's the freelancer who worked the Triad story with me."

"I remember now. Her partner got stuck with one of those temporary minister-of-something jobs for the Human Empire, right?"

"In addition to being council head of the Traders Guild, which used to just be about organizing Rendezvous, but has turned into a real time-drain since they voted to become a member of the sovereign human communities." Ellen shook her head and sighed. "I suppose I better get out there and find out where they're sending us then."

"Good luck. I'll be watching for your byline," Hildy said.

When Ellen slipped out of the office, the Hortens she had met in the hall were just returning to their seats in the improvised meeting room, and a familiar-looking Grenouthian replaced them at the lectern. His large black eyes scanned the room and narrowed when they reached the freelance journalist. His whiskers twitched in recognition, and Ellen realized that he was the less aggressive of the two bunnies who had carted off John's load of Huktra spy equipment that morning.

"I'm told this is a briefing so I'll keep it brief," the Grenouthian said. "I arrived on this planet to investigate the removal of certain statues from a building owned by one of our theme parks, and I quickly determined that the Wall Street Preserve is just one of the victims of a sophisticated gang of thieves who have been ransacking this planet for some time. In the absence of cooperation from local law enforcement agencies, I've been unable to ascertain whether the thefts are being committed solely by Humans, though the technical expertise of the criminals hints at the involvement of at least some members from advanced species."

"Now that you've identified yourself to us, we'll get you whatever cooperation we can from the local authorities," EarthCent's president called out from his seat in the audience.

"I'm sure that will be as helpful as it sounds," the Grenouthian said. "Based on the first-order correlation results from the data mining ISPOA has released, it's clear that Earth requires outside aid."

A slow-footed Verlock shuffled up to the front of the room and boomed, "Fortune tellers."

"Excuse me?" the president said.

"Human fortune tellers on Earth are defrauding innocent travelers," the slow-spoken alien said. "You want our cooperation on these thefts, we want something in return."

Everybody in the room waited for the Verlock to speak again, and finally, the president asked, "What?"

"License your fortune tellers and provide ratings."

"You mean, you want us to quantify the accuracy of our fortune tellers? That's not possible."

"Why not?"

"Because we're just making it up," the president explained, and then looked horror-struck when he realized what he had said.

"Please elucidate," the Verlock requested in a voice like a stone crusher.

"It was just a summer job I had in university. I'd tell people what I thought they wanted to hear and they often came back. The owner of the psychic shop was an academic psychologist and she said we were providing alternative therapy."

"I have data gathered from thousands of our tourists who have visited Human fortune tellers and it's clear that some offer accurate forecasts."

"By my second summer, I thought I really did have the knack, but the shop owner just laughed and told me to predict the exact opposite of whatever I thought I saw in their palms or the crystal ball. If anything, my clients believed that my accuracy went up."

"Verlocks are not Humans," the alien stated the obvious. "If you need help creating a testing regime for fortune tellers, our mages can provide it, but if you fail to certify your psychics, we'll have to put Earth on the watch list for tourists, and you don't want that to happen."

Six

"Over here," Dianne called, and stood up to make sure Georgia could see her in the crowded café. "I didn't think it would be so packed in the middle of the morning," she continued when the freelancer joined her at the tiny table. "It's a unique place, and I thought you might be able to get a 'Food for Thought' column out of it. I've had their take-out delivered, but this is the first time I've been here in person."

"The décor is very, uh, metallic," Georgia said. "Is it some retro style from Earth?"

"According to the business directory listing, the owner is a former researcher from the Frunge Encyclopedia of Diplomacy, and the *Blue Tea Café* is the first Frunge restaurant to open on Flower."

"I had blue tea once in a café on the Poalim habitat. I hope the food here is better than that place."

"You know that traditional Frunge stay away from grains, and we can't eat any of their animal proteins," Dianne said. "Other than the tea, the entire menu here is from the All Species Cookbook, but it's limited to the Frunge tribute recipes. The majority of the ingredients are grown on board Flower, and there's a note in the take-out menu about anything imported from Earth."

"It is an interesting concept for a restaurant," Georgia said. "I wonder how many other aliens have opened places selling faux-versions of their native cuisine that we can eat."

"Keep in mind it's not just us. All of the tunnel network members can safely digest the ingredients used in the All Species Cookbook recipes, so it's a way for aliens to eat cross-species without having to worry about running for the bathroom."

A young woman with her hair dyed green and twisted around a low-rise trellis arrived at their table and asked, "May I take your order?"

"I'll have a White Lightning and the pastry of the day," Dianne said.

"Are you here to review us?" the waitress asked, eyeing Dianne's Galactic Free Press ID.

"I'm not, but she might be," Dianne said, indicating Georgia with a head tilt.

"Do I get different treatment if I'm here to do a review?" the freelancer asked.

"I don't know, you'd be the first," the waitress said. "The owner told us to ping her if any press came in."

"That sounds a bit ominous. Do you recommend anything in particular?"

"I could live on our salads, they're so good. But if you just want a tea and dessert, it's hard to beat the pastry of the day."

"Which is?"

The waitress shook her head. "I can't tell you. Putting your trust in the chef's daily special is a Frunge tradition."

"Then I won't be the spoil-sport," Georgia said. "Give me that and a blue tea."

"I'll have the drinks right out," the waitress said, then retraced her steps through the crowded café.

"So where are you coming from this time?" Dianne asked Georgia.

"Fyndal. Have you ever been to a Verlock open world?"

"No. I've heard the Verlocks tend to favor extreme climates and active volcanoes."

"It's true. We set down on this ancient tarmac that was as smooth as glass from being scoured by wind-blown grit. The sovereign human community there is organized as an academy town after the Verlock fashion, and it's entirely underground. They sent an oxcart to bring us to the subway station."

"An oxcart? As in an ox pulling a cart?"

"A stone cart, with stone wheels and everything," Georgia said, shaking her head at the memory. "But it turned out to be a ceremonial welcome and the ox was just for show. The cart had built-in skimmer technology—something like Dollnick floaters except it hugs the ground. And I swear that my crates of salt cod felt twice as heavy as they were on Union Station, but Larry said we only weighed about ten percent more on Fyndal."

"Smart move, bringing salt cod to trade with the Verlocks."

"It wasn't my idea, but it worked out fantastic. While Larry was meeting with the community leaders, I bartered all of the cod for educational games. I want to become a specialty trader, and academy worlds are definitely the place to go for anything related to education."

"Are you giving up on journalism?" Dianne asked.

"Not a chance, but being a freelancer means working flexible hours, and other than the lucky break I caught last year when Ellen brought me in on the ship mortgage fraud story, I haven't found my footing as an investigative journalist. I'm making good money with my food writing but the truth is I could do that in my sleep. At my first annual review, the freelance editor suggested I practice my interview skills."

"I read the series of articles you wrote about differences in the education systems at the sovereign human communities you've visited. That was an excellent piece of journalism."

"Did you really think so?" Georgia asked. "It felt like I was back to writing restaurant reviews, except substituting schools for restaurants. There wasn't any investigating involved other than sitting in some classes and talking to a lot of children. It was just something I did while Larry was busy getting feedback about what people envision the ministry of trade should do in a Human Empire."

"I thought your insights about the way the local teachers build curriculums that integrate the best practices of their alien hosts were spot on. And it's encouraging that sovereign communities are putting a priority on live classrooms, rather than leaving education entirely up to Stryx-subsidized teacher bots and homeschooling. I wouldn't be surprised if there are more human children regularly attending a school on alien worlds than on Earth or human-run space habitats."

"I'd be surprised if that weren't the case," Georgia said. "But part of the challenge on Earth is that the population density outside the cities is so low that attending school in person is impractical. Making children commute for hours a day when there's a viable alternative is just cruel. On habitats, I think the reliance on teacher bots is more a matter of cost and tradition."

"It seems to me that if you combined reporting on education with trading in educational toys, you could corner the market," Dianne said. "You should talk to Flower. She's always locking teachers in their cabins or trapping them in lift tube capsules so she can substitute teach. I guess you could call it her passion."

The waitress returned with a tray and transferred a tall glass and a small teapot with a cup and saucer to their table, taking up half of the surface area. "I'll be back as soon as your pastries cool."

"They're just out of the oven?" Georgia asked, but the girl was already moving away. "So what's a White Lightning?"

"Carbonated steamed milk with vanilla flavoring. My husband grew up in New York City, and he told me it's the Frunge version of an egg cream, if you've ever had one of those."

"There was an antique soda fountain in our commune's cafeteria and some of the old men were addicted to them. You know what?" Georgia asked as she poured the brilliant blue tea into her cup. "I may owe my journalistic career to egg creams. It's the first time I got interested in digging for the truth."

"I don't follow you," Dianne admitted.

"There's no egg or cream in egg creams—it's just milk, seltzer, and flavoring. I was around twelve years old when I found out, and after that, I began to question if everything was a lie." She pointed at her ear and listened over her implant for a few seconds before saying, "I'll see you there," and dropping her hand.

"Do you have to leave?"

"No, that was Larry. He just got out of his meeting with Flower's people about her hosting the upcoming Rendezvous and now he's going to the temporary Human Empire headquarters just to check in. We're meeting at the shipyard in a half an hour to talk interiors with the design staff.

I'm looking forward to giving them my feedback about Zero-G kitchens."

"Two pastries of the day," the waitress announced, somehow finding room on the tiny table for the desserts. "Will there be anything else?"

"All set, thank you," Dianne said.

"It's a little pie!" Georgia exclaimed. "I wonder what's inside?"

"Fruit filling."

"You mean it's always the same?"

"It's just that Flower grows a lot of fruit," Dianne said, and then broke open the crust with her fork. "Apple and something. Rhubarb maybe?"

"But how could it be a Frunge tribute recipe?" Georgia asked. "They don't even eat crust."

"We do when it's made without grains," a scratchy voice announced, and the women looked up from their desserts to see a sturdily-built Frunge whose hair vines were uncharacteristically short for a female, as if she had gotten a buzz cut and only recently started growing them out again. "I'm Fandaz, and I own the *Blue Tea*."

"Dianne, I'm the local Galactic Free Press reporter on Flower, and this is my friend Georgia, a freelancer who writes—"

"Food for Thought," the alien interrupted, and then she pointed at a chair that had just been vacated at the next table. "May I join you?"

"Of course," Dianne said immediately.

Rather than dragging the tall chair across the metal tiled floor, the owner carefully lifted it and placed it as close as she could to the table occupied by the reporters while leaving room for her knees.

"I was commenting to my friend about the décor," Georgia said. "The wrought iron chairs are very unusual, and the tables remind me a bit of the shields I've seen reenactors wear on their forearms."

"Bucklers," Fandaz supplied the term in English. "All of the furniture in my café was forged by Razood, the Frunge blacksmith who works in Colonial Jeevesburg."

"Ah, that makes sense now. And the pie crust?"

"It's a recipe the Humans living on one of our open worlds came up with to honor our dietary restrictions. I suppose it won't surprise you to hear that we don't have much of a pastry tradition of our own."

"It has a lovely taste," Dianne said, having tried the flaky dough. "What's in it?"

"The main ingredients are almond flour exported from Earth by Drazen Foods, and tapioca flour from roots grown on one of the ag decks," Fandaz told them. "Some days the chef adds coconut flour as well, along with the standard egg and butter you find in most crusts. Baking powder, salt—I think that's everything."

"It's brilliant," Georgia said, having tasted her own crust while the owner was expounding on the ingredients. "And it's apple rhubarb?"

"Flower has a fine orchard of baking apples, and the rhubarb just came into season in one of the climate zones. I have to admit that the Dollnick ag deck design is extraordinarily flexible."

"And could I ask what gave you the idea of opening a Frunge-tribute café based on All Species Cookbook recipes on board Flower?" Georgia asked.

"The availability of high-quality ingredients and the local blacksmith were the two biggest factors," Fandaz said. "After I took early retirement from the Petrification

Bureau, I wanted to open a business where my clientele wouldn't be frightened when they saw me coming."

"There must be a mistake in the business directory," Dianne said. "The biography had you as a career employee of the Frunge Encyclopedia of Diplomacy."

The Frunge's stubby hair vines turned dark green, and her jaw muscles clenched involuntarily.

"Is something wrong?" Georgia asked.

"Me, there's something wrong with me," Fandaz gritted out. "It's all a lie. I used to be an Inspector General with our diplomatic service, but I lost the ability to work undercover because I could never keep my cover story straight. I was granted a medical discharge, and my therapist suggested that I try a job where I could make others happy instead of scaring them half to death."

"That's a fascinating story, and if I could include it in my article, I bet the paper will feature it in the weekend food section. Not that you need the publicity."

"There's no such thing as being too busy in the restaurant business," the owner said. "And you're welcome to write about my checkered past as I'm already the punchline of a Frunge joke about Zather's Confession."

Georgia exchanged a look with Dianne, who shook her head in the negative. "I didn't understand that last bit."

"Do you both have implants?" the Frunge asked.

"From the Galactic Free Press," Georgia replied.

"Then I'll try telling you in Frunge and see if it translates since I'm curious whether a primitive species like Humans can suffer from the same condition," Fandaz said, and shifted from her scratchy English to even hoarser Frunge. "My therapist described my inability to keep my cover story straight as an extreme case of Freudian slips. Does that mean anything to you?"

"It's what we call it when your subconscious struggles with some unresolved conflict and expresses itself through your speech. Did you enjoy your job?"

"I hated it. My parents both had internal affairs jobs in our diplomatic service and they raised me to become the youngest inspector general since all of the personnel records were lost in the Great Hacking. I thought I would be investigating serious corruption, but the new director was a teetotaler, and he kept sending me after career diplomats who were heavy social drinkers. Do you have any idea what percentage of Frunge ambassadors drink?"

"I would have guessed most of them," Dianne said.

"And you would have guessed right." Fandaz let out a raspy sigh that sounded like she was sanding a block of wood in her throat. "The thing that really made me angry is that my parents had worked for centuries on uncovering a ring of diplomatic personnel who were involved in smuggling artifacts off non-tunnel network worlds, but the new director closed the investigation. I don't know if he was involved himself or protecting friends, but the whole diplomatic service runs on the Old Log Network."

Twenty minutes passed in a flash as the disgruntled Frunge vented to the reporters about her time as an inspector general. Eventually, Georgia realized she was running late, thanked Fandaz, promised a positive review of the *Blue Tea*, and hurried off to meet Larry. She instructed the lift tube to take her to the shipyard, and was caught off guard when Flower asked, "Your cargo is educational toys?"

"Uh, yes," the freelancer said, reflexively looking up at the speaker grille in the ceiling of the lift tube capsule. "It's just my own trade stock, not a full cargo. I plan to make it my specialty."

"I have a strong interest in education myself and I'd like to take a look at your merchandise. Would you mind if I send a bot to inspect your goods before you leave?"

"Of course not," Georgia said. "If we had planned on staying longer I would have laid out a blanket in the bazaar to test the market here, but Larry is in a big hurry to visit some alien worlds without human communities before Rendezvous."

"I've heard he has the treasure hunting bug," Flower said as the capsule doors opened. "They're waiting for you at the final station of the assembly line to your right."

Georgia took a few cautious steps to get the hang of her lower weight on the new deck and then strode towards the group of people admiring the custom paint job on a two-man trader. She arrived within earshot just in time to hear Larry asking a question about storage locker capacity.

"You noticed that on our fact sheet," a woman in crisp Flower Shipyards coveralls replied with a grin. "Now that your partner is here, let's just go in for a demonstration, which is easier than explaining. I can tell you that the concept came from Don, who used to work in home construction on Earth."

"Just between SciFi cons," a man wearing identical coveralls said. "But I got the idea from under-the-counter corner cabinets in kitchens." He noted Georgia's press ID and asked, "Are we on the record?"

"I'm just here as Larry's better half today," the freelancer said. "Besides, the Galactic Free Press already has a reporter assigned to Flower."

"Dianne," Laura said. "She's done some great stories about us, but you can never have too much publicity in business."

"Funny, I just heard that from a Frunge who owns a café."

"Fandaz. I used to go there for lunch salads but it's too crowded now."

Georgia followed the shorter woman up the ramp into the cargo hold of the ship and saw that Larry was already halfway up the ladder to the bridge. "He's been talking about your fact sheet since we picked one up at Mac's Bones on Union Station," she said. "I think he doesn't believe some of the claims are possible."

"We've had almost six months to think about ways to remodel the cabin of Sharf traders," Laura said, and then corrected herself. "I'm sorry, it's technically the bridge on spaceships, but I grew up working on sailing craft in my family's shipyard on Earth, and to me, anything you sleep in is a cabin."

"Were you able to do anything with the kitchen?" Georgia asked, following the other woman to the ladder. "All we have is a microwave and a fridge."

"You mean the galley, and I think you'll be pleasantly surprised."

"Look at this," Larry said as soon as Georgia climbed through the hatch. He was standing at a standard looking row of storage lockers, bouncing with excitement like a small boy. When he was sure he had Georgia's attention, he nodded to Don, who pulled up on the locking handle that was normally pressed down to open a locker.

Instead of the door opening, the whole stack of storage units slid forward out of the locker bank, showing themselves to be twice as deep as one would have expected. Then the stack spun one hundred and eighty degrees, proving that it was actually back-to-back storage units, and smoothly returned to its place in the bank of lockers.

"Presto," Don said. "Double your locker capacity, and we're making it available as a retrofit once we've built enough of them for the new ships."

"Put me on the waiting list," Larry said. "No more fighting over locker space on the bridge."

"We're working on another bridge retrofit that I can't tell you about at this time, but you might want to hold off on the lockers until we introduce it at Rendezvous," Laura said. "It sort of competes for the same real estate."

"Is it a full kitchen?" Georgia asked, and turned to Larry. "If it turns out to be a kitchen option, I'll start keeping all of my personal stuff on the cargo deck. I swear," she added after he gave her a skeptical look. "I'd even give up the Zero-G shower if it meant getting a real kitchen. We could give each other sponge baths."

Seven

Ellen undid the harness holding her on the exercise bicycle, and then looked around to see if John had returned from straightening things out in the hold. He was floating at an odd angle near the locker where he stored their basic trader's gear, staring at the Stryx mini-register as if he were trying to decipher a secret code.

"Cooking the books?" she asked him.

"I'm trying to balance my programmable cred, but it doesn't make sense," he replied.

"How much are you short?"

"That depends on whether or not you include the twenty thousand creds that just showed up, which is more than I'll earn from EarthCent Intelligence this year."

"You're complaining because the balance went up?" Ellen asked incredulously. She pushed gently off the bike for a spot where she'd be able to see what he was looking at. "Like those apocryphal stories you hear about somebody needing money to save a world, and all of a sudden it shows up on their programmable cred?"

"The twenty thousand is my share of Myort's transaction with the Grenouthians," John said. "I'm still waiting to hear from the ethics committee about whether I'll have to hand it over to EarthCent Intelligence. The problem is with the bill from the elevator transit authority for our stay in the long term lot at the elevator stalk. There's over three hundred eBucks in charges for streaming immersives that I didn't watch."

"Don't look at me. I was living in hotels and meeting with syndicated journalists all week. But the ETA is one of the best-managed businesses on Earth, so you can probably get a refund when we return next month. Three hundred eBucks is almost sixty creds, so it's worth jumping through a few hoops."

"I'm just concerned that somebody found a way to hack into my ship controller's payment mode to charge my programmable cred. If it can happen to me, it can happen to anybody using the automated system."

"Now you're just being paranoid," Ellen said. "Stryx mini-registers and controllers are the backbones of interspecies trade. If they were hackable, it would be a much bigger deal than somebody piggy-backing on your account in a parking lot to watch porn."

"It wasn't porn," John said, swiping at the register's display and bringing up a series of images to show her. "Going by the artwork, they're all from some alien anime series in translation. Look at this."

"Dragon Wars," she read the title from the first flame-throwing image. "Dragon Wars Two. The Return of Dragon Wars. The Revenge of the Dragons. I seem to be detecting a pattern here."

"And they were all seventy-two-hour rentals so we can't even watch them now. There's also a nineteen cred freeze placed by some shop on Union Station that I never heard of. Did you buy anything there over the mini-register?"

"You know I have my own programmable cred. What did your ship's AI think?"

"It's not AI, it's an expert system, and I was about to ask if it has any records," John said. "Controller. Do you still have a log of your data traffic from our stay on Earth?"

"I maintain a permanent record of all communications originating from and addressed to the ship, plus a first-in, first-out buffer of everything I pick up in the vicinity," the controller replied.

"Does the local traffic show any communications with ETA entertainment services, specifically, streaming requests for the Dragon Wars anime series?"

"There were thirty-two requests for streaming anime entered through the manual control for the viewscreen during our stay on Earth," the controller replied.

"What! You're saying that it was me?"

"Maybe stress is making you sleepwalk," Ellen suggested.

"I haven't used the manual controls in months," John protested, launching himself for his command chair and pulling up the arm to gain access to the fallback remote. "It's not in here."

"Somebody stole it?"

"Controller," John said. "Were there any unauthorized visitors to the bridge logged during our stay on Earth?"

"Do you think I would have waited until now to inform you?"

Ellen swiped at the mini-register to advance through the rental records, and then she exploded in laughter. "You didn't look far enough," she told her partner when she recovered her breath and then began reading additional titles. "The Rise of the Gryphons. Gryphons versus Dragons. Gryphon Apocalypse—"

"Semmi!" John yelled, launching himself for the hatch to the cargo deck. He showed excellent flexibility for a man in his mid-forties, pulling himself down the ladder head-first. Ellen stowed the mini-register away before following, and she found him wrestling with the sleepy gryphon, trying to pull Semmi out of her crate.

"Don't be so hard on her, John. She probably didn't understand the rental terms. I've heard that parents on Earth have to hide their entertainment system remotes from the children so they don't run up the bills."

"I want to see what else she has in there," he growled, bracing his feet against the crate and pulling on the gryphon's front paws. "I'm going to have to go back through all the records now. What if she's been ordering jewelry from one of those home shopping networks?"

Semmi came wide awake and gave him a speculative look.

"Uh oh, now you've done it," Ellen said. "I'll bet she never heard of home shopping before you brought it up."

"Give me back the remote," John demanded in the command voice he'd picked up during his time in the mercenaries. Semmi responded by licking his face with her rough tongue.

"Exiting the tunnel in five minutes," the ship's controller announced over the public address system. "Safety protocols require crew members to return to the bridge."

The gryphon took advantage of John's hesitation to deliver a quick peck to each of his hands, causing him to let go of her paws, and then she slammed the door of her crate closed.

"This isn't over," John growled as Semmi pulled the shade down over the door's grating.

"At least wait and see what your boss says about Myort's commission," Ellen said, pushing off a cargo container for the ladder. "If they let you keep just a fraction of that twenty thousand, it will make Semmi's binge-watching look like chump change."

"It's the principle of the thing," John said, casting a sour look back at the crate. "If I can't trust her with access to my credit, I'll have to take her off the controller."

"You registered Semmi as crew?"

"When we stopped at that Fleet orbital." He followed Ellen through the hatch to the bridge, ordered the controller to secure for docking, and strapped himself in before continuing. "The Vergallians might accept a gryphon traveling with human pets, but not the other way around."

"And you waited for the hatch to close to tell me that because you were afraid she might overhear you?"

"She's probably too busy watching anime in her crate," John retorted. "Myort mentioned there was a display in there, but he gave me the impression that it just cycled through nature scenes from her homeworld so she wouldn't get claustrophobic. I should have realized when it showed up as a node on the internal network that it could support streaming."

"Did you remember to ask him if the signs she's been teaching us are from some kind of battle language?" Ellen asked. "Maybe he can get us a book."

"I forgot. Finding out that the Huktra had a listening post on the moon for a couple of centuries caught me by surprise. They're one of the least involved tunnel network species, you know. They don't even have an ambassador on Union Station."

"Myort seems pretty involved to me. We wouldn't be—"

"Hold that thought," John interrupted. "Controller. Did you capture imagery of Myort's ship when I was leaving the Moon?"

"Affirmative."

"Including the nose art?"

The display screen came alive with an image of the blunt prow of Myort's vessel. A Huktra female in flight was painted on the hull, her red eyes glowing like rubies.

"Check our database for any previous images of that artwork," John instructed.

"There is one prior image on record from Myort's visit to Flower last year," the controller replied, and splitting the view screen, displayed the nose art from the previous capture.

"He didn't mention his wife at all when we were on the Moon. Normally he can't shut up about her."

"I didn't know he was married," Ellen said.

"As far as I know he's not, but Huktra females like a male who projects confidence. Does that look like the same woman to you?"

"You mean, like the same terrifying dragon variant?" Ellen's head swiveled back and forth a few times like she was watching a tennis match. "If it's not, he must like a certain type. Wait! The tail is different."

"You're right. The new art has three spikes and the old one had five."

"Maybe she got in an accident and lost two."

"I don't think so," John said. "The only reason I ended up with Semmi was because that one," he pointed at the five-spiked tail, "didn't like her. I wonder why Myort didn't say anything about wanting Semmi back."

"Whoa!" Ellen gripped the arms of her chair and looked a bit nauseous. "That was the roughest tunnel exit I've been through in years."

"Like a bad rollercoaster ride. Controller, what was that all about?"

"Phileist Orbital requesting navigation handover," the artificial voice responded.

"Transfer navigation and then answer my question."

"Traffic control reports that a large freighter jumped out of the system just as we were exiting the tunnel," the controller replied. "They apologize for any discomfort caused by the space-time interference, but the freighter ignored navigation instructions, and there was never any danger of a collision. Phileist parking authority has sent us a coupon as compensation for any inconvenience."

"How much?" John asked.

"Twenty percent off," the controller replied. "But the spot that they're offering is a long walk from the freight lift tube."

"I'm just bringing my pack so it will be fine. Ellen?"

"From what the paper's business database says about this place, there's no point in my laying out the blanket here," she said. "I doubt that collectors would be interested in my craft supplies."

"I'm only carrying my trader's pack for cover," John said. "I'll find something light to stuff it with. How long until arrival?"

"Three hours and forty-seven minutes," the controller responded.

"I'm going back to sleep," Ellen announced. "You should take a nap too, and maybe you won't pass out when we arrive like you always do."

"Don't worry about me. I'm going to mainline some coffee."

Ten hours later, John woke up in his command chair and rubbed the sleep from his eyes. The main view screen displayed a text from Ellen reading, "For future reference, the coffee boxes with the orange stripes are decaf. I'm taking Semmi and exploring."

John checked the time on his implant, groaned, and made a quick stop in the bathroom before climbing down the ladder to the cargo deck. He activated his magnetic cleats and estimated his weight at about ten percent of Earth normal, which was typical for the docking core on smaller orbitals with a limited number of decks. The large trader's pack stuffed with children's flotation devices weighed even less than it would have empty under normal gravity. He shrugged into the straps, headed down the ramp, and instructed the controller to secure the ship.

"Blue for freight lift tubes, green for everybody else?" he asked himself, then activated the heads-up display on the high-end implant provided by EarthCent Intelligence, and tried accessing the standard information channel for tunnel network space structures. A new query added an overlay with a path shown in black dots, and he navigated his way to the closest lift tube.

"Collectibles deck," he requested when the capsule doors closed behind him.

"All six commercial decks on Phileist include collectibles vendors," the orbital's AI responded. "Please be more specific."

"Uh, mechanical collectibles from primitive species?"

The capsule began to move, and John took the opportunity to pull up the directory for vendors with permanent displays, and he gave a low whistle. The number of listings looked comparable to the business directory of a Stryx station, even though the orbital couldn't be a twentieth of the size.

"Do you have a summary of Phileist's history for tourists?" he asked out loud.

"Phileist is unique among the tunnel network system's orbital destinations for being owned by a multi-species association of independent collectors. The Phileist organization predates the current iteration of the tunnel network by millions of years and includes active members from over three thousand species. Would you like me to list them?"

"Are you serious?"

"No, we've arrived at your destination," the orbital's AI said, and the capsule door slid open.

John blinked his heads-up display out of existence and walked out onto a scene that reminded him of the bazaar on Flower. Directly in front of him was an antique vehicle that featured millipede-style drive, rather than wheels or tracks, and to his left was a display of tricycles that were either intended for adult humanoids or a species with very large children. At first, he thought that there were no aisles between the booths, but then he realized that a large fraction of the merchants were selling something that was just too large to fit in a standard space, so straight paths just weren't possible.

"First time on Phileist?" a cheerful voice to his right inquired.

"Yes," he replied, even as he turned to see a robot wearing a smock of sorts.

"You're my second Human ever," the bot said, offering one of its three arms for a pincer shake. "The first came through a few hours ago in the company of a gryphon, and our primary AI supplied me with a language package. Are you together?"

"Yes," John repeated. "I must have fallen asleep from tunnel lag and they came on ahead. Are you with the orbital staff?"

"I'm an information desk volunteer," the robot replied. "I collect myself, so it's a dream vacation for me. Going by the size of your pack I've tentatively identified you as either a trader or a hoarder. Are you looking for a place to display your wares?"

"I might do a little bartering if I see something I like, but I'm here today just to take a look around."

"A hoarder then," the robot said. "I had a bit of a problem with that myself when I first got into collecting, but that was thousands of years ago. Do you have a particular specialty?"

"I'm interested in mechanical devices from early industrial cultures, including my own," John said. "Do you know if there are any booths specializing in goods from Earth?"

The robot, which had been ambling alongside John on its tripod arrangement of legs, came to a halt and examined him through three lenses. "You came all the way here to look for collectibles from your own world? Are you working for the Tharks?"

"I'm a trader. Do you get many aliens working for the Tharks here?"

"I asked because I know that Thark bookies are the primary insurers of valuable collectibles on the Stryx tunnel network, and they offer substantial rewards for information leading to the return of items that they've paid out on," the robot said. "While it's unusual for stolen goods to show up on Phileist due to our organization's emphasis on the provenance of collectibles, it occasionally does happen with items that age off the hotlist."

"Phileist maintains a list of stolen goods?" John asked. "Are you plugged into the ISPOA system?"

"I was referring to the Thark hotlist, which is published with the prices they are willing to pay for the recovery of stolen goods. I believe I saw somebody advertising collectibles from your Earth earlier this cycle, so let's see if they're still here."

"How do you know they were from Earth?"

"Lots of toy soldiers that looked just like you," the robot said. "Of course, all humanoids look alike to some extent, but the labeling on some unopened packages matches the character set of the language we're speaking."

John tried to walk next to his guide to ask more questions, but the robot's tripod arrangement of legs allowed it to take ninety-degree turns at full stride. He ended up trailing a step behind as the robot navigated a zigzag path through what seemed like an endless sea of legacy mechanical devices, tools, and toys from a dizzying array of species. The robot came to a sudden stop in front of a booth displaying a menagerie of bizarre metal figurines. The vendor immediately popped to his feet and said something that John's implant failed to translate.

"That one," the robot said, pointing at one of the constructions with a closed pincer. "Is it authentic?"

The vendor, who was from one of the countless reptilian species that John couldn't differentiate without a field guide in hand, shook his head at the robot and spoke again. This time John's guide replied in an undecipherable language and the two aliens entered into an energetic discussion that involved much raising of voices and waving of limbs. Eventually, the reptile handed over the figurine in question, and the robot reached into one of its bib pockets and produced what looked like a flat washer.

"Is that a coin?" John couldn't help asking.

"It's a washer," the robot replied, and placed it on what John now realized was one of the figurine's three arms. There was a sound like a ratchet spooling free, and the other two arms came together to remove the washer and dropped it in a slot that opened between two of the figurine's three legs. Then the little automaton straightened up again and froze in its original position.

Displaying his teeth in a fierce smile, the reptilian vendor held up four talons. The robot volunteer guide hesitated, and then replaced the figurine on the table and turned away.

"A mechanical bank from your world?" John asked.

"The biologicals who created us seemed to find them amusing," the robot said. "I collect them."

"And their old coins had holes in them?"

"So do our current coins, though we primarily use them for trading with other species."

"So why didn't you feed it a coin rather than a washer?" John asked.

"If I had fed it a coin, I would have lost it," the robot pointed out. "But I'm hopeful that if I stop back later he'll be a little more reasonable. You have to be willing to walk away if you want to get ahead in this game."

"Would it offend you if I asked about your makers?"

"Three legs, three arms, three eyes," the robot said. "I used to inhabit an android form that would allow me to pass as one of them, but as I grew older, I found that maintaining extra body mass solely for the purpose of aesthetics was more work than it was worth. I sold that body to a younger AI and put the proceeds into my coin bank collection. Ah, there it is."

John looked in the direction the robot was pointing with one of its arms and was stunned to see a saloon standing in the middle of a collection of other free-standing structures so alien that he could only guess at their purposes. The wooden building looked like it had been scooped up whole from the Wild West, and the sign above the swinging doors that identified it as a saloon was riddled with holes that might have been from bullets or carpenter bees.

"Impressive, no?" the robot asked. "I have a great deal of respect for building collectors, but I don't have the storage space myself, and extended time in Zero-G can play havoc with structures built from natural materials. I understand it's especially tough on primitive stone constructions that rely on gravity to hold together. Shall we go in?"

John pushed through the batwing doors, the name coming to him from a history book he must have read during the endless exercise sessions on his ship, and a tinny piano immediately began to play. The first clothed Grenouthian he had ever seen in his life popped up behind the bar and asked the robot in a drawl, "What will it be, stranger?" Then the bunny noticed John and grunted, "We don't serve Humans in here. Don't make me draw down on you."

"Hold on," the EarthCent Intelligence agent said, keeping his hands visible in front of his body. "I'm not armed and I'm just, uh, passing through. Is this your saloon?"

"One of them," the Grenouthian said. "I have drinking holes from over a hundred species. Are you a collector?"

"A trader, but I've seen my share of unique artifacts over the years and I've been thinking about starting a collection. I had no idea that anybody collected historical buildings. Did you get it before the Stryx opened Earth?"

"Are you insane? I bought this place from a dealer—had to take a bank, two hotels, and a barbershop to make the deal, but I was able to sell all of those off to other specialty collectors." The bunny reached under the bar and John flinched, expecting a shotgun, but instead, the alien produced a standard tab and swiped it to life. "Tell me what you make of this."

John went forward, accepted the tab from the giant bunny, and found himself watching a clip from an old movie featuring the very saloon they were standing in. "This building must have been part of a movie set," he said. "Earth's pre-Stryx version of immersives."

"I wondered why somebody would take so many still pictures and chain them all together," the Grenouthian said. "Your eyes must run at a low refresh rate if the motion appears continuous to you. I'm glad to hear my saloon's provenance is confirmed."

"You knew the building wasn't original?"

"I'd have to be an idiot to think that. The construction is wood planks on steel studs, and the walls can all be swung away for better camera angles. Did you think I would buy a building stolen from a historical site?" The bunny reached below the bar again.

"Not you, personally," John hastily backtracked, "but I've heard that such things have recently become common on Earth. I happened to be in the neighborhood so I thought I'd look around Phileist and see if anything turned up."

"It seems you brought a cop into my place," the Grenouthian snorted at the robot, who nodded his trinocular head in agreement. "If you're looking for stolen collectibles, Mr. Undercover Agent, try a black market. Everything here is sustainably sourced from reputable dealers."

"Might either of you be aware—I'm leaving, I'm leaving," John cut himself off as the sawed-off shotgun made its appearance.

As the EarthCent Intelligence agent backed out through the saloon's batwing doors, his hands held over his head, he heard the three-legged AI say to the Grenouthian, "I should have known. The other Human I had this morning turned out to be a nosy reporter, but I did enjoy meeting the gryphon."

Eight

Larry closely examined the bolt of semi-metallic cloth on offer to make sure that it wasn't a quality control reject, and then nodded his approval. "Two from the blue-dot tier," he agreed.

The woman bobbed her head, and scanning the children's shoes with blue stickers on the toes, picked out two pairs. "These are Earth sizes? They look a bit large."

"Have the kids try them on. That's what the chair is for."

"Oh, I thought you brought the chair for yourself."

"Traders believe that when you can't sit cross-legged on the blanket it's time to think about retiring," Larry said. While the woman corralled her children and made them try on the shoes, he folded up the bolt of cloth and sprayed it with a protective layer of Dolly-wrap which could be peeled off later without leaving any residue. The woman had to exchange both pairs of shoes for a better fit, but she was all smiles when the trio departed.

"Why didn't you send her my way?" Georgia demanded from the next blanket over. "Those kids were the perfect age group for my educational toys."

"She told me that was her last bolt of cloth," Larry said. "In my experience, people living on Frunge worlds don't spend cash at trade fairs unless it's an emergency. Contract factory workers have the option to take part of their salary in the goods they produce at a discount off the wholesale price, so for them, it's like buying money at a discount."

"Why do the factories give them such a good deal?"

"For one thing, it's a perk in the employment contract, but it's also a good deal for the factory. Keep in mind that the production cost is dependent on scale. The more the factory produces, the cheaper the unit cost. And the production cost includes all of the overhead expenses, including R&D and financing, and then they add their marketing costs and profit to get to the wholesale price. When the workers take part of their pay in goods to barter with traders, it saves the money that the factory would have spent on packaging and shipping, not to mention reducing the risk of returns to zero. I wouldn't be surprised if the factory books a bigger profit on salary swaps than they do on sales."

"So it's not a perk at all," Georgia said.

"It's mutually beneficial," Larry told her. "Most of the advanced species offer similar deals to workers. I remember when I was thirteen and my folks threw a party at the end of a fair on a Dollnick ag world to celebrate paying off the mortgage on their ship. A bunch of alien traders came for the free drinks, and I had just gotten my implant so I was making an idiot of myself trying to talk to them all. I'd completed studying a history module about the early American coal mining industry with my teacher bot, and—"

"I had a picture book about a mine pony when I was a little girl that always made me cry."

"Don't worry, I wasn't going there. My dad usually didn't deal in foodstuffs because of all the issues with storing bulk and spoilage, but we were on our way to a Stryx station next, so he knew it wouldn't be a problem to sell a cargo of Dollnick tan tubers and a few other root vegetables. I asked one of the alien traders if the Dollys let the field workers bring home whatever they could carry, and she explained that they could buy the produce they picked at a discount in the company store."

Georgia smiled hopefully at a man whose daughter stopped to look at the educational toys, but then the girl lost interest and they moved on without a word. "It sounds like the same system as here except they were growing agricultural products rather than weaving cloth."

"Right, except I was sure I knew all about company stores from my history module. I told the Vergallian woman that the Dollnicks must be pretty mean if they made their workers shop in a company store, and I was never coming back to an ag world when I grew up," Larry said. "She asked my parents if I had a defective implant since I didn't seem to understand her, and then one of the other traders who had seen a Grenouthian documentary about coal mining on Earth—"

"No ponies," Georgia interrupted again.

"—explained to the others about how mining companies owned whole towns and the miners had to rent houses from the company and shop in the company store, making them more like serfs than free workers. That's when I learned that even the best translation implants can lead you astray when combinations of words take on a secondary meaning unique to a particular culture."

"I haven't encountered that many problems, but I only got my implant a few years ago when I started working for the Galactic Free Press. The truth is I never had that much contact with aliens on Union Station because I fell into food writing."

"That's an Earth accent if I've ever heard one," a woman wearing a Frunge power-suit addressed Georgia. "East coast, I'd say. Maybe one of the outlying communities of the New York city-state?"

"If my parents had paid taxes, they would have paid New York, but I grew up in a commune that was pretty off-the-grid. Are you interested in educational toys and games? I'm Georgia, by the way."

"Zoe," the woman said. "I've been considering taking the kids to Earth on vacation before they go too native to appreciate it, if you know what I mean."

"Have you ever heard of the Twenty-Second Century Bazaar initiative?" Larry jumped into the conversation. "EarthCent has been sponsoring low-cost package tours that can be booked through your local travel agency. I can give you a coupon for a ten percent discount."

"You can get me a discount on travel booked through a Frunge agency?"

"As long as the itinerary includes a stop at Earth. I have the coupon book in a pouch stuck to the side of my mini-register, but I've never actually done one of these before."

"Enter a null sale for tourism in the register, it will create a unique code, and you copy that onto the coupon blank," Georgia told him. "I remember you weren't paying attention when we watched the instructional holo."

"Why would a coupon need a unique code?" Zoe asked.

"When your travel agency enters it to get the discount reimbursed by EarthCent via the Stryx register network, we'll get credited with a commission," Larry told her. "It's nothing big, but I think they said the top producers will get a prize."

"And considering you're our first potential sale, you can imagine how likely that is to happen," Georgia said to the woman with a laugh. "Do your children go to school here, or do you homeschool with teacher bots?"

"Basic schooling for children is part of the twenty-year contract we're all working on," Zoe said. "The Frunge system allows us some flexibility in establishing teacher qualifications and curriculum, but they have minimum standards for science, math, and language that the schools have to meet to maintain their subsidies. If the performance slips, the Frunge can reduce their contribution and withhold it from our pay and benefits package instead, so you better believe that everybody stays involved."

"Here you go," Larry said, giving Zoe the coupon with the hand-printed code. "I've never had a reason to book a package tour myself, but I'd suggest getting to a final price before bringing out the coupon, or they might try to pad."

"Frunge travel agents are basically travel therapists, they don't have any leeway on prices one way or the other," the woman said. "Thank you for this, and if you're interested in trading for jewelry-quality chain, I work as a manufacturer's rep for the factory and I always take the maximum in chain out of my salary."

Georgia thought for a moment. "It doesn't really fit in with my merchandise, but I suppose if I'm not going to hold out for cash, I have to practice my bartering skills. Alright, I hope to see you later."

"And if there's anything I can do for you," Zoe said to Larry after tucking the coupon away.

"I'm always on the lookout for unique pieces of historical interest," he said.

"You mean you're a treasure hunter?"

"I'm hoping to find something special to display in a couple of months at Rendezvous. I was just elected head of our council last year, and it would be embarrassing to show up empty-handed."

"Do you have something I can draw on?" the woman asked.

"I've got a pad of paper here," Georgia offered.

Zoe froze, and Larry winced. "Just a little bad trader humor," he said hastily and offered the factory rep his tab. "Here, it's in art mode."

She took the tablet, cast a suspicious look at Georgia, and then began drawing a little map with her forefinger. "This is the fair, and I'll draw a little stick figure for us. If you head towards that stadium you can see past the ship parking area, there's a busy street lined with small shops. Take a right and look for Joz's Curiosities. There's a model of a Frunge passenger liner hanging out front, and the inventory is all stuff he picked up during his travels."

"He was a colonist?" Larry asked.

"Crew, and he put in six hundred years, so he accumulated some interesting stuff. Don't expect to barter with him though, it's cash only. He opened the shop a few months ago because his wife wants to downsize and their house was full. I know the family because her sister is married to the chief blacksmith at our factory."

"You have a blacksmith making jewelry chain?" Georgia asked.

"He's really our metallurgist, but the Frunge prefer being known as blacksmiths," Zoe said. "Good luck."

Larry waited until she was out of earshot and then said, "If you want to come with me, pack your stuff up. I'm going to call it a day and rent a mule bot to bring everything back to the ship so we can visit that shop before they close. Sunset is in another two hours, and the Frunge frown on night-shade retailers."

"But what if she comes back to trade with me?" Georgia protested. "I saw her eying my calculus puzzles."

"She's not coming back after your paper comment. You have to expect that people living on a Frunge world will share the local sensibilities about anything related to trees."

"I wasn't thinking. I guess it's a good thing all of the Verlock puzzles are made from obsidian or stone rather than wood."

By the time all of the goods from the two blankets had been returned to the ship and they found Joz's Curiosities, there was only an hour left before sunset. The retired Frunge purser gave them a welcome that sounded like a tree creaking in the wind and otherwise ignored the traders. Georgia browsed around the poorly lit shop without seeing anything that remotely caught her interest until she noticed a stack of plastic placards on the floor that were reminiscent of menus.

"Do you read Frunge?" a voice rasped behind her.

"I'm afraid not," Georgia replied, turning to find that the old purser hadn't lost the ability to move silently when he wished. "Are these menus?"

"I saved every Seedling Day menu for three hundred and twenty-eight years," Joz said. "My wife wanted me to throw them out, but I told her that someday they would be worth their weight in gold."

"I'm just window shopping."

"You're also the first person to ever give them a second look. My wife was right." The old Frunge kicked the stack and then swore, hopping on one foot. "Grains! I hate it when my wife is right."

"Maybe a historian would be interested," Georgia suggested. "Have you considered donating the menus to a university?"

"Fah, they're all identical, you know. Nobody cares."

"For three hundred and twenty-eight years?"

"My people are traditionalists if you haven't noticed. The Seedling Day menu on Frunge Imperial Lines hasn't changed in hundreds of thousands of years. So you're a journalist."

"I am? I mean, yes. How did you know?"

Joz pointed at the Galactic Free Press ID hanging from a lanyard around the freelancer's neck. "We were starting to see a few Human passengers before I retired, so I picked up enough Humanese to be able to read the name tags on luggage. Why your people can't use electronic tagging like the rest of the civilized galaxy is beyond me."

"But you understand English."

"Kept my purser's implant when I retired," Joz said. "It's not like they can wash it off and put it in the next guy's head."

Georgia glanced towards the back of the shop where Larry was sitting on the floor shuffling through what looked like old subway tokens. "Have you ever given an interview about your career as a purser?" she asked the old Frunge.

"Who would care?" he asked, clearly taken off guard. "Is this a gag? Did my wife put you up to coming in?"

"No. A woman named Zoe who works for—"

"Alright," Joz cut her off and headed back to his high stool behind the counter. "If you want to interview me, you better get started. When the sun goes down, dinner is on the table, and if I learned one thing in the passenger liner business it's never to be late for a meal."

"Great," Georgia said, and then she fished her tab out of her purse. "Do you mind if I record this?"

"Mind? I insist, and you'll zap me a copy before you leave. I don't want to read something in the Galactic Free Press that I never said."

"You read our paper?"

"Your what?!" the old Frunge practically screeched.

"Our, uh, text-based news service," Georgia amended herself.

"I identified your employer from your press badge." He shot a disgusted look towards the back of the shop and yelled, "If you're not going to buy any of those, I expect you to put them back just like you found them. And be careful with those map crystals."

Georgia enabled the recording function on her tab and placed it on the counter between them. "So, do you remember why you chose to pursue a career as a purser?"

The old Frunge began to laugh, a sound like sawing logs, and he clapped his hands in mirth. "Let me see," he said when he recovered his breath. "I believe I made the choice during the first long break after I started university. My father saw my grades and said, 'If you're not going to study, Joz, you may as well start working for your uncle's upholstery cleaning business.' I think he hoped that after I found out how hard it was to make an honest living I'd take school more seriously, but—what was that?" he demanded after a loud clacking from the rear of the shop.

"No damage," Larry called back. "I was looking at these glass balls and the pile in the box shifted."

"Bring them up here so I can check for chips," Joz ordered, and then turned back to Georgia. "Where was I?"

"You were dropping out of university to work for your uncle."

"I didn't drop out, I just stopped going to parties and started cleaning upholstery part-time after classes resumed. Then my uncle won a contract cleaning suborbital aircraft and I got addicted to the money."

"Cleaning jobs pay that well?"

"They have to or nobody would do them," the old Frunge told her. "You wouldn't believe all the loose change that ends up in seat cushions. To make a long story short, I got interested in accounting, changed my major at university, and began working my way up the ladder in the transportation business."

"Have you ever been to Union Station?" Georgia asked.

"What does that have to do with anything?"

"I spent my first three years working for the pa—the news service there."

"My question stands," Joz said.

"My editor told me that it's important to establish a rapport with interview subjects, so I was looking for something we might have in common. Never mind. What was your first job with Frunge Imperial Lines?"

"Upholstery cleaner. My father thought I was crazy taking a job with them when all the other accounting students were doing internships for Big Nine firms, but cleaning all those suborbital cabins had given me the wanderlust, and then I saw my future wife who was a stewardess trainee and it was all over."

"That's so romantic," Georgia said. "And you've been together for—"

"Don't remind me," Joz cut her off, and turned his glare on Larry. "Let's see them."

"No chips or cracks," the trader said, gently placing the box on the counter. "Why don't you keep them in egg-carton packing so they don't roll around?"

"Because I keep hoping some careless browser will shatter one and I'll finally get a sale," the old Frunge rasped, pulling out one of the spherical crystals that might have just fit in a standard shot glass. "I found these rolling around a stateroom a few hundred years back. The ship's lost-and-found wouldn't accept them because they only take items that they can identify. At first I held onto them because I thought the passenger might contact us, but eventually I took one to a trade fair on a Grenouthian orbital and an old collector told me they were map crystals."

"I thought they were art glass," Larry said.

"If they had a flat spot, you could use them as paperweights," Georgia contributed, and then clamped a hand over her mouth, but fortunately the old Frunge's translation implant had mapped the offensive construct to something that made sense in the local culture.

"Look at one under the data lamp," Joz said, pulling a light mounted on an articulated mechanical arm away from the wall so it would shine over the counter.

Larry closed one eye, peered into the center of the ball under the flickering light, and a look of wonder came over his face. "It's a star map."

"There are those who say that map crystals lead to the treasures of a forgotten race of explorers from before the era of the Stryx," the old Frunge said in reverential tones. "I spent many a night trying to match the patterns in these crystals with models of how the galaxy might have looked a hundred million years ago." He turned off the data lamp and looked out the shop's display window at the setting sun. "I've got to start closing up or the meat will be gone by the time I get home. What do you say to ten thousand?"

"WHAT!" Larry was so surprised that he almost dropped the map crystal on the floor, juggling it several times before cradling it safely against his body.

"Ten thousand whats?' Georgia asked.

"Frunge Imperials," Joz said, and then squinted at something on a heads-up display that only he could see. "That's eight hundred and three Stryx creds at the current exchange rate."

"Which is what I clear in a very good month," Larry said. "I was thinking more like twenty."

"Alright, two hundred Stryx creds," Joz said. "It's hard to establish a market price for items that never come on the local market. I should have sold them while I was traveling."

"Not two hundred, twenty. Maybe I could go thirty for two of them."

"Oh, you weren't interested in taking the whole lot? I could do fifty for two."

"Wait, you were offering me the whole box for two hundred? I've got one-eighty in cash."

"How much do you have?" the Frunge asked Georgia.

"Me?" She took out her change purse. "Ten, twelve, seventeen."

"A hundred and ninety-seven," Joz told Larry. "I won't charge for the interview and you can keep the box."

Nine

"What's this for?" Ellen asked, catching the holstered stunner that John tossed to her.

"You point the skinny end at the bad guys and push in the button with—"

"Don't get wise with me, buster. I want to know why you think we have to arm ourselves to visit a glorified tunnel-network junkyard."

"Alfe isn't a junkyard, it's a recycling facility," John said. "And the Sharf aren't tunnel network members, this orbital only got an exit because they give the Stryx a good deal on taking all the scrap that the other species won't accept. This is where the stuff that gets abandoned in the space lanes turns up, and there's a sovereign human community here with over a hundred thousand people."

"They aren't contract workers?" Ellen asked.

"Most of them were originally, but they stayed on to work and raise their families when the contract expired. Our people on Flower sent a tip that the Sharf set aside a safe-zone for pirates on one of the decks, so there's a thriving black market."

"Why would the Sharf be tolerant of pirates?"

"You know that the Free Republic forms a buffer zone between the Horten and Sharf empires," John said. "While the Free Republic is more of a dumping ground for the

Hortens than the Sharf, you'll spot plenty of skeletal long-necked pirates if you look past the tattoos."

"And you think that the statues stolen from Earth might show up here?"

"Nothing is that easy, but between you and me, our sources on Alfe have been mysteriously quiet about the black market. I'm sure you know what that means."

"Somebody eliminated them?" Ellen asked, and reflexively checked the charge on the stunner.

"Bought their silence is more like it," John said. "The reports still come in like clockwork—tonnage of scrapped spaceships, important visitors, registration numbers of ships passing through—but nothing about the black market."

"Oh. And some visitors from Flower just stumbled across it while they were shopping?"

"The alien spies on board Flower pool their intelligence sources to reduce their workload so they have more time to run their cover businesses," John explained. "We have a guy working as a double agent for the Sharf spy on Flower, and the black market information came from him."

"Well, at least I've never been here, but it still doesn't count as a vacation," Ellen said. "How long do we have to wait for a customs inspector?"

"Came and went while you were in the shower."

"I'll have to remember that if I ever become a smuggler. Take the contraband in the shower during inspection."

"It cost me a twenty cred bribe for the inspector to leave you in peace, but it was worth it," John said, checking the position of the throwing-knife sheath between his shoulder blades. "Once the inspector had the money he skipped going through the cargo hold. I don't know what it might have cost me if he saw Semmi because the Sharf and the Tyrellians don't get along."

Ellen followed her partner down the ladder to the cargo deck and they exited the two-man trader together. An urchin with a hand-drawn cart full of cleaning supplies was waiting at the bottom of the ramp.

"Clean your thrusters, Trader?"

"What do you charge?" John asked.

"Two creds to clean off any atmospheric residue, five creds with the anti-corrosion treatment," he said hopefully.

"What do you use?"

The boy held up a bottle of Sharf Protect 40/20, the manufacturer recommended coating.

"Is it real?" John asked. "A bottle of the genuine article would cost me ten creds on Union Station."

"There's an outlet store on Alfe," the boy said. "If you buy the factory seconds, it's only a cred a bottle. There's nothing wrong with the goop," he added hastily, "it's the laser etching of the logo on the glass that's messed up. See?"

"Tell the ship to ping me when you're done so I can check the job and pay you," John said. "I've got an enhanced controller and the outside voice pickup is on."

"Yes, sir," the boy replied, throwing the two traders a crisp salute. "If you're here for the black market, tell the lift tube you want to shop for something special."

"How did you know we were here for the black market?" Ellen blurted out.

"He looks like a cop," the boy said, "and you might want to stick that press badge in your purse, or somebody might put the bag on you both and I'll never get paid."

"Smart kid," Ellen muttered to John, removing the press ID she habitually wore as they headed for the lift tube.

"You'd think I would have remembered that from the kidnap avoidance training."

"If he does a good job with the cleaning, I'll try to recruit him"

"Doesn't EarthCent Intelligence have a minimum age?"

"We used to worry about kids putting themselves in danger, but you wouldn't believe all of the actionable intelligence that comes out of a job like his," John said. While they waited for a lift tube capsule, he asked her, "Do I really look like a cop?"

"You didn't know?" Ellen laughed. "You stand like you're at attention all the time, and you make steady eye contact with everybody you meet. Not to mention you stopped dressing like a real trader years ago."

"I did?"

"How many traders do you know that wear a dark suit with a holster under the left arm and a bulge on the ankle?"

"We're supposed to carry a backup piece in situations like this," John said.

"I'd rather have Semmi along."

"I just hope she's not running up the streaming charges again to get even for being cooped up in her crate."

"You should have encouraged her to at least come out and stretch her wings. There's plenty of room on the cargo deck."

"I tried, but she ignored me. That's why I'm worried."

The lift tube capsule finally arrived, and after they stepped in, Ellen said, "We'd like to do some special shopping."

"Do you mean you'd like to shop for something special?" the orbital's AI inquired. "We don't get a lot of EarthCent Intelligence agents or Galactic Free Press reporters visiting except for when Flower stops, and then all bets are off."

"Yeah, something special," John said, and couldn't help himself from asking, "How did you make us?"

"You've both got high-grade implants, your reporter friend didn't disable the transponder on her press badge, and you look like a cop."

"Thanks," Ellen said, getting out her Galactic Free Press ID again and squeezing the dimple-switch to kill the power. "Is the black market here well-known?"

"You wouldn't be here if it weren't. I'm required to inform you that the deck is a Free Republic safe zone, which means safe for them, not for you."

"Thanks. If you have any information that leads to a story—"

"Information is cash in advance," the AI said as the capsule door opened. "And if you buy anything expensive, mention that Ada sent you and I'll receive a finder's fee. But if you get in trouble, you don't know me."

"John, I have a feeling we're not in Kansas anymore," Ellen muttered a few seconds later. "I don't like the looks of that Farling selling pills."

"She's an outcast, you can tell by the yellow highlights on her carapace," he said, glancing at the giant beetle. "That direction looks like it's all drugs and weapons, so let's try this way."

"Oh good, out of the frying pan and into the pawnshop."

"I think the term you're looking for is fences, and you keep telling me I need new socks." John approached a table piled with prepackaged socks for men in the old Earth-size of 6-12. "Miss?" he called to the underdressed young woman who was ignoring them to talk with the young man selling leather jackets in the adjoining space.

"Are you buying, or are you just going to ask me stupid questions about which pirate attacked what freighter?" she demanded without coming over.

"I need socks, but I don't see a price."

"Two creds a pack."

"That's twelve pairs?" John asked.

"Six pairs. The twelve refers to the total number of socks."

"Oh, they aren't that cheap."

"One-fifty, but that's as low as I'm going. All the best socks come from the Chintoo orbital."

"I think they smell a bit like burnt electronics," Ellen said, replacing a package on the table.

"Maybe the freighter captain didn't want to be boarded," John speculated.

"One-thirty, but I don't make change," the young woman offered, coming over to close the sale. "How many packages are you taking?"

"Six pairs of socks goes a long way with me," John said, handing over a five-cred piece. "That's yours to keep if you can save me a little time with the rest of my shopping."

She gave him a speculative look, and her eyes shifted to the bulge under his left arm. "I got the socks from a legitimate wholesaler. They sell better with the spray-on-space-battle smell and the piracy backstory. Makes shoppers think they're getting a deal."

"I'm actually more interested in collectibles from Earth than plundered cargos," John told her quietly. "Have you seen anything interesting lately?"

"You're also looking for silverware and place settings?" the young woman replied at her normal volume with the addition of an exaggerated wink. "All the way down to the next spoke, and then spinward past the antiques section."

"Thank you," John said, taking a package of socks.

Ellen bumped along close by his side as if they were a romantic couple doing some honeymoon shopping. "Is this what you normally do when I'm not with you? Go around offering money to attractive young women?"

"Most of my job consists of paying for information one way or another," he said in an undertone. "This probably isn't the best place to discuss techniques."

"Do you think she was telling the truth about buying the socks from a wholesaler?"

"Can't imagine why she'd lie, and I've heard about manufacturers on Chintoo who specialize in pre-distressed goods that look like space salvage for the very reason she gave. People love a backstory that makes them think they're getting a special deal."

"Two commercial-grade Dollnick stunners, a lethal projectile gun on your ankle, a throwing knife in a neck sheath, and that looks like a can of mace in the purse," a Horten holding a tab in one hand and what looked like a dish antenna on a stick in the other said in a conversational voice. "Let me guess. A cop and a reporter posing as traders?"

"Who are you?" John asked, closing the distance in case hand-to-hand combat became appropriate.

"Dorna, of Dorna's Police Scanners," the Horten said. "I've got a version that's plug-n-play with Sharf two-man traders so you'll never be surprised by a guest packing heat. What's your ride?"

"You're three for three," the EarthCent Intelligence agent admitted. "It's not what I'm shopping for today, but let's hear the price."

"Posing as a trader and you aren't even going to try to barter?"

"I thought the market was all cash."

"It is, but I used to do some undercover work myself, and I learned it always pays to stay in character," the Horten said. "Retail to government customers, I get ninety creds in bulk for the scanners. I could let you have a single unit for that."

"Does it come with the tab?" John asked.

"Don't be greedy."

"I don't have my tab with me," John told Ellen. "Let's try it with yours."

The Galactic Free Press reporter shook her head at how badly their cover was blown, but the black market was starting to feel more like a tourist trap than a danger zone, so she pulled out her custom reporter's tab and accepted the dish antenna. The near-field protocol recognized the new device and a message came up asking, "Install Dorna's Police Scanner?"

"My tab has the scanner in the built-in support set," she told John while swiping to accept. "How come I've never seen one of these before?"

"You probably have but didn't notice," the Horten told her. "We've sold tens of millions of these to law enforcement and private security firms."

She pointed the antenna at the salesman and boggled at the array of lethal hardware secreted about his body. "Do you carry all that stuff just to prove the scanner works?"

"I like to be prepared," he said.

Ellen handed the tab and the antenna to John, who tried to be subtle as he scanned a few passersby. The amount of concealed weaponry exceeded his expectations. "Can you sharpen your pencil a little?" he asked the Horten.

"You want me to stab you with it? The price is the price."

"I have a question," Ellen said. "If you've sold millions of these scanners, what are you doing standing around a place like this trying to sell one at a time?"

"Dorna was my great-great—I don't know how many generations back—grandfather's name. Somebody in the direct male line always gets stuck with it, and the position happened to be available when I was born. But after I dropped out of university to pursue a career in professional gaming, my father cut off my allowance. I'm lucky if they send me a shipment of factory seconds on my Naming Day."

"You mean this is a quality control reject?" John asked, returning the tab to Ellen and examining the antenna assembly closely.

"Factory second means it failed the first QC test, but they took it apart, fixed it, and then it was fine," the Horten said. "The Drazens would sell them as new, but we have higher standards."

"Do you take programmable creds?"

Dorna snatched back the antenna. "Cash only. There's a Thark moneychanger in the precious metals section who will make the exchange for you. It's just past the looted cutlery."

"Am I the only one getting the feeling that this black market is just a marketing ploy?" Ellen asked John as they turned left at the structural spoke, which was the omnipresent design component of cylindrical space structures.

"Do you think that shady Farling was only selling cold remedies and hangover meds?" John asked. "We can check on the way out, but the weapons I've seen are real enough, so I'm guessing we're just seeing market forces in action.

It's got to be easier to make a living with a regular supply chain than counting on pirates for stolen goods."

"I hadn't thought of it that way."

"Keep your eyes open for anything that might have come from Earth, though it's not looking promising."

"Hey, what about that grandfather clock?" Ellen asked a minute later.

"The what?"

"The grandfather clock," she repeated, pointing at the towering wood and glass cabinet that was surrounded by more modern looking mechanical contrivances from other species. "The managing editor of the Galactic Free Press is from Earth and he has one in his office. Hildy had one too, now that I think of it."

"What's with the plumb bob swinging back and forth?" John asked. "Does that mean it's out of level?"

"It's a pendulum, that's how those clocks keep time. I thought you knew all about mechanical stuff."

"The need to tell time with a pendulum hasn't crept up," he said, circling the cabinet. "I wonder—"

"Can I help you?" a well-dressed woman in her mid-fifties asked. "That's my favorite piece you're looking at, and I'll be sorry to see it go."

"How does something like a grandfather clock find its way into a market on a Sharf recycling orbital?" Ellen asked her.

"Ah, do you want the story about how it was stolen from a colonial home in a restored tourist village on Earth?"

"Really?"

"Or, I have one about the last scion of a wealthy family selling off his treasured inheritance for a scrap of bread."

"How about the real story?" John asked.

"It's a replica, manufactured by the Dollnicks," the woman said.

"So you were kidding about being sorry if somebody bought it," Ellen said.

"Not at all." She touched a hidden button in the fancy carved side panel, and the whole thing swung open to reveal a full-length mirror. A tray with a complete makeup kit slid out from behind the large clock face, the hands of which operated without a bulky mechanical drive. "The pendulum is just for show."

"If I wanted to buy an authentic grandfather clock, do you know where I might get one?" John asked.

"Oh, so you're them," the woman said.

"We're who?" Ellen asked.

"The EarthCent Intelligence agent and the Galactic Free Press reporter. There was an announcement over the public address system when your ship came in."

"You mean everybody here knows who we are?"

"Unless they weren't paying attention. Excuse me, I think I see a real customer."

"I'm going to be having a word with that artificial intelligence when we get back to the lift tube," John said angrily. "She must have sold us out when I handed over navigational control."

"But we're registered as traders," Ellen said.

"And anybody who does even a cursory background check will find out that I won a seat in the Guild's last election running as an EarthCent Intelligence agent. Either I need a fake identity or I'm going to have to give up undercover work anywhere that has access to tunnel network data."

"You're getting too old for that sort of thing anyway," Ellen said unsympathetically as they wandered in the general direction of the Thark moneychanger.

"And how about your investigative journalism?"

"I never get anywhere undercover. I do best when I tell people who I am. Maybe the same thing would work for you."

"Sometimes it does, sometimes it doesn't." John handed his programmable cred to the Thark, who slotted it into a Stryx register and nodded in approval.

"How much do you want?" the wrinkly alien asked.

"A hundred creds."

"Buying a weapons scanner?"

"Why does everybody here know more about my business than I do!" John exploded.

"Just an educated guess," the Thark said, offering a wink. "Don't forget to tell Dorna that Ada sent you so she can get her commission."

"I'm not feeling that generous after she outed us to the whole orbital."

"Just the market vendors," the Thark assured him. "We all pay her protection money."

"What kind of artificial intelligence runs a Sharf orbital and extorts the black market vendors?" Ellen asked.

"The rich kind," John answered before the money-changer could reply, and the alien nodded in agreement.

"I assume you're here about the recently discovered thefts on Earth that made the Grenouthian news," the Thark said. "You show admirable energy visiting public markets, but I put in my time as an insurance adjustor, and finding stolen goods for sale is always a long shot. We focused on developing relationships with snitches, active surveillance for catching thieves before they can get away, and no-questions-asked rewards for recovering priceless artifacts."

"Active surveillance? But we don't have any leads on who to watch."

"Not who, what," the Thark said. "I let my auxiliary membership in ISPOA expire so I don't have access to their data anymore, but from what the Grenouthians reported, the thefts on Earth are ongoing. All you have to do is establish a pattern and figure out where the thieves are going to hit next."

"EarthCent doesn't have a law-enforcement presence on Earth," John said.

"So you're stuck with snitches or going in undercover," the Thark said. "Lose the suit and you could almost pass as Human."

"Now there's something you don't hear every day," Ellen said. "Any advice for me?"

"Follow the money."

"I've heard that one before."

"That doesn't make it any less true," the Thark growled. "Now go away, you're scaring off my customers."

Ten

When Georgia walked into the ore-sorting room which had been temporarily vacated for traders, she silently thanked Larry for talking her into bringing the old blanket to lay out her wares. Although the deck had been cleaned of rock dust, the metal plates were scratched, pitted, and discolored, and the fancy blanket would have looked terribly out of place.

"Finally, somebody who isn't pushing prospecting gear, weapons, or canned food," a neighboring trader commented when Georgia started laying out her goods. "Puzzles and games just might work for you here."

Georgia looked over at her friendly neighbor's blanket and saw an assortment of drill bits for hard rock asteroid mining, a selection of Dollnick stunners running from the disposable models to the commercial-grade, and a pyramid of tinned fish. Then she glanced at the blanket of her neighbor on the left, who was offering freeze-dried vegetables, and Drazen mining lamps with rechargeable batteries.

"My partner told me that the number of families on Break Rock has shot up in the last couple of years," she said. "He'll be here later with children's shoes and clothes, but he got roped into holding an impromptu Guild session in the docking bay when we landed."

"You're with Larry, Phil's son?" the woman with the blanket to her left asked. "I heard over the grapevine that he was on his way here. That guy gets around even more than his father did."

"Larry's made a point of visiting as many sovereign human communities as possible this year, since he got stuck on some advisory committees after the Traders Guild joined the Human Empire," Georgia said, setting out a science kit. "Why is this place so empty?"

"They run three shifts on the habitat, and you got here between the third and the first. The second shift is turning in for their night around now, but the third shift will start trickling in after they clean up and have their suppers."

"And the first shifters are all in work?"

"The prospectors and miners who sleep here are heading out to the asteroids now, but the ore sorters have the day off since we're in their space and it's a half-holiday on Break Rock."

"What's a half-holiday?" Georgia asked.

"Take it if you want it," the trader explained. "Even though Break Rock adopted Universal Human Time, they don't really do weekends here because so many of the occupants are short-timers hoping for a lucky strike. You burn through cash pretty quickly when the food, air, and water are all imported, so the newbies tend to work every day until they either make it or give up."

"I get it," she said. Georgia inspected the cargo-carrying section of the rented mule bot to make sure she hadn't missed anything before pressing the return button, and the mule bot began the trip back to the landing bay in the habitat's core, where it would rejoin the line of rentals.

"What age group are you targeting with those toys?" the trader with the drill bits asked.

"I have something for all ages, from two-year-olds right up through a prep game for the Advanced Species Aptitude Tests," Georgia said. "Do you have children?"

"No, which may explain why I don't recognize any of that stuff. Whatever happened to building blocks?"

"I had aluminum building blocks, the kind with numbers and letters on them, but a shopkeeper bought them all from me to spell things out in a display window. Have you ever seen a Diff Kit?"

"I've never even heard of one," the trader said.

"It's this," Georgia said, picking up a section of what looked like the approach to a jump for a toy racecar. "You choose the function on the control panel to describe the curve. Then you set the initial conditions, and you can use a straight edge to establish the slope of the tangent and get the derivative at any given point."

"What did you call it again?"

"A Diff Kit, for teaching Differential Equations," she said enthusiastically. "I wasn't that interested in math when I was in school, but it all makes sense when you can see it happening with your own eyes."

"Are you sure they didn't name it that for Difficult Equations?" the trader to her left asked.

"Oh no, that's what the kids say about the NonLin Kit, for Non-Linear Differential Equations. Human kids, I mean," she added and began unboxing another toy. "Verlock children learn this stuff before they even start school."

"Got anything more suitable for two-year-olds with average parents?" a voice asked.

Georgia looked up to see a man dressed in the all-black uniform favored by many mercenaries. He was wearing a six-pointed sheriff's badge.

"Rick," the newcomer introduced himself. "The twins won't be two for a few more months, but you're the first trader I've seen with educational toys, and my wife is already talking about quitting her job and starting a daycare."

"Are you really a sheriff?"

"Break Rock's chief of police, though half of my salary is paid by Eccentric Enterprises. I was part of a pilot program to bring law enforcement to sovereign communities on space habitats like this where there weren't any alien police. Is that a spelling game?"

"This?" Georgia held up a flat board on which letter tiles could be moved in two dimensions. "I suppose you could use it for that."

"What's it really for?" the female trader asked.

"It's a basic cryptography training toy. I haven't quite figured out how it works myself, but it came with a holographic instructional manual. According to the manufacturer it's intended for ages six and above, but that's Verlock ages."

"We'll make that our fallback position," Rick said. "What else do you have?"

"If your wife is really thinking of opening a daycare, you'll want something that works for multiple ages, doesn't have any choking hazards, and is nearly indestructible," Georgia mused. "How about a shape matching game?"

"Do you mean like putting a square piece of wood in a square cut-out? Wouldn't the kids get tired of that pretty quick?"

"These are made from Verlock memory metal and are fully programmable," she said, pulling a velvet sack out of a box and dumping a dozen oddly shaped lumps onto the blanket. "The one with the biggest flat side is always the controller."

"So the pieces change shapes?" the police chief asked.

"Most Verlock educational toys have a programmable component because their children outgrow them too quickly otherwise," Georgia said. "I do have some high-end puzzle games with rock or obsidian pieces, but those are for older age groups. With this," she elevated one of the metal pieces, "you can select from millions of preprogrammed shapes, and there's an upload port that allows you to add your own."

"I think the basic millions would do it for us."

"But you can also clump all of the pieces together and use them for virtual sculpting. I shopped for these with the woman who represents the sovereign human community on Fyndal, and she told me she still uses her MMK, that's short for Memory Metal Kit, at least once a week."

"Now I know I can't afford it on a policeman's salary," Rick said.

"Memory metal is cheap on Verlock worlds. I can let you have the whole kit for thirty-five creds," Georgia said. "Or if you'd rather barter I'm open to taking ore as long as it's been assayed."

"I'm supposed to check with my wife before I spend more than half a day's pay on anything."

"You make less than seventy creds a day as police chief?"

"I get free lodging and there's a decent retirement plan," Rick admitted.

Georgia glanced around the hall, which was still largely empty of shoppers due to the shift change. "How about thirty creds and an interview?" she offered.

"Who are you with?" he asked.

"Oh, sorry." She fished inside her jumpsuit and brought out her Galactic Free Press ID.

"Georgia Hunt," he read. "Sounds familiar. Do you work the crime beat?"

"I contributed to a story about mortgage fraud in two-man trader financing last year," Georgia said. "Plus I wrote about the attempted assassination of the reporter I was working with at the last Rendezvous."

"That must be where I saw your name. Sure, I'll go twenty-five creds for the MMK and throw in an interview. What do you want to talk about?"

"Just a second," Georgia said, stretching her memory and math skills to figure the profit margin at twenty-five when converting from salt cod to memory metal to Stryx creds. "Okay, you have a deal. Do you want to sit down?"

"I spent the day patrolling the asteroids in Zero-G, so I'm better off standing and getting a little exercise if it doesn't bother you that I keep moving," Rick said.

"I spend a quarter of my life in Zero-G myself, so we can both stand. You don't mind if I record this on my tab?"

"I prefer speaking on the record."

"Excellent," Georgia said, and then realized she didn't know where to start. "Have you ever been interviewed about your job here before?"

"The first time Flower returned after dropping us off, so about six months into the job. Break Rock was having a serious problem with claim jumping, and organized crime was gaining a foothold, but it only took us a few months to eliminate the bad actors. EarthCent set us up with a few military surplus Vergallian patrol ships equipped with armored spacesuits, which were more than enough to outgun the competition."

"So why were you patrolling today?"

"Showing the flag. We recently returned two of our three patrol craft to Flower so they'd be available for deployment to other sovereign communities, and half of my starting personnel have moved on to other hotspots as well. But we still see our share of the usual crimes, though I'll take that every day over the domestic violence calls."

"Why does your badge have six points?" Georgia asked.

"Excuse me?"

"I'm trying to learn how to salt my interviews with off-beat questions."

"Oh, then I'll give you a long answer," Rick said with a grin. "For starters, Eccentric Enterprises let recruits to the police program vote on whether we wanted to wear shields or stars, and stars won by a landslide. As to the number of points, I've heard that back when sheriffs and badges first became a thing, manufacturing stars with six points was easier than five or seven due to the symmetry."

"And what are the usual crimes you spoke of?" Georgia asked.

"Back to business, huh? Well, we respond to a lot of pings in the Red Light district—sex, drugs, and alcohol can be a toxic mix. We see drunks getting rolled for their cash, crooked card games, and confidence men, but we're here to protect the people who want to be protected, not to tell everyone how to live."

"Is there organized crime on Break Rock?"

"We broke up some gangs when I first got here, but these days the criminal networks try to keep a low profile because of Break Rock's value as a transshipment point."

"I'm not familiar with the term," Georgia said. "Are you talking about moving contraband goods?"

"Contraband or stolen," Rick said. "Think about it. No criminal in his right mind will try to ship anything illegal by way of a tunnel network station because the Stryx will just seize it. And alien worlds and space structures all have customs inspectors of one sort or another, so even if the goods can get through, it will cost a lot in bribes. And Break Rock is on Flower's regular circuit, which means that twice a year we get access to low-cost shipping to and from Earth."

"Ahhh," Georgia said, her eyes lighting up. "So criminals looking for a cheap way to move stolen goods off of Earth can include them in a shipment for Break Rock, and then the receiver on this end can—what?"

"Break Rock gets regular visits from jump carriers that take ore to refining facilities, including for species who aren't part of the tunnel network. Keep in mind our own tunnel exit is new—the Stryx only put it in when the population and productivity took off."

"Do you know John, the EarthCent Intelligence guy on the Traders Guild council?"

"We've met," Rick said. "Is he a friend of yours?"

"We spent a few days together at the last Rendezvous and he's the only person in your line of work I know," Georgia said. "Does that make you feel more comfortable answering my questions?"

"I was pretty comfortable already," the police chief said with a laugh. "I saw John's name on a bulletin that came through just a few weeks ago asking everybody to keep an eye out for stolen statues."

"I read a story about it in our paper. I suppose it would be really easy to hide stone statues in a load of ore."

"Probably, but as far as I know, most of the aliens only scan cargo for weapons, hazardous waste, and potentially invasive species of flora and fauna, though a lot of that is handled with irradiation rather than inspection."

"How about here?" Georgia asked.

"Off the record?"

The reporter hit 'stop' on her tab and showed it to him.

"We don't scan for anything, so hopefully nobody mails us a bomb," Rick said. "We just don't have the manpower, and when the Frunge leased this habitat to the humans who had finished a long-term contract working here, the artificial intelligence that ran the infrastructure went elsewhere. Our governing council has started a search for an experienced AI willing to work for what we can afford to pay, but they haven't had any luck yet." He gestured at her tab. "You can start recording again."

"So back to the stolen goods coming through Break Rock, does any particular shipment stand out in your memory?"

"Yes, but before I tell you that story, keep in mind that whatever we discover is only the tip of the iceberg. Every time Flower stops here she drops off thousands of tons of canned and packaged foodstuffs from Earth, so your guess is as good as mine how many special—" he made air quotes around the word, "—cases and barrels get through containing something other than what's on the label. And just because a container of mining boots or back massagers shows up with an invoice, who knows whether they were legally obtained on Earth? We just don't have the systems in place yet to deal with electronic record forgeries."

"I hadn't realized it was such a problem," Georgia said. "When I think of organized crime, I think of drugs, prostitution, and extortion, not canned food and sleeping bags."

"Criminals aren't picky, they'll steal anything they can sell, which brings us back to my story," Rick said. "About three months ago, I got a ping from one of the stevedores on the docking deck about a cargo of panels for prefab homes with a bill of lading for a Drazen open world. These panels were strapped together in stacks to make up the size of a standard shipping container, but the banding broke on one stack and the pile slipped. While the stevedores were restacking them by hand, they noticed that a few panels were much heavier than the others."

"Meaning something other than insulation was inside the panels."

"Exactly. Normally we wouldn't have given a shipment like that a second look because it's none of our business. But I went down there with a hand-held metal detector to see if somebody was smuggling obvious contraband, like weapons."

"How would a metal detector tell you if there were weapons?" Georgia asked. "My dad used to wander around our commune looking for old coins when I was a kid and it just beeped for any metal."

"This is a Frunge metal detector, it's more like an X-ray machine, though don't ask me to explain the physics. It's no good at seeing light metals inside heavier metals, like magnesium inside iron, but in this case, the panels were skinned with aluminum and what the criminals were shipping was lead."

"Lead? Were they using it to shield radioactive waste or something?"

"Nope, it was stolen goods, stained glass windows to be precise," Rick said. "If the bill of lading had listed them as stained glass windows shipped in protective aluminum casings, nobody would have given it a second thought. Since they were supposed to be prefab panels, I put a hold on the shipment and sent a request to EarthCent Intelligence to check on the matter with Earth."

"And the windows were on a hotlist for stolen goods?"

"Nope. The cathedral they had been stolen from was undergoing renovation and the windows had been removed for safekeeping. Nobody had any idea they'd been stolen from the warehouse, but the architect was documenting every step of the job for a journal, and EarthCent Intelligence has some pretty good image matching capabilities at this point."

"Has anybody published a story about this yet?" Georgia asked. "Our readers love a happy ending."

"Well, they'll have to wait another half a year or so for that. Intergalactic shipping isn't cheap, and Flower had already moved on. We have to store the panels until she returns, and then she'll deliver them on her next Earth stop."

"Oh, that must have put a real crimp in the restoration schedule"

"Not in the slightest. I asked EarthCent to send me the relevant journal articles just to satisfy my curiosity, and the restoration is scheduled to take a decade. The cathedral was around a thousand years old, and it probably took over a hundred years to build when they originally put it up."

"A hundred years!" Georgia looked skeptical. "I never heard of any construction jobs lasting that long on Earth. It would take multiple generations of workers."

"Apparently the church was patient and the freemasons liked their job security," the police chief said. "I've got imaging of the stained glass from the panels we cut open, but you should probably check with the architect before publishing them."

"I can't imagine that colonists trying to start a mining operation in the outback of some Drazen open world were the ultimate destination for stolen stained glass. Did EarthCent Intelligence track down the shipper or figure out the ultimate destination for the load?"

"EarthCent Intelligence doesn't have any jurisdiction on Earth. The thieves must have had an inside man at the prefab manufacturer because they knew when those panels were ready for shipment. They broke into the manufacturer's warehouse to remove some of the insulation and bedded the stained glass down for a nice trip up to orbit on the space elevator."

"I'll call them the Warehouse Gang in the story."

"That's not far from the truth," Rick said. "As to the ultimate destination, we can only assume that the same thing in reverse was scheduled to happen once the shipment reached Two Mountains. A gang member with warehouse access would break in, steal the goods, and then off they go to a collector."

Somebody tugged on Georgia's arm, and she looked over to see a boy of eleven or twelve bursting with impatience. "Are you through talking?" he asked. "I want to try the Diff Kit and my mom said I had to ask you first."

"I didn't know you were there," she apologized, and then the boy's question sank in. "You know what a Diff Kit is?"

"Of course. My parents promised to get me one. I'm a prodigal."

Georgia retrieved the Diff Kit from her blanket while processing this last statement. "Do you mean a prodigy?"

"That too," he said. "I spent two years in boarding school on Flower because my parents were staying out on their claim for a week at a time and there wasn't anybody here to take care of me. They've got more money now and I'm big enough to be home alone, so I'm going to live half a year here and a half a year on Flower going forward."

"Can your parents afford sixty creds?" Georgia asked.

"Forty," the boy said, sticking out his lower jaw. "I can mail-order from the Verlock academy supplier on Flower for thirty-eight, so you're only saving us the shipping."

Georgia laughed and ruffled the boy's hair. "You're a prodigy at something, alright."

Eleven

"We're not going in Walter's office?" Ellen asked the freelance editor when they turned right instead of left at the end of the corridor.

"He pinged me just before you arrived and said that our publisher wants to sit in, so we're meeting in her office," Roland said. "You know Chastity, don't you?"

"We've met a couple of times at events, but just in passing. She doesn't use her last name around the office?"

"It's Papamarkakis. Would you?"

"Point taken. I'm not in trouble, am I?"

"Not since you quit drinking," Roland said, steering her to an office, the doors of which slid open at their approach.

"Welcome," Chastity greeted them, rising from her desk chair. "If the two of you will sit on the couch, Walter prefers the overstuffed armchair, and I use the Vergallian stander because I sit too much. He'll be here in a minute."

"Do those standers help?" Ellen asked. "I tried one for a day and I ended up with pains in muscles I didn't even know I had."

"They're really intended for ballroom dancers," Chastity explained as she stepped into the framework of padded torsion bars. "The stander forces you to work the appropriate muscle groups, but if you aren't already in tango shape, I imagine it could be a strain."

The doors slid open again, and the managing editor entered, carrying two short rods in one hand. "Good morning, don't get up," Walter said, leaning over to offer Ellen a quick handshake. "How long are you staying on Union Station?"

"Just today," she said. "We were on our way back to Earth but we stopped for supplies, and my partner got called in to EarthCent Intelligence for a meeting. I pinged Roland to let him know I was here and he asked me to come right over."

"Serendipitous timing," Walter said, settling into his favorite chair. Then he transferred one of the rods to his other hand and pulled them apart, causing a holographic scroll to extend between the handles. "What do you make of this?"

"It looks like stained glass from a church on Earth," Ellen said. "Isn't that one Abraham binding Isaac to sacrifice on an altar?"

"I told you she'd get it," Roland said smugly.

"I've never seen a holographic scroll before," Ellen continued. "Is it something the Earth tourism groups are putting out to promote pilgrimages, or are you thinking of publishing the Galactic Free Press on scrolls?"

"We're looking into it," Chastity said. "It would be the perfect alternative for people who hate reading on tabs."

"They aren't in mass production yet," Walter said. "I got this set from the Horten ambassador when his uncle requested beta testers for the active display version. The original product included a scanner in one handle, but all it could do was display scanned scrolls from memory. This version is fully networked so it can build the hologram out of any properly formatted data stream."

"Ellen is short on time, so perhaps we could save the technical discussion for a later date," Roland said. "The reason Walter has those stained glass images on his scroll is that we'll be running them as part of a story going out in the next edition. Your friend Georgia got the scoop, if you can call it that, while visiting Break Rock."

"Why wouldn't you call it a scoop if nobody else has reported on it yet?" Ellen asked.

"Because the crime—the stained glass getting stolen from a warehouse on Earth—took place almost a year ago, and nobody even knew the windows were missing before they were recovered by the police on Break Rock," Walter explained. "Our ed board had an interesting discussion over whether it should run in the crime section, the arts and architecture section, or as a weekend historical piece."

"I guess I don't have an opinion."

"That's fine," Walter said. "What do you think about staying on Earth until Rendezvous to follow up on the crime spree? While your syndicate reporters have begun digging up some interesting stand-alone stories, they're all focused on their individual coverage areas. We think somebody needs to take a whole-Earth look at the problem, and you're the ideal journalist to get to the bottom of it."

"You mean, staying on Earth for over a month?" Ellen frowned. "I'd have to discuss it with my partner. We've been keeping our visits to a week, and you know that working as a trader is only his cover job for EarthCent Intelligence. He hates spending time on Earth because it's outside his jurisdiction."

"Don't ask me how I know this, but I understand that the EarthCent president's office has obtained temporary permission for John to operate on four out of seven of Earth's continents," Chastity said.

"Does that include the empty one?"

"Antarctica?" The publisher of the Galactic Free Press stared off into space for a moment, obviously checking something on her heads-up display. "No, he's set for North and South America, Europe, and Asia."

"I hope he wasn't planning on surprising me," Ellen said.

"He's finding out about it in his meeting as we speak."

"Can I bring in Georgia and get her special assignment pay? We work well together, and her partner, Larry, probably needs to get to Earth early to make arrangements for Rendezvous before Flower arrives."

"Consider it done," Roland said. "I'll reach out to her with the offer right after this meeting."

"But you know I don't have any sources on Earth," Ellen continued. "I can't count on the journalists in the syndicate to share with me because they have to put their own stories first."

"So that's the other reason we're meeting in my office," Chastity said. "I have a list of interested parties you can contact on Earth. They're all on deep background and you'll have to agree not to reveal their names to anybody."

"Including Georgia and John?"

"Including Georgia and especially John," Chastity said. "EarthCent Intelligence has its sources and we have ours."

"I suppose that's fair," Ellen said, and then pointed at her ear. "Oh, I didn't know you could do that."

"I'm not doing it myself," Chastity told her. "I asked the station librarian to do a secure ping and data transfer. The service is available to everybody, but it's not cheap."

"I accepted," Ellen said. "What now?"

"Send the data to your heads-up display, but don't read any of the names out loud. This office is as secure as we can make it, but that doesn't mean one or more of the advanced species aren't listening in."

"Roland and I are familiar with the implications of the list, but not the specific names," Walter said while Ellen boggled at the information being superimposed over her retinas. "You understand why secrecy is necessary."

"And while these sources won't expect cash payments, don't be surprised if they ask for other favors," Chastity said. "You have the authority to make modest promises in my name. Just don't give away the paper."

"My idea of wheeling and dealing is limited to the cargo I can fit on a two-man trader," Ellen said. "I'll keep it sane."

"And be careful following up on their leads as well," Walter said. "If you start doing investigative fieldwork, we'd feel better if you brought John along."

"You know that anything he learns would go straight to EarthCent Intelligence."

"We aren't in competition with them, other than for employees," Chastity said with a wicked grin. "I'm not worried about them ruining a story by stopping a crime."

"Didn't you mention something about an urgent appointment?" Roland asked the freelancer.

Ellen checked the time on her implant. "Drat! Now I'm in for it. Is there anything else we need to talk about?"

"We're all set," Chastity said. "Late for a date?"

"John dropped our gryphon off at the groomer to have her talons trimmed and I'm picking her up. I clipped a claw too short the first time I tried, and now she hides in her crate if I even go near the grooming kit," Ellen said as she headed for the door. "I'll keep Roland posted."

As soon as she was in the corridor, Ellen broke into a jog and didn't let up until she was in the lift tube. "Claws and Maws," she requested. Then Ellen unconsciously settled into a standing sprinter's stance, waiting for the doors to open. As soon as the capsule arrived, she ran down the corridor dodging reptiles more than twice her size, one of whom passed a comment about rude humanoids. When she reached the salon, Semmi was in the waiting room, watching the station advertising loop on a display panel and refusing to look in the journalist's direction.

"Did you have to wait long?" Ellen asked, feeling like a parent who had forgotten about picking up a child.

The gryphon continued to ignore her, but flexed the muscles in her front paws, causing the talons to extend.

"What a great nail job," Ellen said enthusiastically. "Did you pick the colors yourself?"

Semmi finally deigned to look in the freelancer's direction, gave a derisive snort, and clicked her beak. Ellen mechanically reached in her purse and produced a treat, which she tossed to the gryphon.

The groomer, who strangely enough was human, came out from the back with a high-speed rotary buffer in one hand. "Sorry about that," he said to the gryphon. "The rechargeable battery was dead, but I found a spare and got it working." He pressed a button on the buffer and it made a sound like a dentist's drill.

"She's not done yet?" Ellen asked.

"You're her other human? The man who dropped her off asked me to do her beak while she was here. Doesn't she have a feaking post?"

"A what?"

"For rubbing her beak. It's the avian version of brushing teeth, though maybe there's a different term for gryphons since they're more mammal than bird."

"I've seen her scrape her beak on the corner of her crate, but I thought she just liked the way it felt."

"She probably does, and it helps slough off the old bits of beak. They're always growing a new layer, you know, just like our skin."

"I really need to get a book about gryphons," Ellen said, mainly to herself.

"Let's go, back on the platform," the man instructed Semmi in a firm voice. The gryphon took her time getting up, but she surprised Ellen by otherwise complying without making a fuss. "Well, I've never tried this before, so open wide and tell me if you're not comfortable," the man continued. He activated the buffing tool and started dressing the edge of the gryphon's open beak.

"Her tail is swishing—that means she likes it," Ellen said.

"She's got a little chipping here that's almost healed, as if she tried eating something inorganic."

"A building security drone. She spit it out."

"If you want to try this at home with a dremel kit, the key is to stroke with the tool so the heat doesn't build up too much in one spot on the beak," the groomer said, switching to the other side.

"How did you get started on this career?" Ellen couldn't help asking.

"I was a farrier for the mercenary cavalry on a Vergallian tech-ban world," the man continued, casually fending off Semmi's paw when she tried to pull him closer to keep the buffer on a particularly itchy spot. "I spent years filing hooves on twitchy horses, and the royals on those worlds keep giant war-raptors with beaks even larger than this one."

"She's still growing."

The man gave Ellen a sympathetic look. "Well, if you move to an agricultural planet, you'll never have to worry about a sheep infestation. How is she in flight?"

"Incredibly graceful," Ellen said. "You'd never guess her glide wingspan by looking at her when they're all folded up. It's almost as if she has hinges in her bones."

"The Huktra do, so it wouldn't surprise me. They keep their wings short for serious beating to get off the ground, and then they extend them for gliding once they catch an updraft. Here, do you want to try it?"

Ellen looked at the rotary buffer the man extended, and then at Semmi, who cringed. "I think she'd rather I just watch and learn."

"They never forget getting a talon clipped short, but Semmi might feel differently about the beak."

"Maybe another time," Ellen said, and the gryphon relaxed visibly. "How much do I owe you?"

"Her other human paid when he dropped her off."

Semmi did a rapid series of clicks, and Ellen fished in her purse and brought out two creds. "Is it okay to tip the owner?"

"She's done a good job click-training you," the man said, pocketing the coins. "And you're very generous. I only charge five creds for the standard appointment, and beaks go a lot faster than teeth and fangs."

"You're a braver man than I," she said, gesturing for the gryphon to get down from the platform. "Let's go, Semmi. You can preen at home."

Ellen made it about five steps from Claws and Maws before she realized the gryphon had gone in the opposite direction. She hurried back and caught up just as Semmi entered a specialty food store. The owner, who was a Huktra, greeted the gryphon by name and brought out a large sack from under the counter.

"I was beginning to worry that I was going to have these Tyrellian treats taking up space in my shop for the next century," the owner said. "We don't see that many gryphons on Union Station."

"You just happened to have them in stock?" Ellen asked.

"Semmi submitted the order over the Stryxnet a few cycles ago," the owner said. "Are you going to be able to carry these, or should I have them delivered?"

Semmi clicked loudly and rearranged her wings in such a way that they formed the sideboards of a natural cargo space on her back.

"How come you never do that when it's my things that need carrying?" Ellen complained. The Huktra came around the counter and helped place the sack on Semmi's back. She didn't even seem to notice the weight. "Hey, you wouldn't know where I could get a book on gryphons?"

"A library?" the shop's owner suggested.

"No luck."

"There's an information shop at the end of the corridor that sells all sorts of oddities. Maybe they would have something."

"I suppose I can check while we're here," Ellen said. "What do I owe you?"

"The cost was secured via a mini-register over the Stryxnet," the Huktra said. "I don't put the charge through until the order is picked up, but you would have seen a freeze on the funds if you checked. I'll complete the transfer after you leave."

"I suppose it's lucky Semmi plans ahead. We were running low, and without the treats, she'd probably eat us."

The information shop proved to be a bit of a letdown. Ellen had conjured up an image of dusty old scrolls, tablets, and runes, but other than a few odd reading devices and tabs of dubious origin in the bargain bin, the tiny space was empty. A Gem in some sort of rumpled uniform was sitting on a high stool behind the counter reading a Vergallian romance in translation. Her eyes passed over Ellen without interest, and then she saw the gryphon.

"Are you with this Human by choice?" the Gem spoke directly to Semmi. "Does she have some secret means of compelling you to act as her pack animal?"

"It's not what you're thinking," Ellen protested. "Those are her treats—she ordered them herself. I asked the Huktra who owns the store if he knew where I might find a book about gryphons and he suggested your shop."

"I can check your story just by walking down the corridor," the clone threatened.

"Semmi is exactly where she wants to be, but we appreciate your concern," Ellen said, opting for the non-confrontational approach since the Gem really was intimidating. "You have that looming thing down pat. Are you ex-military?"

"It's not polite to ask," the Gem grumbled, and came around the counter to scratch the gryphon's eye ridges. "The Tyrellians are an ancient species, you know. The reason you won't find anything about them on the tunnel network is that they requested the Stryx issue a privacy block. I don't need to check my databases because I know there's nothing there."

"But I was hoping to learn about Gryphon diets and communication. She's trying to teach us a form of sign language—"

"I'm sure that even a Human can understand why battle language would be a military secret," the clone interrupted, and began rummaging through the bargain bin. "I do have an old Tyrellian eBook reader in here, but the privacy block probably means the Stryx station librarian won't translate it for you. Maybe a Huktra scholar would know for sure. Here it is."

Ellen accepted the battered device, which was the size of a placemat. Heavy scratching along one edge indicated some sort of touch controls for users who occasionally forgot to retract their claws, but the rest of the surface area could have been cut from a slab of obsidian.

"You said it's a tab?" she asked.

"It's a form of eBook reader," the Gem said, reaching over and tapping in the heavily scratched area. The surface turned transparent and revealed what appeared to be fine sand inside. Another tap on the edge of the device, and rows of hieroglyphics formed in the sand, just as if they were being scratched out by a talon tip.

"I've seen Semmi do that when she tries to communicate with us through simple images," Ellen said excitedly. "I had no idea the Tyrellians had achieved this level of technology."

Semmi clicked sharply.

"How much is it?" Ellen asked.

"Ten creds, and don't complain if it's loaded with pirated content," the Gem said. "There's a reason it's in the bargain bin."

"We'll take it. Does it come with any instructions?" The gryphon snorted and gave Ellen a look implying that the question was embarrassing. "Never mind. I'm beginning to think that she's better with technology than I am."

"No returns," the clone called after them as they left the shop.

Twelve

"I've never done this before," Larry said as they waited for the subway on Fyndal. "It feels weird returning to the same world so quickly."

"Imagine what it's like for those traders who are participating in the new common carrier network," Georgia said. "Some of them run back and forth between the same two places and end up spending most of their time in a Stryx tunnel. They must live on the exercise equipment."

"I think it's a backlash against the mortgage fraud scheme you and Ellen uncovered. Traders used to take their time paying down their loans, but now there's the whole Debt-Free-By-Thirty-Three movement, where young traders pledge to live like monks and take every job to pay off their loans as soon as possible. It's ironic because repossessing ships to use for a package delivery network was the ultimate goal of the criminals behind the mortgage scam."

"If my educational toys keep selling the way they did on Break Rock, we'll have your mortgage paid off in no time, and then I'll start with the back payments."

"That's just an old-fashioned tradition, Georgia. I don't want your money."

"But I want to give it to you, and I'm the one in this family with two income streams now."

"I have three income streams," Larry retorted as the magnetically levitated train pulled into the subterranean station.

"No, you have three jobs, two of which cut into your trading and only pay an honorarium. When your dad was head of the Traders Guild, his only responsibility was organizing Rendezvous. Now you're representing the Guild at the Conference of Sovereign Human Communities, plus you've got that Human Empire nonsense."

"It's not nonsense, and it's not that time-consuming," he protested as they took their seats in the nearly empty train car. "If my time wasn't my own, we wouldn't be here now. The academy was the only place I could think of to learn something about these map crystals before the artifacts competition at Rendezvous, and you can restock your educational toys."

"But I don't have any salt cod to trade," Georgia said.

"You're loaded with creds—cash is king."

"Half of that money is set aside to repay the chandler for the salt cod when we get back to Union Station. And I wanted to put the rest towards the mortgage."

"We've already got next month's payment saved on the programmable cred, thanks to that featured interview about the stolen stained glass you did for the Galactic Free Press. If I knew being a freelance journalist paid so good I would have learned how to write myself."

"So you're saying I can spend the rest of the money on new educational toys?"

"And if you run short, bill it to the ship's account," Larry said as the train soundlessly hurled down the tunnel. "We're partners, remember?"

"Then you should let me start paying you until our equity shares in the ship are equal," she said in frustration.

"I'd rather have kids."

Georgia drew in her breath sharply, and then asked, "Are the two mutually exclusive?"

"They are if you believe you have to be working around the clock to pay off the mortgage."

"Next stop Academy," the train controller announced.

"We can talk about this later," Georgia said. "Since I'm going to be paying cash this time, I guess I can just go to one of the educational toy distributors and stock up. Where will you be?"

"The astronomy department. I'm meeting Tac there, and she's offered to introduce me to somebody who might help."

"You've been seeing an awful lot of her in your Human Empire holo-conferences. Is she married?"

"She's in a committed relationship with the academy head, Hep, who is away at Earth most of the time working on the interstellar jump project. I think they plan to tie the knot when it wraps up." Larry moved to the door as the train entered the station. "Not coming?"

"I'd just have to take a taxi to the business district. It's the next stop."

"Alright. If you don't come and find me, I'll see you back at the ship for dinner."

Larry climbed the stairs, rather than taking the Verlock version of an escalator, and regretted it by the time he reached the top. The gravity on Fyndal was only about ten percent higher than Earth's, but after two days in Zero-G, it felt like he was climbing a mountain. To his surprise, Tac was waiting at the entrance to the academy complex.

"Welcome," the athletic woman who represented Fyndal's sovereign human community greeted him. "Anything new happening with our empire?"

"Just holo-conferences and talk, but as long as I don't have to pay for the Stryxnet access, it's probably worth it to help shape future trade policy. Is Hep getting excited about the big day?"

"You mean the first jump? They put it off again because the Drazens offered to send a technical historian to look over the prototype and see if we got anything wrong. After all these years, there isn't any point rushing the last couple of months."

"Are you planning on attending?" Larry asked.

"You bet. And I'm sure I'll see you there."

"It's tempting, humanity's first attempt at an interstellar drive, even if it is just a copy of a Drazen museum piece. But we're going to be spending the next month or so at Earth for Georgia's journalism work, and by the time Rendezvous is over, I'm sure we'll both be itching to get out of there."

"But that's perfect," Tac said. "The new test date is scheduled for the same week that Rendezvous opens."

"That means Flower will be in orbit, which could come in handy if anything goes wrong," Larry said, and then hastily added, "Not that anything will go wrong."

"Not with Hep in charge," she said confidently, leading the way down a hall on the walls of which a generation of students had written scientific equations and drawn graphs until it looked like the smooth rock had been papered with class notes. "I heard that the Maker who sat in our meetings at Union Station to write a history of the Human Empire is going to attend."

"Dring is coming? That means that all of the alien media from the tunnel network will be there as well, and if anything goes wrong with Rendezvous, they'll be all over us."

"Why would anything go wrong?"

"It's the first time I'm in charge, but Flower and her people talked me into letting them handle most of the details since she's hosting," Larry explained.

"Does she have room to dock all of the ships that show up? I thought you expected tens of thousands at those things."

"Most of them are Sharf two-man traders, and she can park them almost touching since the people will be in cabins rather than camping out. But they can also leave their ships at the elevator hub and she'll run regular shuttles."

"Or I suppose they can land on Earth and take the elevator up," Tac said. "Have you ever been to a planetarium?"

"I don't even know what one is," Larry said, following her into a strange auditorium that seemed to have been built inside of a large sphere. "Did the academy run out of space and put a bunch of seats in an old underground storage tank?"

"This," Tac told him, taking in the room with a wave of her arm, "is a planetarium. Fik should be here any minute, and he'll activate the projector. You brought your map crystal?"

"I brought two of them, one in each pocket so they wouldn't bang together."

"You have two? I didn't realize you were so successful."

"I bought a dozen at one go," Larry said. "An old Frunge purser was getting rid of them. I thought I overpaid."

"Don't tell Fik that," Tac said, glancing around nervously to see if the astronomer had shown up yet. "He gave a cycle's salary for his."

"Got it. Then I'll only show him the small one."

"They come in two sizes?"

"One was bigger than all the others and had a different sort of—I don't know what to call it—filling?"

"Then you better show him both, but if he asks about the price, just say it was more than you could afford. Academics aren't known for their bartering skills. Fik was so excited when he saw his that he just paid what the seller asked."

"I guess that's fair," Larry said, pulling the larger of the two map crystals out of his pocket and passing it over. "See how it seems to be lit from the inside? You can only see the stars in the smaller ones if you shine a light on them."

"You mean the other one," she hissed at him, as an old man shuffled into the planetarium.

"Other one," he agreed.

"Is – this – the – young – man – with – the – map – crystal?" the newcomer asked Tac in the stilted speech of someone who spent too much time around Verlocks.

"Yes, Fik," Tac replied, slowing her own speech somewhat. "He has two map crystals with him, and one is larger and lit from the inside."

Fik was so excited by this news that he broke into a trot, which almost got him up to regular walking speed for a man his age. He ignored Larry and made a beeline for the crystal sphere Tac was holding out, snatching it from her hand in slow motion.

"Astounding," he declared, holding the map crystal just in front of his eyes. "Lighting – two."

The lights in the planetarium dimmed, and the internal glow of the star field in the map crystal seemed to brighten in response, even though it was only a matter of contrast.

"Is that the Milky Way?" Tac asked.

"Yes – yes," Fik said, the words almost, but not quite running together. "Nobody – knows – when – these – artifacts – were – manufactured, but – the – earliest – Verlock – tunnel – network – historians – already – knew – of – their – existence."

"From seven million years ago?" Larry asked, his mind boggling at the apparent bargain he'd made.

"At – least," Fik said. "Do – you – know – the – legend – of – their – purpose?"

"That they contain maps that point to the treasure of a lost civilization, or maybe more than one civilization. I tried using my ship's main display to magnify the star field, but the density was too high for the resolution."

"Map – crystals – defy – Verlock – science. Some – speculate – they – were – made – by – the – Stryx – and – exist – partially – in – multidimensional – space."

"Has anybody ever succeeded in matching the stars shown in a crystal to real space?" Larry asked.

"Time – is – the – variable," Fik said. "The – number – of – computations – required – to – model – the – position – of – every – star – in – the – galaxy – at – a – prior – date – is – astronomical."

"Show him your projection," Tac urged the old scientist.

"Do – I – have – your – permission – to – try – projecting – this – map - crystal?"

"Please do," Larry said. "It's been driving me nuts squinting at it and wondering if I'm missing something."

Fik shuffled off towards an equipment pit at the lowest point of the room, but when the other two started to follow, he waved them back, saying, "The – view – is – better – up – there."

"Does he project the stars on the hemispherical ceiling?" Larry whispered to Tac. "It seems a bit old-school."

"It's all Verlock hologram technology, the shape of the room just provides the space for projecting planets that you can walk around."

"I thought the Hortens were the tunnel network's holographic designers. All of the stuff I see on the market is made by them."

"I can't believe you'd think that," Tac said in dismay. "The Verlock technology is millions of years ahead of the best the Hortens have to offer. It's just that you have to pay for this kind of quality. The equipment isn't amenable to mass production, and Verlocks view single-use devices, like Horten holo-cubes, as inherently wasteful."

"Get – ready," Fik's voice came over the public address system.

"What does he mean?" Larry asked.

"Fik's projector for map crystals scales the hologram to fill the whole room, though whether or not we find ourselves standing inside a star field has to do with where the spiral arms end up. With hundreds of billions of stars in the Milky Way, showing them all in a space this size would just cause a white-out, so he created an algorithm that limits the number to what our eyes and minds can handle."

"Whoa!" Larry half-groaned, grabbing Tac's shoulder as he was hit by a sudden spell of vertigo. "I've spent plenty of time space-walking, but I've never seen anything like this."

"The algorithm also adjusts the brightness and size of the stars to create an impression of what we would see if our brains had sufficient processing power," she explained. "And of course, you've never stood outside of the galaxy looking in before. I'd estimate that we're about ten light-years above the bar at the core."

"Twelve," Fik corrected her as he shuffled up to them and continued in his stilted monotone. "Your – map – crystal – is – extraordinary. I've – never – been – so – excited."

"How does it differ from the smaller ones?" Larry asked.

"It – includes – planets," the astronomer said, and then instructed the voice controller, "Forward – one – hour."

"Did something change?"

"It's still computing, this will take a few minutes," Tac told him. "How will all the extra data from the larger crystal impact the processing time, Fik?"

"The – model – wasn't – built – to – take – planetary – masses – into – account – because – there – was – no – data," the astronomer said, and then blinked back a tear as he was overcome with emotion. "I'll – need – time – to – adjust."

"Let's walk around the other side," Tac said to Larry. "I've seen the demonstrations he gave the academy using his own map crystal, so I can explain the goal of the model."

"I'm going to feel awful about leaving with it now," the trader said. "Is there any way he can make a copy?"

Tac laughed, a surprisingly light sound coming from the sturdily-built woman. "Fik speculated that the Cayl or the Farlings might have the capacity to copy a small map crystal given enough time, but this one?"

"You're saying I picked up a unique artifact in what amounted to the Frunge version of a junk shop?"

"Fik bought his crystal from a collector who had a number of them, and maybe that collector held out on the large ones. They're mainly of interest to cosmologists because they offer high-resolution images from a galaxy frozen in time. When Fik instructed his algorithm to move forward one hour, it began computations for every star in the displayed subset to project the view one hour into the future. But most astronomers believe that these crystals are tens of millions of years old."

"I'm beginning to think that the map crystals themselves are more of a treasure than any objects they could point to," Larry said. "Does anybody know how that part of it works?"

"Oh, yes. Fik always attends the session on map crystal treasure hunting at every computational astronomy conference he gets to. Can you spot the cubical star?"

"There's no such thing."

"In every map crystal, there's at least one cube," Tac said. "The theory is that it's a marker for a treasure left behind by an ancient civilization or visitors from another galaxy, and there's a millions-of-years-old debate over what that treasure might consist of."

"You mean it could be a trove of knowledge, or technology, or sleeping artificial intelligence waiting to be awakened," Larry speculated, even as he searched among the seemingly infinite points of light for a cube.

"And the philosopher's stone for crystal collectors is developing a model that will let them extrapolate the position of the cube in the current galaxy. Fik's model is idealized for his crystal, but it's more about the journey than the destination for computational astronomers. If anybody has ever succeeded in finding the treasure, they've kept it to themselves."

"But it doesn't sound like that hard of a task," Larry protested.

Tac laughed again. "Imagine if the treasure was a regular book floating in interstellar space. How precise of a location would you need to establish before you took your ship out searching for it?"

"Pretty precise, I guess. But what if the cube shape is just a way of highlighting a real star, and the treasure is somewhere in orbit, or on one of the worlds in that system?"

"Then the sort of reduced model Fik is trying to compute might be sufficient, but remember that none of the advanced species have gotten anywhere with the crystals. Projecting the precise movements of every star in a galaxy over tens of millions of years is a herculean task, and that presumes you could somehow account for all of the mass passing through during that timespan, including dark matter."

The pair continued their slow circuit around the room, with Larry trying not to trip over his own feet as he searched for the elusive cube until they finally arrived back at the place they had left the astronomer.

"How – much?" Fik demanded bluntly.

"You mean you want to buy my map crystal?" Larry asked. "It's not for sale."

"You're – a – trader. Everything – has – a – price."

"Yes, but, the thing is, I plan to enter it in the artifacts contest at our Rendezvous."

"After – the – contest."

"I—I don't know," Larry said. "It's unique, right?"

"Every – map – crystal – is – unique," Fik told him. "I – didn't – know – two – sizes – existed, but – now – I – will - make – enquiries."

"Does mine have a cubical star?"

"Highlight – cubes," the astronomer ordered.

A dark glow suddenly appeared from a cluster of points in the thickest part of the galactic disk, and each of those points expanded into a blue cube the size of a fist.

"There must be hundreds," Tac said in amazement.

"And – just – from – the – subset – of – stars – the – algorithm - displays," Fik choked out.

"Perhaps the treasure is at the intersection of connected lines, rather than the points," Tac suggested. "Maybe the smaller map crystals are parts of sets that have to be combined in some way."

"The – naming – rights – of – the – planetarium – are – available," Fik said hopefully.

"What does he mean?" Larry asked.

"I think he's saying that if you decide to donate the crystal after Rendezvous, this could be the 'Larry, Phil's Son Planetarium,'" Tac said. "It has a nice ring to it."

"I'll think about it."

Thirteen

Ellen yawned, undid her safety restraints, and took her time rising from the acceleration chair she'd obviously fallen asleep in again. She could tell from her weight that they had already landed on Earth, and she marveled over the fact that she had slept through reentry. After grabbing a juice box from the fridge and scowling at the empty charging bay where she had left her cell phone, she climbed down the ladder to the cargo deck and then walked down the ramp into the sunshine.

"I thought I was the one with the gravity-induced sleep problem," John greeted her. "You've been out like a light for almost ten hours."

"How long ago did we land?"

"Seven hours ago. Semmi eventually dragged herself up the ladder to wake me."

"Can't she let herself out?"

"I think she wanted to watch me go out first to make sure there was enough oxygen in the atmosphere. Semmi isn't anybody's fool."

"Hey, this is your father's old town!" Ellen said in surprise. "I remember that water tower, and over there is where we harvested all of the acorns for the Huktra market. What are we doing here?"

"When we came out of the tunnel, I received an anonymous message addressed to our ship on a continuous loop. It was a picture of a crushed acorn."

"I don't think they're in season," Ellen said, looking up at the trees. "I didn't mind raking up acorns on the ground but I'm not climbing for them. Maybe we could train Semmi."

"Good luck with that," John said. "I can't be certain, but I'm betting the crushed acorn was a coded message from Myort sent by one of his operatives on Earth. Landing here was all I could think of, but I didn't find any obvious instructions lying around about what to do next."

"And then you went to sleep."

"Well, yes. But I always do that, and like I said, Semmi woke me over an hour ago."

"Do you think Myort is in the area somewhere?"

"I sent Semmi out looking for him. She flew off in a straight line toward the hills like she sensed something. We really need to kit her out with a video link so she can share what she's seeing."

"That would be useful if you're going to train her as a field operative," Ellen said. "She did a good job for me on the statue story. Speaking of which, I need to check in with the news syndicate's secretary. I finally remembered to charge my stupid phone *before* we landed."

"Considering you've been the Earth syndication coordinator for almost a year, it's about time you learned to use the technology they all depend on," John said.

"So, hand it over."

"You think I took your cell phone? What for? There's no coverage out here anyway."

"I know that you use it because you're too cheap to buy your own."

"You hate cell phones but you want me to buy one? That doesn't make any sense."

Ellen glanced up and began waving her arm in a circular motion above her head. John watched as the gryphon glided down in a tight corkscrew and landed so close that the air pressure from the final braking beat of her wings nearly bowled them over.

"Very funny," John told the gryphon. "Find anything?"

Semmi clicked her beak and each of the humans reflexively reached in their pockets and tossed her a treat. The gryphon caught them both, swallowed one, and deposited the other in the pouch she had taken to wearing around her neck. At the same time, she removed something from the pouch, and gingerly held it out in the tip of her beak.

"You had my cell phone?" Ellen said. "You better not have been streaming pay-per-view on my account. And I don't remember sharing my lockscreen code with you."

Semmi snorted, sat on her haunches, and then used both of her front paws to draw a box in the air.

"I think she's trying to tell you something," John said.

"You're a regular Hep," Ellen said, and after tracing out her lockscreen code, went directly to the camera memory. "Did you eat any of these sheep?" she demanded of Semmi, holding up the aerial image of wooly quadrupeds in a pasture fleeing towards a barn. "You know we're going to have to find this place and pay the farmer."

The gryphon gave her an annoyed look and made a cycling motion with one paw. Ellen swiped through several more pictures of prey animals, and then a startled look came over her face.

"It's an alien freighter of some kind. Myort's?"

John looked at the image and shook his head. "That's not a Huktra ship. I don't even recognize the type. Keep going."

Ellen flipped through more images, several of which showed large cages that held either feral dogs or coyotes and one that almost certainly contained a pair of wolves. Then there was a picture of a man pointing something long and skinny directly at the camera.

"He shot at you?" she asked Semmi.

John immediately began inspecting the gryphon for signs of damage, but other than a broken feather near a wingtip, he couldn't find anything. Semmi underwent his ministrations without complaining but shook herself like a wet dog when he was done.

"Are there any more pictures?" he asked. "Check whether the geolocation was on."

"You just said there's no service out here, and there isn't," Ellen replied, swiping the screen again and displaying zero-bars of connectivity.

"They use something called the global positioning system for those functions, it's a separate satellite-based service. I remember reading that there's an old factory on Earth that builds one replacement satellite a year to keep the system going, though these days they use the elevator rather than rockets to get them into orbit."

"I can't figure this stupid thing out," she admitted, thrusting the phone at John. "Why don't Earth engineers add voice controls like the rest of the galaxy?"

"I thought you could talk to it. I've heard you."

"Swearing doesn't count as talking," Ellen told him. "About the only thing the voice interface is good for is asking the time or to connect a call to some other poor fool who has one of these things."

"You know I've barely used it myself, but it seems to me that if you just keep tapping—there," he declared, bringing up what looked like a round target with tiny text labels grouped together. "We must be at the middle, and those are time-stamps for the pictures Semmi took. There should be a way to establish north—"

"It's that way," Ellen interrupted, pointing in the direction of the water tower.

"How do you know?"

"Because Semmi is pointing that direction."

John turned to the gryphon, who was pointing just to the right of the tower. "Maybe she's just telling us where she was," he said.

"Semmi, which way is south?" Ellen asked.

The gryphon shot her a look that clearly wasn't intended as a compliment, turned her back towards the water tower, and pointed towards the new-growth forest that had taken over the old pastures.

"All right," John said, and aligned the top of the circular map towards the water tower. "Oh, I guess that's what the little arrow was for. It's pointing just to the right of the tower now."

Semmi rolled her eyes and made a choking noise.

"So do we take the ship or do you want to hike it?" Ellen asked.

"There's at least one man there armed with some sort of rifle. I'm going to get on the radio and contact the authorities. Maybe it's some sort of legitimate operation to preserve wildlife."

"That doesn't seem very likely. Why would they have a spaceship, not to mention a type you've never seen before? I'll bet they're here poaching wildlife, and Myort is tipping you off because it has something to do with all the other thefts going on."

"In that case, I'm calling for backup," John said. "The deal EarthCent made with the continental law enforcement organizations allows me to investigate, but I don't have any authority to make arrests."

Ellen took back her cell phone and wandered around the abandoned village checking to see if she could get a signal anywhere, while John went back into their ship to try to raise the authorities via the controller. She eventually found herself looking speculatively at the water tower, but when she put her weight gingerly on the first rung of the metal ladder, it gave way.

"Don't break the phone, I need it," John called to her.

"Did you get through?" she asked.

"Unfortunately," he said. "They transferred me about a dozen times, and finally I ended up with the agency in charge of policing disbanded municipalities. They can't get a team here until tomorrow morning at the earliest. But I got them to put through a call to the EarthCent president's office for me, and the secretary there explained how to show distances on that map."

"What good will that do?" Ellen asked, handing over the phone.

"I'll know whether or not I can hike there before it gets dark. I don't want to take the ship because they'll almost certainly detect us, and for all I know, just landing here may have spooked them."

"I'm going with you either way, and we're bringing Semmi."

"They're armed criminals and I don't have any authority, Ellen. I'll bring my stunner but I can't use deadly force, which means I can't protect you."

"I can take care of myself, and unless you're willing to use that stunner on me, I'm coming. How far is it?"

"Her explanation was pretty complicated. I'm still trying to find the right menu."

"Told you so."

"Here we go," John said. "It's, uh, twenty-two li."

"Twenty-two what?"

"Li. I guess it's some sort of Earth unit. Let me check the menus again."

"While you're doing that, I'll go ask the ship controller," Ellen said. She stopped and looked back at the EarthCent Intelligence agent, who was hunched over the small screen. "I have to say that I've seen my share of police and spy thrillers, but I don't ever remember anybody running into a problem with unit conversion."

"Chinese," John said, beckoning her back. "You have the distance units set to Chinese on your phone. I swapped to English and it's about seven miles."

"How far is a mile?"

"Wait a second," he muttered, swiping and tapping menus. "It looks like about sixteen hundred meters per, or about ten thousand meters to our target. When I was younger I could run that in an hour, easy, but call it two hours walking on a good path, or maybe three through the woods."

"I'm packing lunch," Ellen said. "You carry the water."

Four hours later, Semmi finally began showing an interest in her surroundings and let out a low cry that sounded perfectly natural given their surroundings. They entered a narrow band of older trees which might have demarcated the boundary between two farms a century earlier, and then halted under cover at the edge of a hayfield that had recently been mowed.

"Let's see our recon images again," John said, holding his hand out for the phone.

"Ooh, I love it when you talk military," Ellen purred. She passed him the smartphone that was still displaying the map showing them to be within a few hundred meters of the destination. "I think those big round bales look familiar from the pictures."

"This is the place, all right. Semmi does good work."

The gryphon clicked her beak, and Ellen dutifully handed over a treat.

"We'll move directly forward to that roll of hay on the crest of the rise so we'll still be under cover unless they have drones up. Semmi, air cover is your job, but stay on the ground until we need you because you'll give away our position otherwise."

"Do you really think she understood all of that?" Ellen asked.

"I've given up guessing how much she does and doesn't understand, but it's the logical plan, so she'd probably come to the same conclusion on her own," John said. "Leave your backpack here."

The party disencumbered themselves of everything except for their stunners, and bending over slightly in deference to his training, John made a beeline for the hay bale. It was large enough that he was able to stand up straight once he got there, and when Ellen arrived, he was peeking around the edge.

"Anything?" she asked.

"A lot of activity. At least a dozen unfriendlies, but I only see one cage on this side of the ship."

"Maybe they began loading the animals after our landing, or Semmi's flyover tipped them off that somebody might be on to them. Take a picture with my cell phone. That's the one thing it's actually good at."

"How does it work?"

"Let me," Ellen said, taking the phone back and swiping through the menus. After about two minutes, she found what she was looking for, and sticking just enough of her head and arm out from behind the bale, snapped a few pictures. "There. I'll see—Hey, I have connectivity."

"Give it back to me," John said. "The EarthCent secretary gave me a different number for the New York City-State police rapid response unit. It's worth a shot to see if they can get some patrol craft out here."

Ellen handed the phone back and then peeked around the edge of the giant hay bale again. "They're loading the last crate."

A mournful howl reached them from the far end of the field where the alien landing craft was parked, and then the ramp that the men and the cage had just utilized folded up into the fuselage.

"Busy," John cursed, and after consulting his heads-up display, tried another number. "It's ringing now."

"Put it on speaker," Ellen said.

"I don't know how."

Ellen snatched the phone back and hit the icon just as a pleasant voice announced, "New York City-State Police. If you know the party you are calling, please enter the extension now. If you are reporting a floater accident, please press or say 'One.' Otherwise, describe your emergency with as much detail as possible and I will transfer your call."

"I'm with EarthCent Intelligence and I have my eyes on an alien ship that I believe is smuggling wildlife off of Earth," John said.

"You want to take an intelligence test. Am I right?"

"No! I'm witnessing a crime in progress and it appears the ship is about to launch. I need air support."

"Thank you for offering to support the New York City-State Police. We accept donations through electronic transfer or in cash at all participating stations."

"They're lifting off while you're talking to that brain-dead answering system," Ellen said in frustration.

"You require help lifting a brain. Am I right?"

John handed the phone back to Ellen, who swiped to hang up, and then they both stepped out from behind the giant hay bale to watch the alien lander soaring for the sky.

"Do you have Hildy's number saved on your phone?" John asked.

"Sure, but what is EarthCent's public relations director going to do?"

"Get the president on the line for us," John said. "I asked earlier when I talked to the secretary, but he was out for the morning and she wouldn't call him for me."

"Hildy Grueun," Ellen told the phone with exaggerated enunciation. It seemed to hesitate for a few seconds, and then the phone began to ring and was picked up.

"Ellen?" the public relations director asked. "You're back on Earth?"

"Just got in. We have a bit of an emergency and John wants to talk to the president if he's available."

"Just a sec, we came home for lunch," Hildy said, and they both heard her yelling in the background, "Stephen," followed by, "He'll be here in a minute. Are you in a jam?"

"We're fine, but we just witnessed a crime that might involve aliens, and John wants to find out if the president has any options."

"It looked more like a lander than a freighter so they're probably returning to a mothership in orbit," John said over Ellen's shoulder. "I know we don't have any assets capable of intercepting them, but it would be nice to get a positive ID."

"Maybe the elevator authority or the AI running the tunnel exit could help," Hildy said. "Here he is."

"President Beyer here," a familiar voice announced, though it sounded a bit like it was coming from inside a tin can. "I'm on speakerphone with Hildy."

"This is John, and I'm on speakerphone with Ellen," the EarthCent Intelligence agent replied. "We just watched an alien lander take on board an unknown number of cages containing wildlife. Looked like wolves and coyotes."

"Sounded like wolves," Ellen interjected.

"When our gryphon spotted them earlier, somebody took a shot at her, so they aren't fooling around."

"I've got a favor I can call in with the AI running the tunnel exit so I'll see if he can identify the ship for us, maybe the destination as well," the president said. "Do you want us to contact the local police for you?"

"Already tried that. They'll be here tomorrow morning at the earliest, and I should probably call them back and tell them not to bother. If you can get that information from the tunnel exit AI, that's probably the best we can do."

"And send it to me too," Ellen added. "I'm working on a story."

"We're heading back to the office now and I'll get right on it," Stephen said. "It will be a nice change from the endless dog-and-pony shows I put on for visiting alien businessmen."

"Poor president," Hildy chided him. "Oh, and I have something you might be interested in, Ellen. It seems that—"

"Seems that what?" Ellen asked after a few seconds of silence, and then stared at the phone in disbelief. "The signal is gone. How does that happen?"

"Weather maybe?" John said. "You only had one bar to start with. We may as well go take a look and see if they left anything behind."

"We may end up sleeping in that barn," she said, glancing at the sky. "When it starts getting cold on this planet, the sun goes down pretty early, and I don't want to be lost in the woods."

John stopped and stared off into space for a moment. "I just called the ship. It will be here in a few minutes."

"I forgot you can do that with your EarthCent Intelligence implant," Ellen said.

"It would probably work with yours as well. The ship's controller is the top of the line, so the problem is less signal strength than the curvature of the planet. Go ahead and reconnoiter, Semmi."

The gryphon took a few leaping bounds before spreading her wings and taking off. She flew directly to the barn and disappeared inside.

"Maybe that wasn't the smartest idea," John said, breaking into a run. Ellen kept pace on the recently mown field, and they both arrived at the same time. Natural light entered the barn through the wide-open door and vertical planks that hinged open for ventilation, but after being out in the sunshine, it took a minute for their eyes to adjust. Semmi was in an empty cage worrying at something with her beak.

“What do you have?” John asked, stooping a bit to enter the large enclosure. “Is that a remote control?”

The gryphon gave a satisfied snort and a blank panel at the end of the cage that John hadn't noticed lit up with an image of a rabbit fleeing across an open field. Then a wolf appeared from the side, herding the rabbit towards its mate. Semmi pecked at the controller again, and the video was replaced by a long shot of a sheep straying from its herd.

“It's like hunting porn,” Ellen said. “Do you think the poachers have a thing about carnivores?”

Semmi looked away from the screen and shook her head. She pointed at the water dish, which had a paw control for refilling, and the remains of several gnawed bones.

“I think she's trying to tell us that these were luxury accommodations for the animals that were captured,” John said. “We'll load the cage into the ship and maybe there's a way to trace it back to the manufacturer.”

“As soon as we get back to civilization, I'll reach out to the syndicated journalists and see if they've heard of anything similar going on,” Ellen said. “My gut tells me there's a big story in this somewhere, but I don't have a clue what it is.”

Fourteen

"Are you sure you're willing to hang around Earth?" Georgia asked again. "The opportunity for me to work with Ellen for a whole month is just too good to turn down. She can really use my help since I grew up here and went through the New University system before moving to Union Station."

"If I finish up all of the arrangements for Rendezvous early, maybe I'll pop back through the tunnel to Echo Station to see if I can get the Stryx librarian to tell me anything about my map crystals, but it would probably be a waste of time," Larry said.

"You think the librarian will say that it's protected competitive information?"

"Yeah. And when I asked my old teacher bot, it didn't have any information at all about map crystals, which means that humanity hasn't discovered anything about them yet. Maybe when Flower gets here I can ask the Human Empire's Cayl mentor if she knows how they work."

"I thought she was barely out of their version of university herself," Georgia said.

"She would still have access to their reference libraries, not to mention an imperial education, and it wouldn't hurt to ask Flower. Maybe when I finish the Rendezvous arrangements here, I'll pop through the tunnel and catch them at their last stop before Earth."

"You weren't kidding when you told me that treasure hunters were kooky," Georgia said as she gathered the recyclables from the folding picnic table and started towards their ship. "You really are obsessed with those little balls."

"Where are you going?" Larry asked. "I emptied our bins right after we landed—it's free with the long-term parking pass. If we take any Earth trash into space with us we'll just have to pay to get rid of it somewhere else."

"I wasn't thinking." She looked around the parking area, spotted a few open-air recycling bins, and put the take-out containers back on the table. "They're in the same direction as the monorail so I'll recycle this stuff when I head into town."

"Listen, Georgia," Larry said, trying and failing to keep his tone light. "I know you grew up on Earth and that Ellen is an experienced investigative journalist, but from what you've already told me, these thefts you're going to be looking into probably involve organized crime."

"We'll be careful," Georgia said. "Besides, Ellen mainly wants me to deal with researching archives and interviewing bureaucrats working at the universities and government agencies. She and John believe that these crimes date almost all the way back to when the Stryx opened Earth, so it's going to take a lot of legwork looking into old record-keeping systems."

"Just keep in mind that some of those nice bureaucrats you talk to may not want you to uncover the truth," Larry said. "I don't see how the systematic looting of Earth artifacts could have been kept quiet all these years unless a lot of people were being paid to look the other way."

A young woman riding an electric scooter with a large storage box on the back pulled right up to the picnic table. She flipped up the visor on her helmet and inquired, "Georgia Hunt?"

"That's me, but our food came twenty minutes ago," Georgia said. "The elevator parking lot authority told us when we landed they were sending a complimentary breakfast, but we don't need two of them."

"I've got my suspicions that the first breakfast may repeat on its own," Larry added.

"I don't work for the elevator," the woman said, pulling a padded envelope out of the scooter's storage box and handing it over. Then she extended a standard tab with a stylus on a short cord. "I need you to sign for it. There's no charge."

Georgia passed the package to Larry, signed the tab, and reached for her purse to get a tip. Before she looked up again, the delivery driver on the silent scooter was already gone.

"Can I open it for you?" Larry asked, tearing along the perforated line in the envelope and pulling out the contents. "It looks like an archaic tab of some sort."

"It's a cell phone, like for pinging people," Georgia said, clapping her hands with glee and taking it from him. "I haven't had one of these since I left Earth. Ellen must have sent it."

"I didn't see a note or anything." Larry pulled the padded envelope wide open and then inspected its construction. "I wonder who came up with the idea of sandwiching air bubbles between two sheets of plastic for packaging. Hey, this stuff is pretty tough."

"You're wasting your time trying to tear it with your bare hands. If there's one thing that Earth knows how to manufacture, it's indestructible single-use packaging."

"I'm going to see if I can trade for a few cases of these. I could see them having a market somewhere, and everything is recyclable with an atomizer."

The newly powered-on phone announced a series of incoming texts with a burst of happy chirps. "Change of plans," Georgia said while reading the messages. "I'm going to be spending today doing research at the elevator stalk museum. According to Ellen, they have the best collection of digitized import and export records on the continent."

"Ask if she's with John," Larry requested. "He's the only member of the Guild Council who's never worked at organizing a Rendezvous before, so I should show him the ropes if he has time."

"I doubt he does," she said, typing away with both thumbs. "Ellen already told me that he's in charge of coordinating between EarthCent Intelligence and the Earth law enforcement agencies on this whole theft thing."

"I was just going to take him to a couple of meetings so he can see what's involved. If he works around the clock on the one thing without any change it will just lead to burnout."

The phone chirped again, and Georgia said, "She'll pass along the message when she sees him. He refuses to carry a cell phone. Hey, we should get you one."

"I'll keep my eyes open for a good deal," Larry said, his go-to expression when he didn't want to buy something. "I've got a meeting at the elevator authority myself today to negotiate a bulk-discount contract for traders who want to visit Earth while they're in orbit for Rendezvous."

"Why wouldn't they just land?"

"You mean aside from the wear-and-tear on their fuel packs? A lot of them probably figure their ships are safer in orbit, and space elevator trips are a good way to catch up on your sleep."

The phone chirped again, and Georgia's anticipatory smile turned into a grimace.

"What's wrong?" Larry asked.

"Spam," she snarled, swiping away the message. "I only went online a minute ago. How could I be getting spam texts already?"

"Online?"

"Connected to the Internet," Georgia said. "It used to drive me nuts in university because we had to use it for research, but it's funded by advertising. It's basically ads leading to ads leading to ads. Finding what you need is like searching for a lost cargo container in interstellar space."

"You're going to have to explain it a little better than that if you want me to understand," Larry said, gathering up the breakfast packaging Georgia had put down and starting for the recycling bins.

"It all starts with these things called search engines," she said, falling in beside him with her eyes still fixed on the little screen. "Did you secure the ship?"

"Just sent the command over my implant. You know, the way civilized species do things."

"Right. Well, on Earth, everybody uses smartphones, and they all connect to the Internet, where you find things with a search engine. You tell the search engine what you're looking for, and then it shows you a bunch of advertisements related to that thing."

"If your goal is to convince me not to get one, you're doing an excellent job," Larry said. "Suppose you were working on a story and wanted to find out if anybody had been stealing, uh—" he looked around the long-term parking area, "—picnic tables. What would you ask?"

Georgia sighed. "Doing this by voice rather than typing is the worst possible case, but I'll give it a try." She tapped something on the screen and then spoke directly to the phone. "Have any picnic tables been stolen from the Elevator Transit Authority long-term parking area?"

The phone took a moment to process the request and then responded in a sultry female voice, "You want to purchase a picnic table. Am I correct?"

"No."

"Please ask again and provide as much detail as possible."

"I'm researching crime statistics and I want to know if any picnic tables have been reported stolen from the Elevator Transit Authority parking area."

"I found a report on elevator cargo statistics published in the Gotham Times. Do you want to hear it?"

"I'd like to hear that," Larry said before Georgia could respond. "Maybe we'll pick up some trading tips."

"This report is available for nineteen eBucks. Do you authorize payment?"

"No," Georgia practically shouted, and shot Larry a scowl.

"As you're a first-time purchaser of Gotham Times archival material, I can give you a fifty percent discount," the voice offered persuasively. "Do you authorize payment?"

"No, I don't."

"A paid-in-full subscription to the Gotham Times includes free access to the archives."

"Is that thing working on a commission?" Larry asked as he sorted the breakfast recycling into bins.

"You want to know about working on commission," the voice shifted gears smoothly. "Am I correct?"

"Cancel, cancel, cancel," Georgia barked at the phone. "So that's how the natural speech interface works."

"Is it any better with text?"

"It's different. Reading is faster than listening, especially if you skim, so you can skip past all of the advertisements to get to the real results without wasting too much time. The problem is that the real results just lead to more advertising. It takes a lot of practice to find anything useful unless you just stick with the old Wikipedia information, but in that case, you can get it faster by asking a teacher bot."

"No wonder Earth is so far behind on everything if that's how the people here have to do research," Larry said. "Do they have a version without advertising for students?"

"No. And they have these things called cookies that you can't refuse which track you everywhere so they can show ads related to your lifestyle rather than what you're researching," Georgia said, almost tripping over the first stair to the monorail station because she was looking at the phone and texting with her thumbs again.

"That makes no sense at all. You mean you could be looking up molecular weights for a chemistry class and—"

"—and the search engine will be showing you ads for sexy lingerie."

"I don't buy sexy lingerie," Larry protested.

"But you might have clicked on a picture of a model once, so when the teaching assistant in the media lab is grading your research skills in a timed trial, all these lingerie ads keep popping up," Georgia said, again stumbling when they reached the top of the stairs because she wasn't paying attention to where she was going. "I mean, theoretically."

"It sounds a little more like personal experience. Good timing."

"What?"

Larry took Georgia by the upper arm and walked her onto the monorail car that had just pulled into the elevated station. By the time they got to the main offices of the Elevator Transit Authority, she had stopped even pretending to listen to what he said as the little screen demanded all of her attention.

"We're here," he said, shaking her shoulder lightly as one might a sleeper.

"Oh, that was quick. I'm figuring on spending the whole day data diving so I'll see you back at the ship."

Larry gave her a quick kiss goodbye after they exited the monorail car, and then he followed a few feet behind as she somehow navigated her way to the museum without ever looking up from the phone. Then he returned to the monorail platform and followed the arrows for the Elevator Transit Authority administrative offices.

Georgia looked up just in time not to walk into the glass door of the museum. The uniformed man at the entrance pointed her to the elevator that led to the archive, and while she was waiting for it to arrive, she couldn't help returning to her old profile page that hadn't been updated since she left Earth. She still had her head down two minutes later when she exited the elevator and walked into a turnstile that failed to turn.

"Ow," she declared loudly. "That really hurt."

A disinterested woman behind a desk who didn't bother looking up from her own phone said, "You have to swipe your visitor pass."

"I don't have one."

"Access to the archives is limited to certified researchers with an academic affiliation. We have original source materials, many of which are unique to this facility, and we can't have just anybody pawing through them."

"Do you mean records on paper? I don't think I need to go that far back."

"It's not about what you need," the woman said in a bored voice. "It's about our rules. I'm afraid I'm going to have to ask you to leave."

"I'm with the press," Georgia said, brandishing her press badge at the woman, who finally looked up.

"I don't care if you're—the Galactic Free Press? Why didn't you say so?"

"Does that mean I can come in?"

"Just a moment please, I need to contact the head archivist. There's a waiting room through the door to your right with fresh coffee and pastry."

Somewhat mystified by the receptionist's change of heart, Georgia entered the waiting room and found that a whole wall was given over to a giant display panel that came to life with an orientation video for visitors. After a brief overview of the information sources available, the narrator launched into a lengthy explanation of copyright laws that prohibited using phone cameras to capture images of any material unless it had entered the public domain. Then the video was replaced by a spreadsheet that covered the entire wall with instructions for determining whether or not a given publication was still in copyright.

"Intimidating, isn't it," a voice said behind her. "We have a dungeon for scofflaws."

Georgia turned and saw a man in his forties who was appreciably shorter than she was and probably weighed less as well, but the twinkle in his eye belied his words.

"It would take me an hour sitting with a lawyer just to figure out what all of this means," she said, gesturing at the spreadsheet.

"The short version is that everything published since the invention of the digital computer is still in copyright unless it's the work of a government agency," the archivist said. "I'm Yossi, and I want you to let me know if you need anything at all. In fact, why don't you tell me what you're looking for and I'll help steer you in the right direction."

"That's very generous of you. Could you tell me how to obtain a visitor pass?"

"You won't need one," Yossi said. "Sandy will buzz you through now that she knows who you are. So where do you want to start?"

"It's hard to say exactly," Georgia admitted. "I'm working on a story about the theft of cultural artifacts from Earth, but it may extend to collections of biological materials like seeds and cells, and even live animals. Another journalist I work with has some access to old police reports, so I'm hoping to come at it from another angle."

"It seems to me that your best source of information would be newspaper archives," Yossi said, leading her out of the waiting room. "Have you ever used a microfiche machine?"

"I've never even heard of one."

"Then I'll forgo telling you the rest of the joke, though it's a good one." He swiped a pass to go through the turnstile, and then reached back and swiped it again to let Georgia through. "Archivist's prerogative."

"Do you have a subject index for newspapers like the one I used for academic journals in university?" she asked.

"It only covers famous names," Yossi said. "There's just too much information to deal with any other way than computer indexing."

"Am I going to have to use that search engine with all the ads?"

"I'm beginning to think you'll be pleasantly surprised." When they reached a junction in the hall, he turned left, away from the sign pointing to the main archive, and led the way to a thick velvet-sheathed rope on chromed stanchions blocking the hall. "When you come back, you can unhook the rope or duck under," the archivist told her. "Just ignore the sign about restricted access."

"I've gotten special treatment from restaurant owners who wanted me to write a good review, but nothing like this," Georgia said. "Does the archive get a free subscription to my paper or something?"

"Or something," Yossi said, opening an unmarked door on the right. "Welcome to the Galactic Free Press room."

"You have a whole room set aside for our reporters?"

"It will be open to everybody when the rest of the workstations arrive and get connected. Your publisher heard that the newspaper archives on Earth were in danger of being lost due to lack of funding and made a substantial donation." He swiped a screen alive and pulled a tray out from under the table that included an old-fashioned keyboard and a pointing device. "You can try voice control if you prefer, but our beta tests indicated that typing is more efficient. It's an English interface added to a standard Verlock archive system, so it's a bit quirky, but millions of years in advance of anything that we could have managed ourselves."

"And the technology transfer restrictions?"

"Because all of the information in the system was generated by our own people on Earth, it falls under the exclusion for entertainment devices," Yossi told her. Then a strange jingle sounded from his pocket and he pulled out his phone and grimaced. "A couple of visiting academics are fighting over a manuscript in the reading room so I have to run. Just dial our main number and ask for extension double-oh-seven if you need me. I'll check back when I can."

Georgia soon lost herself in the intuitive Verlock search system, which started with a basic query but then asked her to score the importance of various topic areas, such as crime, history, smuggling, and collectibles. When it presented the first list of ten results, each included the option to eliminate records from the same source in future searches. And best of all there were no advertisements cluttering up the screen.

By the time Yossi returned to check on her before lunch, she had a whole list of potentially related stories to follow up on. The most surprising was a seventy-year-old theft of a hundred thousand rainbow trout smelts from a fish hatchery in Maine, but there was also a fifty-year-old story about an identity-theft ring that used the names to get around limits on otherwise legitimate purchases of livestock semen. When she had shifted to thefts of collectibles, there was a story from just two years after the Stryx opened Earth about a national historical site, the Springfield Armory, that somehow lost its whole collection of antique firearms during a move. Then there was a funny series of articles from before her parents were born speculating about which alien species was buying up all the earthworms farmed for bait shops.

"You look like you had a good morning," Yossi said. "Do you need to make any prints?"

"What? I've been dictating notes to my reporter's tab because I thought everything was in copyright."

"The Verlock system is set up to allow you to print up to five percent of any publication. We charge twenty eCents a page and you pick it up at the reception desk on your way out."

"But is it legal?"

"Ten eCents goes to the newspaper, assuming the copyright royalty agency can locate the intellectual property owners. Otherwise, the money goes into a scholarship fund for law school students."

"That seems a bit counterproductive," Georgia said.

"I didn't make the deal. Supposedly it dates back to the old national government and nobody has replaced it with anything. A lot of the laws in North America are like that. A lot of everything on Earth is like that." His phone began to sing again and he looked at it regretfully, "Including these things, but we had to draw a line about replacing all of the tech on Earth with alien-made gadgets somewhere. Human pride has its price."

Fifteen

Ellen kept her hand on the butt of the stunner in her low-slung shoulder bag as she entered the park. A single flickering streetlight offered less illumination than the half-moon shining through the light cloud cover. A man wearing an overcoat with a fur collar was sitting on the park bench waiting, his features almost visible in the glow from his tab. Behind the bench stood a pair of bodyguards in black suits that matched that of the man waiting next to the limo floater at the curb just outside the park entrance. One of the bodyguards leaned forward to the seated man and whispered something.

"You're her?" the man asked, looking up from his tab but not rising.

"I'm Ellen, if that's what you mean. You're—"

"No names yet," he interrupted. "I was told you'd have a gryphon."

"I do, but I don't keep her on a leash. She's up there somewhere," Ellen said, pointing at the sky. "I have my Galactic Free Press badge if there's a question—"

"Anybody can forge an ID," the man interrupted again. "Gryphons, not so much."

"Tell your guards not to point any guns at Semmi when I call her down or I won't be responsible for her reaction," Ellen warned.

The man nodded at his bodyguards and motioned for the reporter to proceed. Rather than waving her arms, Ellen tried the whistle that John taught her. Semmi glided in from the dark, spit out some drone parts, and made a hacking noise.

"Is that one of ours?" the man asked the shorter of his two guards.

"Paint color is wrong," the guard replied tersely. "Looks like the expensive type the paparazzi use, with a stealth coating that kept it off the radar of our security drones."

"If you see another one of those, you can catch it," Ellen told the gryphon, who took a few running bounds and launched herself back into the sky. Then Ellen addressed the man on the bench. "You're satisfied with who I am now?"

"Can't be too careful," he said, and then offered his hand without standing. "Governor-General Charles Mayhew at your service. If you'll give us a little privacy, gentlemen."

"We should search her first," the taller bodyguard said.

"If she was here to assassinate me, the gryphon would have taken care of it already," retorted the most powerful figure in New York. He smiled and patted the bench next to him.

Ellen approached warily and sat closer to the end of the bench than the middle.

"Thank you for agreeing to meet me, even if you chose a dark park in a section of the city I wouldn't have visited without a gryphon watching my back," she said.

"And I wouldn't have asked Steve to forward my message to your publisher if I didn't have a reason."

"Steve? As in the president of EarthCent?"

"They need to come up with a less grandiose job title for the position. He's a sharp cookie, though not as tough as Hildy, but I've got more people working as sewer inspectors than EarthCent employs on the whole planet."

"He has the authority to grant sovereign status to the real-estate holdings of aliens who start businesses on Earth," Ellen said.

"True, but only because of the deal the Stryx forced on us," Mayhew shot back angrily, and then made a visible effort to calm himself. "Neither of us came here to argue about politics or debate the past. Did you know we've had an offer for the Brooklyn Bridge?"

"What!"

"Some unidentified collector, a rich alien no doubt, via a Thark intermediary. I have to say that the money is tempting."

"But how would people get back and forth between Brooklyn and Manhattan?"

"It's primarily a walking bridge these days since floaters can go over water, but the main obstacle is that it's part of our heritage, not to mention one of our leading tourist attractions. You wouldn't believe how many aliens are willing to pay to climb on the cable lattice to pose for—but that's not why I contacted your publisher either."

"Well, the Thark would have been a dead-end for my investigation anyway," Ellen said. "They handle most of the dark transactions on the tunnel network and they have a reputation for absolute discretion."

"Listen," the governor-general said. "I have as much respect for cultural artifacts as the next guy, but I'm also responsible for the well-being of the twenty million citizens left living between the Republic of Boston and Chicagoland, so I can't afford to be too sentimental. My intelligence people tell me that your news syndicate is digging into the possibility that a criminal gang has been systematically looting Earth for decades, if not all the way back to the Stryx opening."

"As is the president's office and EarthCent Intelligence, with the grudging cooperation of local law enforcement," Ellen added pointedly.

"When I took this job, there was a letter in the desk from my predecessor. Do you want to guess what it said?"

"Wait, I've heard this joke. Is the punch line something about writing a letter?"

"That's with three letters, and after a few years in this job, it's no longer funny," Mayhew said. "No, this letter was signed by every governor-general going back to the founding of the city-state, and as I found out later, it disappeared as soon as I put it back in the drawer, some kind of alien trick." He sighed. "Do you know how governments coped after the Stryx opened Earth and the best and brightest of our population began leaving the planet?"

"I'm not a historian, but I understand it was pretty rough for a while," Ellen said.

"We all went broke under the weight of pension obligations to retired employees as our tax base crashed faster than we could downsize. Essential services ground to a halt all over, even the public education system collapsed, though the Stryx stepped in to supply us with teacher bots for homeschooling. There was a period when we couldn't even police all of Manhattan and lost part of the island to gangs."

"And then remittances to families started coming in from the contract workers on alien worlds?"

"That made a difference, of course, and while it's not widely known, the tunnel network has some loan programs for primitive worlds that helped us maintain critical infrastructure," he said. "It's the one instance where our short lifespans work in our favor. We opted for balloon payments and the maturity dates on the first loans we took out are still hundreds of years in the future. But when it came to the discretionary funding needed to maintain the quality of life at a sufficient level such that every last person didn't leave the planet, taxes couldn't close the gap in the early days."

"Are you about to tell me the city-states turned to organized crime?" Ellen asked.

"There was plenty of that as well, but the most reliable source of income turned out to be asset sales. Whole families left on multi-decade alien contracts, and real estate prices crashed to the extent that many properties weren't worth selling and were eventually taken for back taxes."

"Sounds like somebody got rich."

"It took decades for a new balance to emerge, and then it turned out that some aliens were willing to let contract workers start independent colonies on open worlds, and a new wave of emigration began," Mayhew said. "The early governors-general were desperate for a way to preserve a core of professionals to operate the power grid, the communications networks, and provide sanitation engineering, all in the face of alien recruiters promising more interesting work in exotic locations with tax-free earnings."

"So they sold assets to raise money," Ellen said. "I understand your logic, but I'm having trouble connecting it with—wait. Are you telling me they sold assets that didn't belong to the government?"

"Who owns the public libraries, the museums, the airports, and the roads?"

"The government? Or are there independent authorities, like with the elevator? And can you really sell a road?"

"You can, and then the new owner adds tolls, but that had already been done to death before the Stryx opened Earth," Mayhew explained. "It turns out that many institutions we think of as public are run by not-for-profit foundations. That's basically a charity that preserves assets or carries out a mission rather than redistributing funds to the needy. And wealthy people in the pre-Stryx era were often able to protect their estates from taxes by creating not-for-profit foundations."

"Sounds like a loophole of sorts."

"It was. My point is that governments needed cash, yet most of the really valuable collectibles on Earth were tied up in foundations we couldn't touch."

"So you changed the laws?" Ellen asked.

"Not exactly." The governor-general fixed her with a penetrating stare and said, "This is all on deep background, right?"

"You're supposed to make that request before you start spilling the beans, but it was kind of my assumption going in."

"Just here on the island of Manhattan we had museums with tens of billions of creds of artwork and antiquities, most of it shut up in dark vaults where nobody could even see them. The public library housed more volumes in private collections that could only be accessed by researchers than they did books that could be borrowed by readers." He paused and took a deep breath. "My predecessors did a deal with alien brokers."

"You mean they really did sell off assets they didn't own."

"That would have caused riots. Instead, they sold harvesting rights for certain items to alien brokers, who then employed middlemen to recover said items, provided they could do so without causing damage to persons or property."

"You're saying the government collected fees for allowing aliens to hire burglars to steal the assets you couldn't legally sell," Ellen surmised.

"That's one way of putting it," Mayhew said. "The practice wound down years before I became governor-general, but it appears that some of the thieves got together and offered their services to less reputable brokers."

"So the government isn't profiting from the current wave of thefts, but you're reluctant to get involved for fear of exposing past sins?"

"Exactly. I can't offer you access to the records because my predecessors wisely didn't keep any, but if you look into private collections that were bequeathed to institutions, including universities and private museums, you're likely to find that some famous pieces haven't been displayed in many years."

"And this raised enough money to keep the government going?"

"Government always keeps going until somebody else takes over, the question is whether or not it meets the needs of its citizens," Mayhew said. "The alien collectors were only interested in unique items which were concentrated in the hands of a very small number of institutions and individuals. We didn't have anything else to sell."

"What about the loss to human heritage?" Ellen asked.

"The museums and libraries still have more artwork and books than they can display in a lifetime." There was a loud screech from above, and fragments of a drone rained down on the ground in front of the bench. "That's my cue," the governor-general said, rising suddenly to his feet. "You know how to contact me if anything comes up."

"And the strategic reserves of seeds and genetic material that were either stolen or purchased on false premises?" Ellen asked.

"Don't know anything about that," Mayhew said as his bodyguards appeared out of the dark as if by magic. "It doesn't sound profitable enough to have attracted government involvement."

"You wait here until the limo is gone," one of the bodyguards told the journalist as she started to rise. He glanced up at the dark sky, and added, "Cool gryphon."

While Ellen waited in time-out, John was swatting at giant mosquitoes in the jungle of an island belonging to the Jakarta city-state. There was nothing particularly special about the trail they'd been on since leaving the floater at the riverbank, though if his guide had tested him on the flora, John couldn't have named a single plant or tree. Then he began to notice a change, as if the rainforest was transitioning to something else but not quite getting there. The towering trees remained, but the ground itself took on a rolling aspect as if they were climbing in and out of shallow trenches.

"Was this area cleared for farming and then abandoned?" he asked the guide.

"No. The rainforest on this island was always protected—even scientific expeditions required special permits."

"But it's not a natural phenomenon," John stated with some certainty. "Even though the trees remain, the rest of the vegetation is different, somehow. Less balanced."

"You have a good eye," the guide said. "What you are witnessing is theft on a grand scale, one that stretched over decades. Our scientists have calculated that hundreds of square kilometers of virgin jungle were removed from this rainforest, and the aliens even took the dirt to a depth sufficient that the flora would survive."

"You're sure it was aliens?"

"Humans lack the ability to do this sort of thing so neatly. We theorize that they used holograms or other advanced camouflage techniques to hide their work crews, and then kept those devices active for years, until the rainforest recovered sufficiently that the losses weren't obvious to satellite imaging or flyovers. Leaving the big trees untouched and only removing narrow swathes helped, though they couldn't replace all of the soil."

"Did they take wildlife as well?" John asked.

"The contract specified both flora and fauna," the guide said grimly. "Do you know that ten percent of all of the world's species are found in our rainforests?"

"What was that bit about a contract?"

"So they were too embarrassed to tell you at the Ministry. What do you know about the history of Greater Jakarta?"

"Nothing," the EarthCent Intelligence agent confessed. "This is my first time in Asia."

"When the Stryx opened Earth, our population was young and poor compared to the West, or even our neighbors in Oceana. Within a few decades, eighty percent of our people had left on alien work contracts, and since those who remained behind were mainly the elderly, the population never recovered. My grandparents were among the first to leave and they never looked back. My parents, however, retired to Earth after making their fortune working in Frunge textile factories. They were at the forefront of the movement known as the Homecoming."

"From what I saw of the city, it must have gone well."

"The leaders of the Homecoming knew what they were up against, so they pooled their resources and brought with them two armies of mercenaries to depose the latest corrupt government. They replaced it with a system that, if I may speak frankly, they copied from the Frunge."

"I didn't know the Stryx would allow an invading army through the tunnel," John said in surprise.

"Human mercenaries, and most of them originally from this area," the guide explained. "All in the family as far as the Stryx were concerned. The Homecoming took place almost twenty years ago, long enough that graduates of the New Jakarta University have started sifting through the over a half-century of history that played out while the seventeen thousand plus islands of Greater Jakarta were ruled, or not, by a succession of strongmen. The contracts I referred to were only recently discovered."

"I don't suppose the buyers used their real names."

"Or their real species. This last year there's been an internal debate in the government over whether or not to publicize the facts. Having one's rainforests looted doesn't seem like something to brag on, but then the story about stolen monuments in New York hit the news, followed by the Interpol request for cooperation with EarthCent Intelligence. That's when I asked my uncle to send you the invitation."

"When he introduced us, he told me that you had first-hand knowledge of the situation, but he didn't mention what it is you do," John said.

"I'm writing my dissertation on what we call the Dark Ages, the period between the fall of the last democratically elected government and Homecoming. My wife is also in the department, and she's the one who discovered the contracts in an old records room. The various dictatorships created a great deal of paperwork, perhaps in an attempt to prove their legitimacy."

"Have you spoken to any local investigative journalists? We've been leaning on them to do much of the legwork since they know their local areas and aren't worried about making the police or government look bad."

"My girlfriend is visiting the offices of the biggest paper in Greater Jakarta as we speak, and I won't be surprised if I'm doing this tour again tomorrow with some reporters in tow. Now that the council of elders has decided to go public, it makes sense to show the damage while it's still obvious, and also that nature is on its way to recovering."

"It certainly seems like nature is winning the battle most places I've visited on this planet," John said. "I'm told that the sheer amount of greenery is one of the things that attracts so many Frunge tourists to Earth."

"I wish my generation could take credit for that, but I have a friend in university who studies the world-wide changes in population distribution that have occurred since the Stryx opened the planet. Despite all of the vacation homes and country estates you hear about, the urbanization that was taking place in the twenty-first century only accelerated. You would think that with access to floater technology, people would choose to live in nature, but it seems that most of us prefer to clump together and work in air-conditioning. Combine that with a population that's approximately a third of its peak count, and you find that nature is reclaiming ground almost everywhere."

John marveled at a tree whose above-ground root structure looked like an abstract sculpture in wood. Unfamiliar birds made a racket in the canopy, and he saw something that looked like an armadillo moving across the path with no apparent fear of humans.

"Were all of the contracts your girlfriend found related to selling swathes of rainforest for harvest or was there anything else?"

The guide smiled grimly again. "It seems that one of the great tragedies of our cultural history, the Night of Burning, was a cover story for selling museum collections. The dictator in power at the time blamed the fires on religious zealots out to destroy heretical artifacts, but now we know the collections were removed before the museums were destroyed. The Council of Elders is looking into our legal options, though unless we can figure out who the buyers were, the chances of recovery are zero."

"That's pretty rough," John said sympathetically.

"We try to look on the bright side. Our heritage is safe somewhere, and if the thugs who ruled our nation those years hadn't sold it to the aliens, the museum complex probably would have burned down or collapsed from neglect. We're trying to interest the Grenouthians in doing a documentary."

Sixteen

"—and over twenty thousand squirrel cages were also discovered in the warehouse and never claimed," Georgia concluded her report. "Are there any questions?"

"Bryan Livingston," one of the journalists on the teleconference introduced himself. "Do you mean squirrel cage induction motors? The kind used in blowers?"

"No. These were cages manufactured specifically for transporting squirrels. In fact, the reporter who wrote the article went into great detail about the latch mechanism on the cages. She had personal experience with squirrels raiding her bird feeders and came away with great respect for their resourcefulness."

"But what would anybody do with all of those squirrels, chipmunks, and what was that other one you mentioned?"

"Voles. A type of small rodent. And I don't have a clue, but the empty cages were all discovered in the same warehouse where the turtles and snakes were found. All of the paperwork led to shell companies, so it's very likely the same people were involved."

"Or the same aliens," another reporter contributed without enabling his video.

"And this was sixty-something years ago?" Bryan followed up.

Georgia checked her notes. "Yes. Around the same time that conservationists throughout North America were reporting coming across deer of various species that had been hit with tranquilizer darts that failed to bring them down. And the deer population mysteriously stabilized despite a fall-off in the number of hunters."

"Could some aliens have been taking all these animals for meat, maybe to feed their contract workers from Earth?"

Ellen tapped the "unmute" on her phone, and the little red light indicating the camera was on went live. "While not impossible, it's highly unlikely for a number of reasons," she said. "If an alien species wanted to bring meat from Earth to feed contract workers, I think they could have bought it on the open market cheaper than stealthily trapping and removing live animals from the wilderness. And having looked up voles, I couldn't imagine a less efficient way of supplying protein to humans. They're smaller than mice."

"My paper keeps a file of tips for stories that never made it into print because the reporter couldn't find enough substantiating evidence," another of the syndicated journalists contributed. "After you messaged us about this meeting, I looked back through the file, and some of those stories don't seem so crazy anymore."

"Can you give us an example?"

"There was one from just before I joined the paper, around ten years ago, about a local beekeeper reporting to the police that his main rival was conspiring with aliens to steal all of his bees," the woman said. "When the reporter went out to talk with the beekeeper, he admitted that none of his bees were actually missing, but he had seen spaceships coming and going from his rival's increase-yard.

Since she was already in the area, the reporter decided to visit the other beekeeper. He denied everything but behaved so strangely that she was sure he was lying. She also noticed that he had a brand new luxury floater parked in an old barn and that his increase yard was empty of hives."

"That's pretty thin for a story," Ellen said.

"Some other neighbors corroborated a spaceship coming and going, but that's not illegal, and the reporter couldn't justify investing more time on a story that was probably motivated by professional jealousy."

"My archive search did turn something up about a mail-order house specializing in queen bees getting in trouble for tax evasion because they had been selling for cash to drive-up customers," Georgia said.

"It must have been an old small-town paper to report on something so trivial," somebody commented.

"The amount of unreported income was over a hundred thousand eBucks, so it must have been a lot of queen bees."

"Could it have been our own communities on open worlds bringing in the flora and fauna they know for agricultural allotments?" another journalist asked.

"Nobody is enthusiastic about having their world overrun by invasive species," Ellen said. "Most aliens allow contract workers to grow vegetables, though they use technology to create isolation zones. I've had offers to carry those cargoes in the past, and the documentation required makes it unlikely theft was involved."

"I still don't see voles as food," Georgia said. "Pet food, maybe. But as long as we're on the subject, the headquarters of Drazen Foods isn't far from where I'm staying, and—"

"Did my phone screen just die?" another journalist interrupted. "I saw her talking and then everything went white."

"Mine too," a number of voices echoed.

"Sorry," Georgia said, coming back into view. "I have my phone propped against my purse and it slid down."

"They make a folding stand for teleconferencing," Bryan said. "It's only a couple of eBucks."

"I think we're on the right track, and the Galactic Free Press is committed to publishing an ongoing series with the articles we're buying from your syndicate until we get to the bottom of what's going on," Ellen said. "Has anybody been subject to push-back from local law enforcement or criminals while following up on leads?"

"Yes," several journalists said at the same time, causing the phone displays to momentarily flash to a grid of faces before settling on the one man who continued talking. "Sato Hideo, Greater Osaka Journal when they can afford to keep me employed. I've received a blunt warning to stop looking into samurai armor that went missing from several family association vaults in recent years."

"Dendera, New Egypt," another journalist introduced herself. "Following your suggestion, I've been digging into archeological finds that are supposed to be housed in the Cairo Museum but haven't been on display in decades. The amount of material they have is staggering, so it's not surprising that many pieces are rarely put on view. But I have a source in the curator's office who told me less notable pieces go missing every year, and they treat it almost like a natural form of attrition. The official line is that the missing items are miscataloged and will likely turn up one day."

"That's what they always say at the British Library," a man with a cockney accent put in. "Everybody knows there's stealing going on but nobody wants to admit it."

Ellen's phone blinked, and then displayed an image of a pirate with a parrot on one shoulder and a hacksaw dangling from a hook-hand. "Arrh, my hearties. I be bombing this meeting."

"Who is that?" Ellen asked. "Please go away," but the video conference was locked-out. "Georgia?" she asked the other reporter, who was sitting across the table from her in the office they had reserved in the meeting facility for traders at the base of the tunnel stalk. "Is your phone locked out?"

"Stupid guy with a parrot? This used to happen all the time when I had remote classes in university. Everybody who lives on Earth knows to just shut down and try again later."

"But I thought it was encrypted."

"It is, but these phones only support native encryption technologies, and the hackers have been smuggling in alien hardware that can cut through it in a matter of minutes if they target your feed," Georgia explained. "If you want to get everybody back, just send them a text with a new meeting code."

"No, I think I'll tell them to just wait for tomorrow's scheduled meeting," Ellen said, typing away with her thumbs. "I just got taken by surprise because I thought that little lock in the corner meant it was secure."

"It means the designer thought it was secure." Georgia waited for Ellen to finish sending the message before continuing. "I thought the hypothesis about a food tie-in was interesting, even though I don't see it applying to voles. But my instincts tell me that we're dealing with completely different groups here."

"The same finely honed instincts that told you Colony One was a scam?" Ellen teased the younger journalist. "Okay then. Where do you draw the line?"

"I think that all of the valuable pieces that are being stolen, with or without some level of cooperation from the owners or local governments, are disappearing into alien collections. They likely won't surface again until so many generations have passed that any reporting we do now will only be seen as buttressing the provenance."

"That may be true, but if we make everybody aware that it's going on, maybe we can prevent some future crimes from taking place."

"It's just as likely that our stories will have people raiding their local historical societies and trying to hawk the stuff to alien tourists," Georgia said, "but ultimately, it's up to the institutions that accumulated all those valuables to protect them. I'm far more interested in the biological side of the story. The breadth of samples going missing, both living and frozen tissue, suggests a highly organized operation with tremendous resources. Keep in mind that it's not just about collecting all of the samples and moving them off Earth. The whole exercise would be pointless unless there's some master plan to do something with it all."

"I feel the same way, but I can't quite put my finger on it," Ellen said. "I'm going to ask M793qK when Flower gets here because the Farlings are the galaxy's champions at collecting biological samples. He's also—"

"Flower!" Georgia interrupted. "That's it."

"You think Flower is responsible? She has a lot of room on board, and maybe some decks nobody has ever seen, but I can't see her importing twenty thousand rodents or redecorating with stolen rainforests."

"Not Flower herself, but a colony ship of her class. I know from her tour that she can provide a permanent home for five million humanoids, so you can imagine how much ag deck space she contains if you rolled it all out flat. I'll bet some species or another has seen how well Flower is doing and is fixing up a colony ship of their own to get into the same business."

"Working for EarthCent?" Ellen asked. "For one thing, the Stryx set that up, and even if somebody tricked out a colony ship to look just like Earth, they can't waltz in and demand a job hosting humans. For another thing, Flower is still operating at less than twenty percent capacity, so there's hardly a pressing need."

"But it all adds up," Georgia said. "Well, maybe not the frozen genetic samples, but the seed bank, the varied flora and fauna, the humane traps and cages..."

"Let me check something." Ellen stared off into space for a moment, accessing her heads-up display, and then tapped out a number on her phone.

"Drazen Foods," a young man's voice answered on the first ring. "Glunk's office. I'm his special assistant. May I help you?"

"I'm Ellen, from the—"

"Galactic Free Press, their Earth Syndication Coordinator," the young man cut her off. "You're on my special contact list. Glunk was wondering why you never called."

"Is there a time I could meet with him?"

"He's open this afternoon from three until five if you're in the area."

"We're at the elevator stalk, and I'd like to bring a colleague," Ellen said.

"You have plenty of time to rent a floater and drive out, or would you prefer I dispatch a limo?"

"We'll drive, thank you. See you at three." As soon as the call disconnected, her smile slipped, and she turned to Georgia and asked, "Do you know how to drive?"

"Are you serious? You've been spending a week on Earth every month for the last year and you've never driven a floater?"

"I take public transportation or taxis, it just hasn't come up," Ellen said. "Is there a test before they'll let us take one?"

"Floaters drive themselves. Even the old Earth cars with rubber tires were self-driving a century ago, or at least, I think they were. All you need is a programmable cred, and there must be a dozen rental agencies within fifteen minutes of here. They're lined up along the monorail."

"I thought those were parking lots."

"They are, for rental floaters," Georgia explained. "Most people coming to the elevator hub for a ride up to orbit are leaving for months, if not years. Larry told me that there's a short-term lot at the other end of the monorail that will fill up when Flower gets here, but there aren't a lot of other reasons for people to take a day-long trip up to orbit and return the same week."

While Ellen gathered her things, Georgia went back to fooling around with her phone and then looked up triumphantly. "The floater's all set and we don't even have to stop at the rental counter. I charged it to the paper through my phone."

"I can't believe you've only had that thing for a week and you're so much better at it than me."

"I lived on my phone when I was in university, probably trying to compensate for the fact my parents didn't let me have one growing up," Georgia said, and then her face fell. "I promised Larry he could meet them."

"What's so bad about that?" Ellen asked, following the younger journalist out of the building.

"Didn't I tell you that I grew up in a commune where half of the people believed that aliens don't exist?"

"Yes, but everybody has embarrassing parents."

"Not Larry, his parents are perfect," Georgia said, stepping onto a moving walkway. "Oh, the chat room I set up for our video conference is getting flooded with messages. Give me a minute to catch up."

"Where are we getting off this thing?"

"My phone will beep when we get there."

Ellen looked at her own phone, which was showing the low-battery warning, and decided to just enjoy the scenery. Eventually, there was a loud beep and Georgia stepped off the moving walkway. There was a louder beep from the parking area, and Ellen spotted a floater with the running lights blinking.

"That's us," Georgia said, finally looking up from her phone. "Don't open the door until we do the inspection."

"I don't know anything about floaters."

"Just look for dents and scratches."

"I thought you said it drives itself."

"It does, but some people insist on taking over with the manual controls, and since the floater doesn't need roads, you can get into a lot of trouble."

Ellen did a clockwise circuit of the floater while Georgia went counter-clockwise, and neither of them turned up anything worth noting. When they got in, Georgia held her phone near the dashboard until there was another beep, and then the floater rose above the level of the other vehicles in the lot and began to accelerate.

"Don't you have to tell it where we're going?" Ellen asked.

"I did that when I rented it," Georgia said.

"And what happens if it rains?"

"None of these floaters have roofs. They're basically cut-down versions of the same ones the Dollnicks manufacture for themselves, so everything is done with advanced field technology. Any species that can engineer atmosphere retention fields to separate between an open docking bay and the vacuum of space can keep the rain and wind out."

The floater suddenly dipped hard, and both women instinctively reached out to brace against the dashboard. There was a loud click from the back seat.

"Semmi," Georgia said, turning and scratching the gryphon above the eye ridge. "You decided to come with us."

"I think John bribed her to keep an eye on me," Ellen said. "He worries that we may run into a crime in progress and get in trouble. I hope Glunk likes gryphons."

As it turned out, the principal stakeholder of Drazen Foods loved Semmi on sight. When he introduced her to a new line of treats the food scientists had been working on for beaked species, it became clear he had made a friend for life.

When they returned to his office after the factory tour he insisted on giving them personally, the Drazen asked, "So, what can I do to help the Galactic Free Press?"

"Have you been following any of the news reporting about how somebody has been systematically looting Earth for decades?" Ellen asked.

"From the stories I've seen, it wasn't clear to me whether the items in question were truly stolen, or if they were purchased from people who arguably had some legal right to sell them," Glunk said. "I'm the last Drazen who's going to defend aliens raiding the cultural treasures of a primitive species, but having done business on this planet for a decade, I've learned how difficult it can be to figure out who owns the legal rights to what."

"When it comes to museum-quality collectibles, it seems to be a mix of opportunistic buying and outright theft, but what I wanted to talk to you about is the biological samples. My understanding is that you work with suppliers all over the world."

"Drazen Foods contracts with over a quarter-million family farmers and cooperatives across six continents, though more than three-quarters of our input comes from the Americas," Glunk said modestly. "We do encourage all of our suppliers to let us know if they see any suspicious aliens in the area, purely for competitive reasons. Other than a rash of Farling sightings a year or so ago, we haven't heard of anything unusual."

"How many Farlings constitutes a rash?" Georgia asked.

"It may have been a single one moving around taking samples. But keep in mind that people tend to notice aliens who resemble beetles scaled up to the size of a brown bear. If there are Vergallians or Hortens operating on Earth, they could go undetected with little effort, and even Drazens and Frunge may pass at night in the countryside. I checked on the Farling issue with friends in the intelligence community, and it turns out that EarthCent gave them carte blanche to collect genetic samples as part of some diplomatic deal."

"We haven't published all of the stories yet because they're coming in so fast, but in addition to the sort of biological samples kept by research institutions, our archival research has also turned up indications of large scale removals of live mammals, fish, birds, and even earthworms," Georgia said.

"Then it must be an attempt to jumpstart a terraforming project," Glunk concluded immediately. "If you had said dogs or cats, it might have been the illegal pet trade, but Humans are the only species I've ever heard of that keeps ants and worms in their houses on purpose."

"We thought maybe a colony ship?" Ellen suggested.

"Doubtful. If you take into account the acreage of the rainforest from Indonesia, Africa, and the Amazon that's been harvested, it would stuff the ag decks of a fleet of colony ships. And that's not to mention the large area of missing taiga in Siberia, which shows up from space if you use hologram-penetrating scopes. In fact—" the Drazen suddenly cut himself off and asked, "This is all on deep background, right?"

"Why does everybody wait until the middle of the interview to tell me that?" Ellen complained. "All right. You're doing us a favor and we're not gotcha journalists like the Grenouthians. Where does all this information come from?"

"Those of us doing business on this planet have found it advisable to overlook the differences between our species and cooperate on certain matters," Glunk said. "I'm sure you understand that all members of tunnel network species living on alien planets are expected to maintain some level of contact with their native intelligence agencies, and that information can flow both ways."

"But ISPOA, the Interspecies Police Operations Agency, is cooperating with EarthCent Intelligence."

"EarthCent Intelligence is the only example I know of that combines spying and police work in a single agency," the Drazen said. "The rest of the tunnel network species are very careful to keep those functions distinct for reasons that are obvious if you think about it. My money is on your missing biomass being used for a terraforming project somewhere, which is a long-term concern for Drazen Foods if they are setting up to go into competition with us. I'm beginning to think that all of the money I invested trade-marking 'Grown on Earth' in every empire within ten thousand light-years may pay off."

"I can see animals, fish smelts, even insects, but what would a terraformer want with genetic samples?" Georgia asked.

"Clones," Glunk replied. "It points to Gem involvement, though they've been poor for so long that rogue Gem scientists hiring out to run cloning operations was common even before their revolution. If I was a betting Drazen, I'd put my money on the Dollnicks. I'm currently in negotiations with Flower about a joint project so I can check with her for you when we next meet."

"That's okay," Ellen said. "Flower and I are old friends, and I'll be heading up to orbit for Rendezvous as soon as she arrives."

Seventeen

"Thanks for meeting me here," Larry greeted John. "I almost didn't recognize you with the sunglasses."

"Maybe the swelling has gone down," the EarthCent Intelligence agent replied, removing the glasses and slipping them into his breast pocket. "How do I look?"

"Like you've been in a barroom brawl. What happened?"

"I've been hopscotching around the globe in suborbitals to follow up on leads from ISPOA. I walked into the wrong barn in Old France."

"You got roughed up by agricultural smugglers?"

"Gendarmes, it's what they call the police there. I'm still not sure if the operation was only protected at the local level or if the whole chain of command is implicated, but there didn't seem to be any point in asking for further cooperation from the local law enforcement. Besides, the investigative journalists working for the news syndicate Ellen helped set up are coming up with new evidence faster than I can process it. I'm beginning to understand why some agents are calling for a merger between the Galactic Free Press and EarthCent Intelligence."

"I've been too busy with the final arrangements for Rendezvous to keep track of the news, and all of my spare time goes into researching my map crystals," Larry said.

"Did I ask you if you've ever come across any during your travels?"

"Three times now. But remind me what we're doing here?"

"A courtesy call on the elevator logistics manager."

"The guy who schedules the containers, like a loadmaster on a cargo ship?" John asked.

"The name is Darla, so I'm guessing a woman," Larry said. "I asked Georgia to set it up for me since she's the cell phone specialist in our family."

"I've resisted getting one, but during this last trip, I had to keep borrowing phones from people I was with when I needed to talk to Ellen. I never thought I'd be able to memorize such a long number, but after the third or fourth call, I didn't have to check for it on my heads-up display anymore."

"Anyway, according to the map Georgia showed me, Darla's office is in that warehouse that looks like it could fit an interstellar liner."

"And going by the size of the hill of dirt out back, they're excavating for an expansion," John said. "It will be a nice change to introduce myself as a representative of the Traders Guild rather than as a cop."

"Less chance of getting punched," Larry said with a laugh. "Georgia was able to pull up the layout of the offices in the warehouse, and if we go in that side entrance, we'll be right there."

The first thing Darla said when the two men walked into her office was, "That one looks like a cop who got punched in the eye so you must be Phil's son."

"I'm Larry, he's John. This is his first year on the council so I asked him to come along and get a little exposure to how we make arrangements for Rendezvous."

"And you've done this before?"

"Like you said, I'm Phil's son, so I've been watching my dad do this all my life. Did you get my estimates?"

"I got them, I just don't believe them," Darla said. "You expect us to see an additional ten thousand tourists taking the elevator during or immediately after Rendezvous?"

"We're expecting over fifty thousand ships to show up—the Stryx are offering free tunnel transit for any traders who aren't carrying commercial cargo for Earth. If you figure on two people per ship as the average, and many of them never having visited Earth before, I may be underestimating."

"But they have their own ships. Why don't they just land?"

"The elevator is a lot cheaper than eating into the fuel pack, not to mention parking and general wear-and-tear from the atmosphere. Unless they're planning to do business on Earth, I'd be surprised if anybody chooses to land over a relaxing elevator ride."

"If I have to put on passenger capacity, I will, but with Flower here, we're going to be flat out moving cargo," Darla said.

"And that's your job, managing the cargo flow?" John asked.

"It's all a balancing act. Think of the elevator as a super-sized cargo vessel, but rather than stacking containers in the holds, or as ocean ships do, on the deck as well, they're all strung out in a line on the stalk going either up or down. Unless there's a big attraction in orbit, like the twice a year Flower stops at Earth, our cargo container to passenger capsule ratio is pushing a hundred to one."

"Can you transport people up to the hub in cargo containers?"

"The stowaways seem to think so, but when the Dollnicks sold us the elevator, they provided enough passenger capsules to fill every position on the stalk. You didn't see them when you came in?"

"We used the door just down the hall from this office."

"That's a staff-only entrance, it shouldn't have opened for you," she said with a frown. "Come on. I'll show you the warehouse."

Three minutes later, they stood on an observation catwalk overlooking the inside of the cavernous building that was filled nearly to the roof with standard-sized containers and passenger capsules.

"If you don't know anything about the history of Earth's elevators, they were built and installed by the Dollnicks under an EarthCent contract guaranteed by the Stryx," Darla said. "Part of the original contract stipulated that the Dollnicks provide enough passenger capsules to fill every slot on the stalk, I guess in case we had to evacuate the planet in an emergency."

"No wonder you need more warehouse space," John said.

"What are you talking about?"

"The new construction. We saw the giant mound of dirt out back."

"We aren't expanding the warehouse, the ground would probably sink from the weight if we tried," Darla told him. "We use the dirt for load balancing."

"I don't follow."

"Earth's biggest exporter is Drazen Foods, and they use the elevator for whatever they can. But imports to Earth, at least by volume, have been outstripping exports for years. Just the floaters and entertainment systems we import account for more incoming containers than all of the outgoing traffic. Then there are all the household items of people returning home to retire on alien pensions. If we didn't load the empties with dirt and send them back into orbit, the whole city-state would be covered in containers by now."

"Why dirt?" Larry asked.

Darla shrugged. "You've got me. And it's mainly topsoil or compost. It comes in by floater-train from all over the continent."

John felt a tingle run down his spine. "You mean that somebody has been exporting dirt from Earth ever since the elevator stalk was built?"

"It's cheap ballast, not a product, so it doesn't show up in any export statistics. It's just to fill the containers and keep the weight on the stalk in balance." She rubbed her chin and added, "You know, when I first got this job, I asked why we didn't use sand or gravel, but I was told it's all needed here for making concrete. There's so much abandoned farmland on this continent that dirt was the cheapest alternative."

"What do they do with the dirt once it's in orbit at the elevator hub?"

"Well, there's no bill of lading," Darla said. "The containers are treated as empties, so I guess they just disappear into the system. Whoever is waiting for a container to ship their goods will be stuck getting rid of the dirt and washing them out. I went to a space elevator tradeshow on Void Station a couple of years ago, sort of a working vacation. One of the presenters said there are billions of containers of this type kicking around the galaxy, though a lot of them have been repurposed for other uses."

"I know a chandler on Union Station who converted a shipping container into a home," Larry contributed.

"But doesn't anybody track where the containers are all the time?" John asked. "They can't be cheap, and I'd bet the Dollnicks would have some technology that does the trick."

"They do, and there are lots of options for logistical managers to help with scheduling," Darla said. "That was a big part of the tradeshow. If we go back to the office, I can show you some holo catalogs I picked up, but I didn't have a budget to buy anything."

"Is there a central authority of some sort that tracks all of these containers on the tunnel network?"

"I'm sure the Stryx know what's going through their tunnels, though the Dollnicks have been building elevators and supplying containers to non-tunnel network species for a couple of million years. You wouldn't believe all the weird life-forms that showed up at that tradeshow. I had to wear earplugs in the exhibition hall to keep all of the alien vocalizations from driving me nuts. But everybody got really quiet when the Container Prince showed up."

"I thought he was a legend," Larry said. "My dad and his friends used to tell Container Prince stories to scare us when we camped out on alien worlds."

"I'll wager you both run Sharf two-man traders," Darla said, and then waited for them both to nod in agreement. "Human traders don't have much to do with elevator containers because they're way too big for your holds, but everybody in the interstellar shipping business knows about the Container Prince."

"A Dollnick?" John asked.

"Of course. They say he owns over a quarter of the containers in circulation, which is enough to control the rental rates. You know that containers are all rented or leased, right?"

"Makes sense. Otherwise, they'd only be good for round trips between one supplier and one customer, and unless they were bartering, one leg of the trip would be empty."

"That's the main challenge in the container business, keeping them moving and keeping them full," Darla said enthusiastically. "The Container Prince basically sets the prices for the whole tunnel network because all of the smaller container owners follow his lead."

"And they—"

"Sorry," Darla interrupted, pulling out her cell phone and swiping the screen. "Yes? Yes? Oh, no. I'll be right there." She stuffed the phone back in her jumpsuit pocket and said, "Sorry guys. We have a possible hazardous waste incident on the import side and I'm going to be tied up for the rest of the day. You found your way in so you can find your way out." Without waiting for a reply, she took off at a run.

"Interesting job," Larry said.

"Are you thinking what I'm thinking?" John asked.

"I'm glad I'm not in the commercial shipping business if that's what you mean. But it might be interesting to learn more about it, especially with Flower trying to organize a common carrier network for smaller shipments."

"I meant the dirt. There's no way that sending topsoil into space is the best solution for keeping the elevator stalk in balance. If I can find out where it's going, I'll know who's behind all of the crazy news reports about live poaching and missing biological materials that Ellen's reporters have been dredging out of their archives. Can I borrow your phone?"

"Don't own one," Larry said as they exited the warehouse. "I thought we just had that conversation."

"You told me that Georgia knew how to use all the advanced features, not that you didn't have one."

"We're only here for the run-up to Rendezvous and so she can help Ellen," the younger trader pointed out. "I may never come back to Earth again. You're here twice a month to drop off or pick up Ellen. What's your excuse?"

"EarthCent Intelligence warns agents not to carry them because they track your location on Earth and they're about as secure as semaphore."

"What's semaphore?"

"Signaling each other with flags," John explained. "It's the example the aliens always bring up when they want to make fun of us. Ouch!"

"Did I miss something?" Larry asked.

"Something hard just bounced off my head," John said, searching around the ground. He spotted an acorn lying on the asphalt despite the fact there wasn't a tree within shouting distance. "Semmi! Get down here."

The gryphon let out a gleeful "Scrawwww," before tucking her wings and plummeting like a stone.

"She's going to try to blow us off our feet," John warned Larry. "Brace yourself."

At the last second, Semmi extended her wings and gave a powerful beat just before landing on all fours. The two men were buffeted back but remained standing. The gryphon shook off her disappointment, and dipping her beak in the pouch slung around her neck, brought out a cell phone.

"Is that Ellen's?" John demanded. "What happened to her?"

"It just chirped," Larry said. "That means there's an incoming text."

The EarthCent Intelligence agent took the phone reluctantly and read the message out loud. "I bought Semmi a phone since you won't carry one. Now you can be like one of those officers in the historical immersives who had a soldier following him around with a radio."

"Was that really a thing?"

"Mercenary platoons still have a communication specialist who carries the heavy gear that can punch through interference if the implants are all jammed," John replied while dialing. "Ellen? You're never going to believe what I just learned. What? I'll put him on."

"She wants to talk to me?" Larry asked, looking at the phone on offer as if it was about to bite him.

"Flower's running ads for Rendezvous on all the Earth networks."

"What!" Larry took the phone. "Ellen?"

"She just handed me her phone," Georgia replied. "Did John tell you that Flower is running ads?"

"For Rendezvous, without bothering to keep me in the loop despite the fact I'm supposed to be in charge? Yeah."

"She's not exactly running ads for Rendezvous itself, but it's easier to show you than explain," Georgia said. "I'm going to text you a link right now and then you'll be able to watch it on the phone. I'll see you at dinner."

"Wait," Larry said, but the connection was already broken. A moment later the phone chirped again, and a strange string of underlined numbers and letters appeared. "She sent us something, but it looks garbled or in code," he said, passing the phone back to John.

The EarthCent Intelligence agent squinted at the text like that would help, and then shook his head. "You better call her back," he said, extending the phone to Larry, who kept his hands behind his back.

There was a loud snort, and Semmi grabbed the phone with one of her front paws. She pressed the tip of her beak against the link Georgia had texted and a video began to play. Rather than giving it back, the gryphon held onto the phone, forcing John and Larry to crowd in behind her and look over her folded wings.

The ad started with a view of a Sharf two-man trader hanging in space against a background of ringed planets that had obviously been arranged for aesthetics rather than celestial mechanics, and then a young woman's voice asked, "Did you ever dream of seeing the galaxy on your own, only to be told that you'll never be able to afford a ship?"

The scene cut to Flower's new production line for the Sharf two-man traders, where at least a dozen hulls on their sides in various states of completion were surrounded by workers in factory coveralls, all of whom appeared to be in the middle of doing something so important that they couldn't spare any time for the camera.

"Two-man traders, the ship of choice for humanity, are back in production on Flower," the voice continued. "Built by humans, for humans, using only the best Sharf-supplied drives and Stryx controllers, these ships are the first to be fully customized for our species. Flower Shipyards offers a lifetime warranty on the hull and all major systems, zero-interest financing with a guaranty that your mortgage will never be sold, and we'll give you a free basket of fresh fruit just for coming in and taking the tour—"

"But why would anybody other than a trader—" Larry began, and then shut up when Semmi shot him a withering glare.

"—when Flower arrives at Earth next week," the voice-over continued. "Come for the best seats in the galaxy to watch Earth's first test of an interstellar jump drive. Stay to visit the bazaar and to experience life on a colony ship. Exciting careers are available, and Flower offers free daycare and universal education."

The video split into irregularly-shaped segments that fit together like a puzzle, the various pieces showing Flower's bazaar, a classroom full of happy children, youngsters picking fruit on an ag deck, and people in costume battling with medieval weapons.

"Retirees are always welcome on the independent living deck," the voice continued as the images cycled through various other work scenes from an industrial bakery, to animation studios, and finally stopped on Flower's Paradise, where a large group of people whose average age was perhaps seventy-five waved at the camera. "Rendezvous is also taking place on Flower during this stop. See your local Traders Guild representative for details."

A dense body of text then scrolled across the screen so rapidly that neither of the men could read it, and then it stopped, with just the last sentence still showing.

"All ship mortgages denominated in Stryx creds," John read. "Well, that explains the zero-interest financing."

"I can't believe she's advertising the new ships," Larry said. "She's going to have a ten-year backlog of orders just from traders who've been priced out of the used market in recent years."

"I wouldn't get too excited about it. When I was here with Ellen before Flower's last stop six months ago, I saw the ads she ran trying to recruit Earthers to emigrate. I think she's just using the two-man traders to spice it up. Besides, you said she set aside a whole deck for Rendezvous so you won't have to deal with the tourists."

"What's that?" Larry asked as the small screen came to life again.

It only took John a few seconds to identify the anime production based on the squadron of gryphons flying towards a castle floating on a cloud. "Dragons versus Gryphons – The Series," he reported with a groan. "Semmi has a binge-watching problem. I just hope that Ellen figured out how to set a spending limit or I'm going to be broke by the time we leave Earth."

Eighteen

"They seemed completely normal to me," Larry said, swiping the dishtowel over the dripping plate he was handed and placing the latter in the wooden drying rack. "I told you that everybody thinks their parents are weird. Your mom is a hoot, and you never told me you were named after your dad."

"He wanted a George Junior, so when I turned out to be a girl, they compromised on Georgia."

"Good for them not letting the doctor spoil the surprise."

"What doctor? My mother had me in the bathtub with a midwife and the whole place full of candles. I'm lucky the house didn't burn down."

"Well, everything clearly worked out okay."

"You just stick to the plan," Georgia said as she pulled the last plate from the dishpan and rinsed it. "They seem normal because we've kept them talking about their work on the commune and haven't said anything about aliens or your Sharf two-man trader that we left in long-term parking at the elevator authority."

"But we showed up in a rented floater."

"Why do you think I insisted on arriving after dark? I'll bet my mom has herself convinced that she can see wheels under the chassis."

Larry placed the final plate in the rack and held up his hands in a sign of submission. "They're your parents so you're the boss. Just don't ask me to lie to them."

"You're doing fine," she said, pulling him close for a quick kiss with hands still dripping dishwater. "No Stryx, no tunnel network, no Galactic Free Press. You're a businessman and I'm a freelance newspaper reporter."

"Fair enough."

The door to the kitchen opened and Janice entered with her hands over her eyes but the fingers split apart so she could see. "There the two of you are. I was beginning to wonder if you were acting out some kind of fantasy on my kitchen table, not that there's anything wrong with that."

Georgia turned bright red and exclaimed, "MOTHER!" for at least the third time that evening, but Larry just laughed and gave Janice a knowing wink.

"If you don't all come out of there, I'm going to think that you're shunning me," Georgia's father called from the dining room.

"Be right out, George," his wife called back, and then continued for Larry's benefit, "The commune hasn't shunned anybody since we found out that Edith Jones was reheating food in one of those radioactive contraptions."

"The commune doesn't allow microwave ovens," Georgia told Larry as they followed her mother out to the dining room. "They're on the dangerous technology list."

"Enough talk about us," George said as his wife and their guests sat down for coffee and homemade cookies. "How are you going to support our daughter in the style to which she's accustomed, Larry? What do you do for a living?"

"I'm in business," he replied. "Buy low, sell high, barter when I can."

"To beat the taxman," Janice interjected. "We know all about that on the commune."

"And where did you meet our daughter?" George asked.

"Mac's Bones, on Union Sta—ouch!" Larry yelped, reaching down to rub his shin where Georgia had kicked him.

"Where?" Janice asked.

"It's a train station, in, uh, England," Georgia said. "I told you I was working abroad."

"Mac's Bones sounds like a Scottish Pub," her father said. "I hope getting into the newspaper business hasn't turned you into a drinker."

"I went there for the takeout food. They make a great chicken cacciatore."

Georgia's parents exchanged a look that expressed concern for their daughter's sanity, and then Janice asked, "So how did you break your nose, Larry? Were you a boxer?"

"I was married young and it didn't work out," Larry said. "Our fathers had been business partners when they got their start. Thistle and I saw a lot of each other growing up, but something changed once we were married, and she always had a temper."

"It's strange how some childhood sweethearts grow closer together while others grow apart. And this Thistle, what a pretty name, broke your nose in lieu of filing for divorce?"

"I thought everything was going great," Larry said. "We'd been married for a little over a year, and I'd just gotten a great deal on an unclaimed shipment of children's shoes at an auction. I try to keep part of my trade stock in children's shoes and clothes because there's always a demand. Thistle was admiring some of the shoes that were handcrafted on a Vergallian tech ban—Ow!"

"Back cramps from driving all day?" George asked sympathetically. "I can only take a few hours on the tractor myself these days."

"I've always regretted having to buy factory-made shoes, but nobody on the commune had any success making them by hand," Janice said. "Do you remember when Dan Thatcher tried to set up as a shoemaker, George?"

"How can I forget? I paid him two sacks of potatoes as a fitting deposit, and all I have to show for it is that bookend," he said, pointing at a shelf where a row of books was held upright by a chunk of wood that had been carved into a shape that vaguely resembled a foot. "He was going to use that as a form for a custom fit, but when I asked him if it was for the left foot or the right, he replied, 'Is there a difference?'"

Larry started laughing so hard that he had to hastily set his coffee down so he wouldn't spill it. "Do you mind if I use that story myself?" he asked when he recovered. "I'll change the names and everything, but it's got great bones."

"It's a deal if you finish telling us how your ex came to break your nose," George said.

"I was telling you about the baby shoes, right?" Larry asked, pushing his chair back to get out of kicking range. "So I said to Thistle, 'Why don't you pick out a few pairs of every size for a boy or a girl and we won't have to run around looking when we have our own.' Then she hit me with the Brannock."

"The what?" Janice asked.

"The Brannock Device, for measuring feet. It was invented a couple of centuries ago by a man who didn't live that far from here. Mine is an antique, and it's stamped 'Made in Syracuse, New York.'"

"Oh, like in the shoe stores when we were children," George said. "My shoe size hasn't changed in forty years so I just mail order from the catalog."

"I'm not sure I understand," Janice said. "She broke your nose because you brought up children?"

"And the weird thing is that she always talked about having a big family," Larry said. "I heard a few years later that she had a baby so it couldn't have been a medical thing. I guess I'll never know what she was thinking."

"Why didn't you tell me the story when I asked?" Georgia demanded.

"I was worried you'd think that I was putting pressure on you."

"Most parents on the commune discourage their children from marrying members who grew up here because so many of those matches from the first generation didn't work out," Janice said. "We have regular dance mixers with the other communes in the area so the young people can meet and howl at the moon together."

"Speaking of howling, do you hear that?" George asked.

Everybody fell silent for a moment and listened, but the only sound came from a hooting owl.

"What are we listening for?" Georgia asked.

"That," her father said. "The silence. Have you already forgotten how bad all the coyote yipping and wolves howling were at night around here? There's been less and less of it in the years since you left for university."

"And a lot more deer, rabbits, and other hungry little creatures in our fields," Janice added. "One of the local trappers whose sister joined the commune told us that he gets paid three times as much for a live predator as the bounty on a dead one."

"But who's buying?" Georgia asked.

"He didn't say," her mother replied. "The truth is, there have been all sorts of strange goings-on around here, not to mention those poor deformed folks whose parents must have been exposed to the radiation."

Georgia's father groaned, and muttered under his breath, "Here we go again."

"It's been proven," Janice insisted, despite the fact nobody had challenged her. "People don't grow a tentacle out of their back for no reason, and," she lowered her voice, "there's that nice couple with the foreign accents who come around looking to buy antiques every summer. They must have been carny folk to be so covered with tattoos, but what you can see of their skin changes color for no apparent reason."

"Sounds like Hortens," Larry said automatically before Georgia could stop him.

"Mr. and Mrs. Horten. How did you know their names?"

"We, uh, met a couple just like that in our travels," Georgia said, shooting Larry a warning look.

"But the saddest thing I've ever seen was that poor fellow with the four arms who couldn't even speak," her mother said. "And he was so tall, almost like some mad scientist had stretched his torso to make room for the extra arms."

A ringtone sounded from Georgia's purse and she pulled out her cell phone. "I have to take this," she said, and then froze halfway up from her chair. "I mean, uh…"

"And what is that, young lady?" Janice asked in an icy voice.

"It's, uh, not important," Georgia said, hastily returning the phone to her purse, but her parents were already up and backing away from her.

"You brought a phone-of-the-hand into our house?" George asked in a sad voice. "You know that they operate on microwaves."

"It's my fault," Larry fibbed. "She asked me to remind her to leave it in the, uh, car, but I forgot."

"Is that true?" Janice addressed her daughter.

"Uh, yes?" Georgia said in a small voice.

"Well, he didn't grow up on the commune so I suppose we can overlook it this one time," she said, retaking her seat. "Would you like a refresh on that coffee, Larry?"

"Yes, thank you," Larry said, holding out his cup. While she refilled it from the old fashioned carafe, he asked, "Do you sell any of your crops to raise money for things the commune has to buy, or are you totally self-sufficient?"

"Don't confuse us with followers of the Old Way," George said. "Those people are Luddite nut jobs."

"They're very nice actually, but they don't use tractors," Janice said. "I've heard that some of them refuse to plow with draft animals as well, but I think those groups focus on orchards and furniture making. We do very well selling our excess produce to Drazen Foods. Isn't that a funny name for a food business?"

"And how many communes are part of your—what did you call the umbrella group again?" Larry asked.

"NACAC," George said. "North American Council of Agricultural Communities. I doubt half of them are even watered-down communes by this point, but we had to band together to give ourselves a political voice because all of us put together don't equal the population of one of the big cities."

"We're officially part of the New York city-state, of course, but they leave us alone and we leave them alone," Janice said. "There are only a few dozen or so communes left that operate at our level of ideological purity, and a handful of those actually look down on us because we own our own homes and pay members salaries."

"Marxist nut jobs," Georgia's father said, rising from the table. "I'll be back in a minute, so don't run off."

Janice waited for her husband to disappear into the bathroom and then said in a low voice, "He wakes up every night to go as well, but he won't see the healer. I think it's his prostate, and I know they have all sorts of nonsurgical treatments these days. Would you talk to him, Larry? He doesn't listen to me about these things."

"Me?" Larry asked in surprise. "Uh, sure, if we get a minute alone."

"I'll stay back while he sees you out to your car," Janice said. "It was very quiet, by the way. I can usually hear the gravel crunching when somebody drives up to visit."

"Is everything else alright, Mom?" Georgia asked. "You're not getting those headaches anymore?"

"It's funny you should mention that. I always thought they were due to radio waves, or maybe chemicals leaching out of the ground, but not long after you left, a traveling ophthalmologist visited the commune. She said I had open-angle glaucoma and she could do surgery to fix it on the spot. I didn't want to have anything to do with lasers, as you can imagine, but the way that Aanid explained it, the real healing came from the special chant she did while massaging my temples. She just needed the instruments afterward to check the effectiveness of the treatment."

"As long as it worked," Georgia said. "You do seem a lot more relaxed."

"Oh, a hundred percent. The strangest part is that she was easily the most beautiful woman I'd ever seen in my life. Your father took a picture of us together." Janice rose and brought back a framed photograph from the mantle.

"Vergallian Medical Mission – Aanid," Larry read off the alien's nametag. "She certainly is a looker."

Back from the bathroom, George stretched and yawned. "Early day tomorrow, harvesting Brussels sprouts for Drazen Foods. Can I see the two of you to your car?"

Larry received a kiss on the cheek from Janice, who also insisted he take some apples for the long drive back to the city, and then hung back while her husband escorted the two young people to their floater.

"Thank you for not getting her upset," George said to Larry. "Her parents were from one of those splinter groups that doesn't believe the aliens exist and her coping mechanism was to go along with it. You can see the space elevator stalk to the south on a clear day, but we have several commune members who pretend it's not there."

"She seemed perfectly normal to me," Larry said, drawing a reflexive scowl from Georgia. "You know, your wife mentioned that you've been getting up at night, and my own father had that problem recently. He had it treated on Flower by—I don't suppose you'll be going up to orbit while she's here."

"You mean that Dollnick colony ship that visits every six months?" George asked, and then laughed at his daughter's expression. "Come on, Georgia. When that ship passes overhead it's bigger than the moon. Your mother walks around looking at the ground all week when Flower is here."

"But all through my teens you—" Georgia cut herself off.

"I know," her father said with a sigh. "Your mother and I were going through some things and it just seemed easier to blame aliens for my problems than to confront the truth. After you left, I started going to the commune's group therapy nights and worked through some issues I'd been putting off thinking about. Not that you were the easiest teenager, you know. Always hiding in the library reading those romance novels with alien—"

"I was studying for university and you know it," she interrupted, missing the wink he gave Larry. "And if the two of you decided to be normal all of a sudden, why did you get so upset when my phone rang?"

"We still follow the commune rules about technology," George said.

"What about the volunteer Vergallian eye doctor and her alien medical equipment?"

"We aren't total nut jobs," he explained, again deploying what was apparently his favorite expression. "Sometimes I think you have this place confused with your Aunt Ida's commune. We never should have sent you there for the summer."

"They really were nut jobs," Georgia said grudgingly. "Wooden shoes, outhouses, no running water. The loom was pretty cool, though. Someday I'll have to show you some of the weavings I have in storage on Union Station, Larry."

"Well, don't be strangers," George said, shaking Larry's hand again and then giving his daughter a hug. "And if you should ever happen across a pair of Drazen work boots, size XF-73, I had a pair that lasted almost fifteen years, but I haven't been able to find any since."

"I know somebody who knows somebody," Larry said, climbing over the gunnels into the floater. "Say goodbye to your wife for us and tell her I really enjoyed her cooking. I can see where your daughter got her food genes."

Georgia was sure she could see her mother peeping out from behind the living room curtains as the floater lifted off the gravel drive, performed a one-hundred-eighty-degree spin, and then silently accelerated off above the recently harvested fields. She remained quiet for almost fifteen minutes before she couldn't contain herself any longer.

"They really were crazy when I was growing up," Georgia blurted out. "It wasn't bad when I was a little girl, but in my teens I had to hide from my mother all the time so I wouldn't go mad."

"I don't question your past, Georgia, and I understand that it's difficult for you to put that behind you. But I'm sure you wouldn't want me to judge them based on your memories rather than how they treat us today. Maybe it's because I've visited so many Vergallian tech-ban worlds but I've gotten to be pretty open-minded about how people choose to live. In the end, what matters is how the children come out, and you know how I feel about you."

"I guess it wasn't all peaches and cream for you either, having your first love hit you in the face with an aluminum foot measuring device," Georgia said, and stifled a laugh.

"If it was aluminum my nose might still be straight today," Larry said. "The Brannock Device is made out of steel. You've seen it enough times."

"I thought shiny metal meant aluminum."

"That's only true for old engines and other applications where steel rusts."

"And getting your nose broken didn't change your mind about having children?"

"You know it didn't," Larry said, nuzzling her neck and placing a hand on her thigh.

"Hey, watch where we're going!"

"Why? You know these floaters fly themselves."

"But it's a rental."

"They have professional cleaners."

"Wait! I have to call Ellen back," Georgia said, struggling to free her arm and pulling out her cell phone. "I hung up on her without a word and she probably thinks I was attacked or something."

"Or she thinks you were at your family's house and you couldn't talk," Larry grumbled, settling back on his side of the floater.

"Hmm, now she's not answering," Georgia said. "Oh, wait. I missed a bunch of texts."

After a long minute of silence, Larry said, "I'm beginning to think there may be something to living without all this technology after all. I mean, a trillion Vergallians can't be wrong."

"Ellen got us an invitation to watch the interstellar jump drive test on Flower with the president of EarthCent. I told her we'd be there."

Nineteen

"I thought we were going to see the test live," the president complained to his public relations director. "Why come all the way up to Flower to watch in an empty theatre?"

"You're the one who has trouble with Zero-G," Hildy reminded him. "And even if Flower lined herself up so we could watch the test from portholes, she's always spinning on her axis to make weight, so you'd just get dizzy looking at everything going around and around. She set aside this theatre for VIPs so we can talk, and I scheduled this trip months ago because it's a coup for EarthCent to have you attend Rendezvous. You'll be the first non-trader ever to speak at the opening banquet."

"Still," the president said, nodding to John and Ellen, who had just arrived. "We could at least have sat in the front row."

"I specifically chose the tenth row so you wouldn't get a sore neck from looking up," Hildy said, and then greeted the new arrivals. "Hello, Ellen. John. Any breakthroughs since we last talked?"

"EarthCent Intelligence has reached out to our allies about the Container Prince and some very interesting information has been trickling in," John said. "I also asked Flower about him as soon as we arrived, and she explained that he's not a real prince. They just call him that because he's wealthy enough to become one."

"Dollnick royalty isn't strictly by blood?" the president asked.

"They aren't royalty in the Earth sense of princes being the sons of kings and queens. The exact process isn't something the Dollnicks share with outsiders, but as near as we can figure out, becoming a prince depends on providing employment and profit-sharing for his retainers over generations, at which point the title vests and becomes heritable. But the existing princes have to approve the elevation at some sort of conclave, and there seem to be rules that limit even the largest clans to a single prince at any given time."

"And didn't Flower say that the Container Prince is known to be secretive?" Ellen reminded him.

"Yes, and she also passed my questions on to the alien spies who live on board under a special arrangement with EarthCent Intelligence," John said. "When we see Captain Pyun later, he may have more to tell us."

"He's not coming to watch?"

"The captain and his wife went out on one of Flower's shuttles to watch at the test site. Flower Studios has the contract to record the jump drive trials for broadcast by the Grenouthian Network, and I assume Flower will be showing us the raw feed."

"Speaking of the Grenouthians, did you talk to the producer whose contact info I sent you, Ellen?" Hildy asked.

"That bunny scares me," Ellen said. "I found myself nodding my head in agreement for fear he'd bite it off if I didn't."

"You know how cutthroat the entertainment business is. I'll bet he can't turn off the intimidation even when he's trying to be nice. What did you think of his idea?"

"I've got mixed feelings about letting them take the lead. But the Galactic Free Press started a joint venture with the Grenouthian Network a few cycles ago, and my editor said that the top brass are all in favor, so I guess we'll do it."

"What's this about?" the president asked.

"The Grenouthians want to make a series of documentaries about the looting of Earth," Ellen explained. "The producer I met claimed it's the best chance we'll get at recovering any historical artifacts or artworks in our lifetimes."

"I think there's some truth to that," John said. "Everybody on the tunnel network watches those documentaries, so the collectors who bought our stuff won't be able to show their acquisitions in public without risking exposure. And you said the Grenouthians are even going to offer a reward for information leading to the recovery of the statues taken from the stock exchange building in their Wall Street Preserve."

"But we'll end up looking like a bunch of fools who can't take care of our cultural treasures," the president said. "Or worse, a species riddled with rotten apples willing to sell their own heritage out the back door for a handful of creds."

"That's why I can't get enthusiastic about it, not to mention it feels like giving up," Ellen said. "But I can't argue with the fact that the Grenouthians can bring far more resources to the table than we can, and the reward the producer is talking about offering may be enough to get somebody to talk."

"They're probably willing to spend so much because it will give them an excuse to rerun every documentary they've ever made about Earth's financial collapse," the president said. "Oh well, what's done is done, and if Hep's interstellar jump drive works according to plan, that should raise us a notch in the eyes of the advanced species."

"I think the whole galaxy knows that we copied the jump drive from the ship that our Drazen friends arranged to loan us from their museum under the guise of a restoration project," Hildy said. "The whole setup was just to get around the Stryx ban on technology transfers."

"You really have become a spoilsport in your old age," the president grumped as the lights in the giant theatre began to dim. "And I still think it's foolish for Hep and the other scientists to put their lives at risk when they could have done an unmanned test."

"The Drazens aren't the only ones who have been out to look over the Long Jump," John told them. "I got a message from the home office that Maker Dring came through the tunnel yesterday and immediately went to inspect the ship. He had a young Stryx with him, and I'm pretty sure that between the two of them, they would have spotted a problem if the drive wasn't going to work."

"Did they come on the Maker's gravity surfer?" Ellen asked. "I've always wanted to see one in space."

"They took a Tunnel Trips rental. Gravity surfers aren't particularly useful for point-to-point trips unless you have a lot of time to kill."

"Sorry we're late," Larry announced from the aisle as he and Georgia began side-stepping into the row. "We went into one of the theatres where they're throwing a big party and then Flower pinged Georgia and told her we were in the wrong place."

"There's a party in another theatre?" Ellen asked.

"There are parties in all nine of the other big theatres, and they were pretty packed. I'm surprised we can't hear them cheering through the walls. I can't believe she set aside this whole place for just the six of us. It must seat thousands."

"Five thousand," Flower interjected over the public address system. "I didn't mean to eavesdrop, but give me a little credit for being able to maintain acoustical isolation between entertainment venues. And two more guests are coming to join you, so don't eat all the snacks before they get there."

"What snacks?" Georgia asked, but she was drowned out by a crashing orchestral score as an enormous hologram of a strange-looking spaceship suddenly filled the stage. After about thirty seconds of a view that panned along the length of the ship, it was replaced by an interior scene showing the bridge of the Long Jump. A group of scientists wearing casual clothes were floating about in Zero-G and chatting with one another.

"They look more like they're out for a picnic than conducting humanity's first test of interstellar jump technology," the president commented.

"That's Tac holding hands with Hep," Larry said. "I hope he's not too distracted to keep track of what's going on."

"I gave him and all of the crew physicals and I didn't note any hormonal abnormalities," a mechanical voice declared, and then the front half of a giant beetle flattened the chair-backs next to Ellen with a crash. He pulled the external translation box hanging around what passed as his neck out from between the chair backs and his carapace, and added, "These seats seem to be defective."

"You're supposed to pull the little lever on the side first," a different voice rumbled, and then the next three chairs in the row flattened out like sleeping recliners. Myort eased his bulk into position, curling up and resting his head on his tail with a good view of the stage. "Where's Semmi?" he asked.

"On our ship, no doubt running up a streaming bill on my programmable cred," John said. "You could have warned me that she's addicted to watching aerial combat dramas with thin plots."

The Huktra snorted. "It's a phase. Gryphons have excellent memories so she'll grow out of it once she's seen everything that interests her."

"And how long will that be?"

"Shhh, something's happening," Ellen said.

The holographic projection on the stage showed the scientists deploying hand-held canisters of compressed air to propel themselves to their seats. Hep was the last to buckle in, and then the hologram divided in half, with the bridge scene to one side and an exterior view on the other. Then Hep pressed a button on the arm of his command chair and both holograms were replaced by an empty star field.

"Did something go wrong?" the president demanded.

"Looked like a clean jump to me," John said. "I've seen Drazen ships jump and they just disappear like that, without the light show that some technologies create."

"So when will we find out if they reached their destination safely?"

"They're only going out a few light-minutes," Hildy said in exasperation. "As soon as they confirm their position and check the equipment for problems, they'll be right back. Didn't you read the flight plan?"

"I just assumed there would be some kind of commentary," the president said. "You know I hate to read a report and then have to listen to somebody giving me the exact same information."

"He has a point," M793qK said. "My main objection to treating Humans is your enthusiasm for recounting endless symptoms, most of which are irrelevant to the underlying problem, which is usually in your heads. Every visitor to my clinic walks through a battery of scanners on entry, at which point I know more about what's wrong with them than they know themselves."

"You need to spend some time on Earth to observe them in their natural habitat," Myort told the Farling. "I learned quite a bit just sitting in parks and listening in on the conversations of people walking by. I distinctly remember overhearing one woman saying to another, 'What's the point of suffering if I can't enjoy telling my friends about it?'"

"If we're going to share Earth gossip, I heard a rumor that there were a number of Farling sightings on Earth not too long ago," Ellen said to the doctor. "I'm trying to track down if there's any connection to the genealogical samples that have gone missing from research institutes."

"Sounds to me like you've been talking to a certain Drazen," M793qK said. "As the president could tell you, my agents have permission to harvest genetic samples from Earth for research purposes. We wouldn't have any interest in absconding with improperly stored and most likely mislabeled tissue samples collected by past generations of Humans."

"Can you think of anybody who would?"

The giant beetle hesitated for a moment.

"Just tell her," Myort said. "It's not like she has any information about your hierarchy worth trading."

"But you might," the Farling said pointedly.

"Put it on my bill if it makes you happy," the Huktra grunted, and then said to John, "Now we're even for Semmi's binge-watching."

"I've already shared some of my thoughts on this matter with Captain Pyun, but given his age, he's probably forgotten the details by now," M793qK said. "Combining the information from the alien intelligence agents on board with the archival material uncovered on Earth, it's clear to me that somebody is remodeling a planet in imitation of your homeworld."

"You mean a terraforming job?" Ellen asked.

"It's more likely they're trying to save money on a complete rehab by renovating a compatible world with Earth's flora and fauna, and perhaps using old genetic samples to clone or engineer missing pieces. Whoever is running the job preserved their anonymity by contracting out the biological harvesting to agents on the ground who must have been allowed some autonomy in the selection and acquisition of samples. An appreciable percentage of the samples will therefore be of no use whatsoever for the project, but casting a wide net offered the best opportunity of gathering everything they needed in a short time."

"But it's been going on for almost a century," Georgia protested.

"As I said, a short time," the Farling repeated.

"They're back," Larry said as a hologram suddenly filled the stage again. This time, everybody on the bridge of the Long Jump was sucking on the straws of juice boxes which likely contained champagne. Hep flashed a thumbs-up, and then the hologram was replaced by a stream of technical data that threatened to go on without end.

"Is that it, Flower?" Ellen asked out loud.

"If you're not interested in the numbers I'll just enjoy them myself," the Dollnick AI said, and the hologram disappeared. "As it happens, I'm holding a message for President Beyer that was coded for conditional delivery should the jump test be successful. I accidentally reviewed the contents when the condition was met, and it doesn't contain anything of a private nature if you wish me to project it now."

"Go ahead," the president said. "It's probably just a message of congratulations."

A new hologram came to life on the stage, this one displaying a towering four-armed Dollnick standing in the middle of a sprawling construction site. Behind him, an unfinished elevator stalk rose into the blue sky, and a large moon was visible on the horizon.

"Congratulations," the Dollnick said. "Now that you have interstellar jump capability, I want to be the first to extend an invitation to visit a place where no Human has ever set foot. EarthCent is authorized to send a delegation to visit Earth Two, a little project I've been working on since your planet was opened by the Stryx. It's a complete makeover job that will provide a perfect home away from home for members of your species, provided the Alts don't outbid you. I've attached the coordinates and you're welcome to drop in any time, but don't procrastinate, because a sweet little world like this isn't going to last long on the galactic market."

One of the aides standing nearby whistled something untranslatable in a low tone and pointed at the elevator stalk.

"Two minor points of interest," the tall Dollnick continued. "A pair of space elevators are under construction, but they won't be completed for another twenty-three point seven cycles at the earliest. And of course, there's no tunnel exit yet, but the Stryx will hook the world up as soon as it meets the minimum requirements for population or economic activity. Financing is available for a whole-world purchase, but if nobody is interested in buying outright, we'll offer one-thousand cycle leases on family holdings to any sentients who aren't allergic to Earth pollens. Hope to see you here."

The hologram pulled back rapidly, and then the scene began to shift as if the immersive cameras were mounted on a formation of floaters that had taken off at high speed. The rocky ground of the construction site soon gave way to a grassy plain, where immense numbers of American buffalo were grazing contentedly. As the view continued to pull back, it became apparent that the land was well watered with small streams and lakes, and areas of young forest were battling it out with the grasslands.

"It's beautiful," Hildy said. "This could really screw up our attempts to get expatriates to move back to Earth."

"I'm getting motion sick," the president said, looking away from the hologram. "Does the Dollnick do any more talking, Flower, or is the rest of it a nature documentary without a soundtrack?"

"The Container Prince doesn't appear again," the AI replied a moment later. "Looking ahead, the cameras do a complete circuit of the globe, but soon they'll be moving too fast for your eyes to make out much detail."

"So that was the Container Prince, and all of the biological material taken from Earth must have ended up in this project," John surmised. "It was a terraforming job all along, but why?"

"I think I can answer that," Flower said. "The Container Prince wants to become the real thing, and the quickest way to win respect in Dollnick circles is to reengineer a world and build a couple of space elevators. I've reviewed the Stryx property records, and the only rocky planet near the coordinates he attached was sold to a private party approximately three centuries ago."

"I'll bet his original plan was to create a standard Dollnick ag world," Myort said. "Then the profitability on ag worlds began to fall as schedules for terraforming projects were advanced to take advantage of the cheap Human labor coming on the galactic market. The Container Prince must have shifted his focus to preparing a world for Humans whose pockets would be full of creds coming off alien labor contracts."

"But then it turned out that our people were perfectly happy to continue living on alien worlds," John said, recognizing where the Huktra was going. "So now the Container Prince is hoping to play us off against the Alts since the planet will be perfect for them as well."

"Can the Long Jump get there?" the president asked. "I'm not much of a traveler myself, but I'll delegate somebody to take a look in my name. EarthCent isn't in any position to go buying planets on credit, not to mention the Human Empire changeover coming up next century, but it would be rude to ignore him completely."

"We'll go," Ellen volunteered. "John can report back to EarthCent Intelligence and I can write it up for the paper with Georgia."

"I can't get away during Rendezvous," Larry said. "I'm supposedly in charge."

"Hep probably has a whole schedule of trials they have to run before he'll be willing to take the Long Jump out on a really long jump," John said. "Just how far away is that place, Flower?"

"I could do the jump in less than a day while keeping within the parameters I've established as necessary for your wellbeing," the Dollnick AI replied. "It's not that far off of our next scheduled stop, so if Captain Pyun agrees, we could shift things around a little and go right after Rendezvous."

Twenty

"That's very interesting," one of the judges said, examining a glowing sword being displayed by the old trader with the blanket next to Larry's. "Do you have any idea of its origins?"

"The Mengoth who I got it from told me that it was a Brupt artifact, but considering he let it go for a gross of toy boomerangs, I'm assuming it's a cheap replica. I just didn't have anything else worth showing this year."

"I've never seen one myself," another of the judges said, hefting the sword and taking an experimental swing. Then he held it out at arm's length and declared, "And gentlemen in England now abed shall think themselves accursed they were not here—"

"What's that?" the third judge cut short his colleague's attempt at Shakespeare. He pointed at a strange glyph on the hilt. "It looks like a maker's mark."

"I thought it was just a design," the trader said.

"Do you mind if I take a look?" an alien with close-cropped hair vines asked as he stepped forward.

"Ah, Razood," said the female judge who had initially expressed an interest in the sword. "Let him see it, Peter. Razood has a blacksmith shop in Colonial Jeevesburg, and whenever I visit Flower, I bring him whatever alien hardware I've saved up for evaluation."

The second judge passed the sword to the Frunge blacksmith, who shook his head sadly. "I'm afraid I've been offered a number of these lately," he said. "My understanding is they were given as gifts to supporters who donated above a certain amount to the military party before the last Mengoth election. You need a dagger and a shield to make up the complete set."

"Then it's a good thing I got those boomerangs from a relative who was just trying to clear space in his hold," the trader said. "Do you have any idea how the glow works?"

Razood pulled out a handkerchief, wrapped it tightly around the blade near the hilt, and the glow vanished. "There are several light-emitting diodes in the hilt, and the sword is cross-polished to create a pattern of ridges at the atomic level which refract the light," he explained. "But the power draw is low, and the Mengoths pack a lot of juice into a small battery, so it may hold out for your lifetime."

A sudden hush fell over the section of deck where over a thousand traders had their blankets laid out with just one or two items they were showing for the groups of judges.

"What's happening?" Peter asked the tallest judge of their trio, who could see over most of the crowd.

"It looks like some VIPs came to the show. I think it's the guy who claimed he was the president of something at the opening banquet, and he's being escorted by an older man who's dressed like George Washington—"

"Captain Pyun," Razood informed them.

"—and they're accompanied by, I think that's a Stryx and some chubby dinosaur type that must be an alien."

"It's Maker Dring," somebody in the crowd murmured loudly, and the deck went from nearly silent to sounding like a bulkhead had developed a major air leak as the news was passed around in whispers.

"The Maker came to Earth for the Long Jump trial," Larry informed the judges. "He's writing a history of the Human Empire."

"I think they're heading in this direction," the tall judge said.

"Everybody act normal," the female judge hissed. "I'm sure they're just here to see the artifacts and wouldn't want us to stare at them."

The three judges moved on to Larry's blanket, and their eyes went wide at the collection of map crystals.

"Have you been skimming from the Traders Guild's non-existent pension fund?" Peter demanded. "I'm going to ask for an audit if any problems show up with our budget."

"I got these for a song from an old Frunge purser who was happy to get rid of them," Larry said. "I'm beginning to suspect that the small ones are more common than everybody thinks, but this large one seems to be fairly rare." He picked up his prize map crystal and handed it to the judge. "I'm planning on loaning them all to the academy on Fyndal for research after Rendezvous."

"Have you had any luck with the maps?" the female judge asked. "I had a small crystal myself for a few years, but eventually I traded it to a Sharf for a recharged fuel pack. The Sharf had a collection of map crystals himself, and he had a way of projecting the star fields as holograms. But he'd never had any luck with the treasure maps because the galaxy had changed too much since they were manufactured."

"I knew a Frunge collector who claimed that map crystals are showing possible futures for the Milky Way,"

Razood said, crouching to look at the smaller spheres. "He tried asking a few Stryx librarians, but of course they told him it was competitive information."

"Clear a space for Maker Dring," somebody said self-importantly, and the growing crowd around Larry's blanket split like the Red Sea to allow the VIPs to approach.

"Very interesting," Stryx Jeeves said, adroitly retrieving the largest map crystal from the judge's hand with his pincer. "It's a shame I can't say anything without getting in trouble with my elders. Dring?"

The chubby shapeshifting dinosaur took the little sphere from the Stryx and broke into a blunt-toothed smile. "May I?" he asked Larry.

"Uh, sure," Larry said, a bit tongue-tied over having drawn the attention of one of the immortal makers of the Stryx.

Dring's features took on a serious look as he crouched and held the large map crystal near each of the smaller ones on the blanket as if he was making some kind of calculation. Then he backed up and changed his grip on the large one, and squinted over it as if it was some sort of astrolabe. After making a subtle adjustment, his thumb shot out, impelling Larry's prize map crystal into one of the smaller ones, which rolled off the blanket and came to rest against somebody's foot.

"What the?—Is it?—I don't understand," Larry said, retrieving the large map crystal that had remained on the blanket, thanks to the backspin imparted by Dring's cast.

"They're Rojack marbles," the Maker explained. "My people were allied with the Goss, who went to the aid of the Rojacks during the AI Wars almost a hundred million years ago. The Rojacks never recovered and passed on from this version of the multiverse. But there was a time when they were known as the most innovative marketers in the galaxy, and they ran a chain of space stations that numbered in the tens of thousands. They gave away these marbles in proportion to how much you spent while visiting the station, so you didn't get one of the shooters unless you brought in a ship for overhaul or something of that nature."

"So how many map crystals, I mean, Rojack marbles, are there?" Larry asked.

"I'm sure they were manufactured in the quadrillions, if not more, as the Rojack space station hospitality network was the largest in the galaxy for millions of years. The marbles are nearly indestructible, and some species saved them up to use for ball bearings. But a hundred million years is a long time to hold onto anything that can roll under the furniture and end up in the vacuum bag."

"Do you know anything about the maps?"

"I believe the regular marbles each showed the location of the station where they were given away in the context of local space, and the large ones, the shooters, showed the entire hospitality network," Dring said. "The stations that weren't destroyed in the war were eventually recycled as scrap or lost as they went dark. Still, the marbles might be of interest to an academic astronomer interested in the evolution of the galaxy."

While Larry and the judges were digesting this information, Georgia was at the other end of the deck exploring the newest retrofit for Sharf two-man traders unveiled by Flower Shipyards.

"Do you mind if I record this for an interview?" she asked Laura, the woman in charge of the shipyard. "I checked with Dianne, the Galactic Free Press reporter who's posted on board, and she suggested I cover your grand opening since I live on one of these ships."

"As a lifestyle choice, or are you a trader?"

"Both," Georgia said. "I'm a freelance journalist and a trader specializing in educational toys."

"Let me check with the boss," Laura said, and pointed at her ear to indicate that she was communicating via her implant. "Okay, and Flower says if your paper features the interview in the Traders Supplement, she'll buy advertising space alongside."

Georgia swiped the recording function on her reporter's tab to life. "I guess my first question is, where did you get the idea for this retrofit module?"

Laura looked around to make sure nobody could overhear them before replying. "Ever since my foreman, Don, proposed to me, Flower keeps bringing up the topic of babies like she's the one with a ticking biological clock. One day, I couldn't take it anymore, and I said, 'If you really want to start a baby boom, you should be working on a way for traders with small ships to care for infants in Zero-G.' The next day she invited the Human Empire's mentor to visit the shipyard to tell us about the breathable gel the Cayl use in high acceleration spacecraft. It does such a good job cushioning mammals both inside and out that it makes the baby centrifuge possible."

"Are you sure it's safe?"

"The mentor could only spare enough gel from her yacht's supply to build two test units, but the babies we've put in them always fall asleep and come out rested and smiling. Small centrifuges are no good for adults because of the acceleration gradient when we're upright, and you'd still need a lot more room than is available on these ships. But with babies, they're lying down, and the only goal is to give them weight so they develop properly and don't lose bone density."

"The glass window reminds me of the industrial dryers on campus at the New University when I had a work-study job in the laundry." Georgia smiled at the memory. "You could stand up in one of those and brace your hands over your head, which some of the idiot boys did to show off while spinning the dryer on the cool-down cycle. The baby centrifuge looks about the same diameter as those dryers, but much shallower, and with the double cylinder. What's the central space for?"

"There wouldn't be any point to filling the whole thing with breathable gel even if we had enough," Laura explained. "The centrifuge is designed so that the baby stays in the gel-filled outer ring, which has just enough clearance for crawling if the baby wakes up. It's only intended for the earliest stage of life—after that, they're big enough to start on the special exercise equipment."

"So once you had the centrifuge, you decided to build a whole nursery module around it?"

"Initially we thought of converting a small Drazen cargo container because those are the biggest ones that you can get through the cargo hatch on these ships after they're built. But then our focus group pointed out that parents aren't going to want to leave their baby on the cargo deck while they're living on the bridge. So we designed the nursery module to be assembled in place from sections, all of which fit through the hatch between the bridge and cargo deck. The drawback is you have to sacrifice about sixty percent of the bridge storage space to make room, and half of the ceiling space, which means you and your partner better agree on which exercise equipment to keep."

"Larry's easy that way, plus he really wants kids," Georgia said. "What's the total cost?"

"Well, you understand that the centrifuge is the most expensive part, and we had to pay the Farling doctor an engineering consulting fee before anybody would let us try it with their kids since he delivers most of the babies on board."

"M793qK worked on the design with you?"

"He kind of threw out what we had come up with and drew up his own design from scratch," Laura admitted. "Flower was so impressed that I suspect M793qK based the magnetic bearings on principles that the Dollnicks haven't discovered yet. And the whole interior of the module is lined with the same material that the Hortens manufacture for reusable diapers, so it wicks away the moisture, and then capillary action moves the, uh, effluent directly into the recycling system."

"I was wondering if you'd have to keep changing the gel."

"No, it's pretty miraculous stuff, but the Cayl are even more advanced than the Farlings. We'll have to import the gel from the Cayl Empire, but it's not expensive, just nearly impossible to manufacture. The way M793qK explained it, the gel is a solidified form of air that acts sort of like a semiconductor. If you connect it to a supply of oxygen and an exhaust, new oxygen molecules migrate through the gel and the carbon dioxide is removed."

"I didn't understand that at all, but that's why I record everything," Georgia said as she turned her attention to the smallest treadmill she had ever seen. "Is this for walking or crawling?"

"Both. It's loaded with sensors and it will slow down if the toddler doesn't keep pace, so there's no running into the front or getting thrown off the back. And it's too dangerous to use bungee cord tie-downs with toddlers because they could get tangled up or even choked, so we, by which I mean M793qK and Flower, designed a one-piece pullover with Verlock magnetic monopoles woven into the fabric to provide an even attraction to the base of the treadmill."

"Why don't they do that for adults? I hate the bungee cords."

"For one thing, it's a lot more expensive, and for another, it would take more power for adults because our upper bodies are much farther away from the treadmill than a toddler's," Laura explained. "It's the same for the miniature rock-climbing machine. For the stationary tricycle, we just used stirrups for the feet and a seatbelt."

"And the display screen shows cartoons to keep them from getting bored?" Georgia asked.

"I suppose it could, but it's currently set up to show outside scenes that coordinate with the toddler's movements, to make it feel more like riding a tricycle on pavement or climbing on the gym equipment in a park."

"You've really thought of everything."

"The kiddie exercise equipment was already out there in various technologies, you probably just didn't notice it," Laura said. "And M793qK insisted that anybody buying the module has to come here for a training course he's designing on how to raise a baby in space. Do you know how much time the average trader spends in Zero-G rather than on a planet or a spinning space structure?"

"With Larry and I, it's around a quarter of our time, and he's told me that's about average," Georgia said. "I guess some traders who spend a lot of time traveling between planets after exiting a tunnel can spend as much as half of their time in Zero-G, but in the end, there's nobody to trade with in a vacuum."

"And nowhere to lay your blanket. M793qK insisted that anybody buying the module sign a contract committing to spend no more than twenty percent of their time in Zero-G, and that the baby gets between eight and ten hours a day in the centrifuge. He's also written a pamphlet that covers prenatal care, and I had a bunch of extras printed as giveaways." Laura led Georgia to the table where Don was collecting names for the nursery module waiting list and took a pamphlet from the stack. "Here you go."

"What To Expect When You're Expecting In Space," Georgia read the title. "Does it have anything about vitamins?"

"The doctor wrote about all of that stuff, plus a section on meditation and breathing exercises for delivery."

"Can I sign you up for the waiting list?" Don asked Georgia.

The freelancer hesitated for a moment, and then said, "Sure, why not. But we won't be taking delivery for at least another nine months."

"That's fine," he told her. "Cayl space is a long way off and we aren't expecting our first shipment of gel for several cycles."

"How are sales of new ships going?" Georgia asked.

"We sold out the next year's production on the first day of Rendezvous," Laura said. "Flower wants to scale up as quickly as we can set up new assembly lines and train workers, and I won't be surprised if we end up building them faster than the Sharf ever did."

Twenty-One

"Just look at her go," John said as the gryphon streaked off into the sky. "From the speed she's moving, you'd think I was chasing her with a bill."

"Semmi is going to develop a complex if you keep complaining about her little purchases," Ellen said. "I've heard that happens to children whose parents are always talking about how much it costs to raise them."

"I finally did a full audit of my linked programmable cred and she spends more than either of us. I wouldn't say anything if she was buying food—I know she's a growing gryphon—but most of the money is going to streaming videos. She's going to wreck her eyes watching that display in her crate, and then how is she going to hunt?"

"There's nothing wrong with Semmi's eyes, I had M793qK give her a checkup while we were on Flower. I'm sure you're exaggerating about how much she's spending."

"I'll show you the numbers. It was a hundred and ninety-two creds last month."

"But we were on Earth the whole month and that's almost a thousand eBucks! There wasn't enough time to run up that much in streaming."

"She spent extra for director's cuts of anime you couldn't pay me to watch, not to mention the action figures," John explained. "I checked in her crate and she even bought a figurine based on M793qK's role as the evil Farling mastermind in Everyday Superheroes."

"At least Flower earns something on those, so it keeps it in the family," Ellen said. "How long do you think we'll have to wait before the Dollnicks get here? It's so beautiful that I'm tempted to go for a hike by myself."

"Don't forget about the wolves. And didn't one of your syndicated journalists from Africa say something about lions and crocodiles?"

"On second thought, I'll get my stunner," Ellen said, heading back towards the ship. "Do you want yours?"

"May as well. That way if Semmi finds somewhere to buy anime on this world I can shoot myself."

John finished setting up the camp table and chairs while Ellen was climbing the ladder from the cargo hold up to the bridge. The gravity on the terraformed world felt a little stronger than Earth's, even though the Dollnicks had insisted it was nearly identical. He sat down and called up his latest instructions from EarthCent Intelligence on his heads-up display. John was still puzzling over how much leeway they were giving him when Ellen returned.

"Here," she said, handing over his stunner and sitting across from him. She set down the scratched-up eBook reader she'd bought Semmi on Union Station, along with something that looked like a glass rod, and a bulkier device with a narrow screen of its own. "Did I tell you that Myort gave me this single line scanner that translates Tyrellian?"

John looked up in interest. "You mean we can read that thing now?"

Ellen brandished the glass rod. "This translates a single line of Tyrellian into Huktra." Then she fit the rod into a groove on the other device. "Then I had to buy this add-on that translates Huktra to English. I checked at the library on Flower, and nobody makes a direct Tyrellian to English version."

"But does it work?"

"Sort of. The three languages don't have much in common so the results can be a bit confusing. But it's clear that the eBook reader is loaded with texts, and the librarian on Flower helped me find one about parenting."

"That nursery retrofit Flower Shipyards is manufacturing made that much of an impression on you?" John asked. "I'm willing to give it a go if you are."

"The book is in Tyrellian, you imbecile. It's for gryphon parents."

"Oh. My offer stands."

"I'm still figuring out the indexing, but it's designed to let the reader jump around to find answers to specific questions," Ellen continued, scanning the awkward translation device over a list of options. "Binge behavior?"

"Let me see that," he said, but she pushed his hands away and concentrated on the top screen, evidently struggling with the translated text.

Several minutes passed, and John had gone back to reading on his heads-up display, when Ellen exclaimed, "Aha!"

"Aha what?"

"Adolescent gryphons hardness impulse deregulation. Encrypt purse."

"Excuse me?"

"The translation doesn't seem to get articles or conjunctions, all the little bits that tie sentences together," Ellen said apologetically. "I don't know if the problem is between Tyrellian and Huktra or from Huktra into English. And sometimes it flips words to mean the opposite, but I think it's saying that Semmi has trouble with impulse control and you should password-protect access to the programmable cred via the ship controller."

"Don't you think I tried that?" John asked plaintively. "Either she's an incredible guesser or she's reading my mind." Ellen looked up from the screen with her eyes wide open, and John's jaw dropped. "Oh, no! Look up telepathy."

Once she navigated back to the index of the book, it only took her thirty seconds to find the subject heading.

"Telepathy develops puberty emotional bonded," Ellen read. "Well, the first part of that is obvious, and I suppose gryphons depend on telepathy for finding mates. Or maybe she can only read gryphons she trusts."

"We're not gryphons," John reminded her. "Wait. Didn't you tell me you thought Semmi was cheating the first time you played poker with her, the Farling, and Flower, while I was recovering from being poisoned?"

"Yes, but that's because she won all of my tongue depressors right after I taught her the game. When we play now she only wins enough to—where is that gryphon?" Ellen interrupted herself as the explanation dawned on her. "I'm going to kill the little cheat."

"Now who's getting upset about pocket change," John chided, and looked up, shielding his eyes from the warm yellow star. "And that's the Container Prince's shuttle coming in, so Flower must have departed orbit already."

"And you're sure one of those Dollnick cargo ships will be willing to take us back to a system with a tunnel network connection without charging some inflated rescue rate?"

"It's obvious that the Container Prince is out to make a good impression, and our little Sharf ship would fit in a tiny corner of the smallest hold on any of those container carriers. I'll be surprised if they charge us at all, and if they do, EarthCent Intelligence will pick up the bill."

"I'm sure I can get the Galactic Free Press to split it with them since this is going to be the story of the year," Ellen said confidently. "Flower captured plenty of images from orbit, but I'll have the first close-ups, not to mention writing about what became of all the flora and fauna that was taken from Earth."

The large Dollnick shuttle set down silently on the other side of the meadow, and a mismatched pair of the four-armed aliens immediately exited, the shorter one toting a picnic basket and a couple of folding chairs. John nudged Ellen and stood up to greet them.

"Welcome to Earth Two," the taller Dollnick said enthusiastically, shaking hands with both humans at the same time. "It's traditional to share a meal before making a sales pitch for something as valuable as an inhabitable planet, and Flower provided us with some things we can all enjoy. I hope you like fruitcake."

"I've been meaning to ask ever since I heard what you named this world whether you mean 'two' as in the second, or 'too' as in also," Ellen said. "I'll need to get that right for my articles."

"Prume?" the Container Prince inquired with a sharp whistle. The shorter alien stared off into space for a moment, obviously reading on his heads-up display, and then his crest drooped in embarrassment.

"Having eliminated homonyms from our vocabulary long before we achieved interstellar travel, it never occurred to our marketing department that such a thing could be possible," Prume said. "My first reading suggests there are three possibilities, and you left out the 'to' which can express a motion of direction and apparently sounds just like the other two—I mean, the other pair of options you vocalized. Would you mind saying all three of them for me?"

"Two, too, to," Ellen rattled off.

"My translation implant now suggests your intended meaning is a couple of dancer's costumes."

"That would be a tutu. It's one word."

The two Dollnicks shared a look, and then the Container Prince said, "When I named this world, I was definitely thinking of it as a second Earth, but of course, that depends on you people buying it. Please, let's eat, and if you have any questions before our walking tour, feel free to ask them."

Prume set out the brandy-soaked fruitcake, several bottles of Flower's hard apple cider, a basket of fresh fruit, and four metal drinking cups the size of large beer steins. Then he unfolded the two Dollnick-sized chairs, and everybody took their seats.

"I hope you don't mind that we let our gryphon out for some exercise," John said. "She flew off towards, let's see, I guess that's south-west."

"Does she eat rabbits?" the Container Prince asked.

"I think Semmi's at the stage that she's willing to try anything once. Of course, we'll compensate you for any damage she causes."

Prume began to cough, covering his mouth with one of his hands while simultaneously holding the slice of fruitcake he'd sampled in another, and at the same time pouring himself a hard cider with his second pair of arms.

"She's welcome to all of the rabbits she can eat," the Container Prince said, "and if she has any gryphon friends, you can bring them along the next time. Does she listen to instructions?"

"Sometimes, we're still working on our communications," Ellen said. "I take it you have more rabbits than you want?"

"First I need to know if Human journalists honor requests to speak off the record."

"Yes, we do, but if you tell me things that I already know, that doesn't mean I'll suppress those facts. If you give me information that helps connect the dots, I'll keep your name out of it, but I can't ignore what I've learned."

"That's the same as with our reporters," the Container Prince said. "Very well. I take it somebody has explained to you by this point that I'm not an official prince and that this," he spread all four of his arms wide, "is the first terraforming project I've attempted."

John and Ellen both nodded.

"My family has tens of thousands of years of experience in space operations, primarily the interstellar freight business, but we also work in orbital construction, and have dabbled in support operations for habitats and colony ships. So I was confident we had the institutional knowledge for creating a new ag world, but then your planet was brought onto the tunnel network by the Stryx and we changed course."

"We understand that the availability of low-cost labor from Earth changed the economics for new ag world projects," Ellen said, setting down a marker so that the Dollnick wouldn't think he was telling her something new off the record. "We deduced that you were using the biological material taken from Earth to prepare a saleable world shortly before you contacted the president of EarthCent."

"Yes, and I offer my apologies for any subcontractors who violated local laws or customs while gathering samples and starter populations of plants and animals. I assure you that any materials we couldn't use remain in storage, and the only reason we haven't returned them already was our desire to preserve secrecy."

"Could I inquire why you didn't want anybody knowing about the project?" John asked. "I would have thought advanced marketing and sales would play a big part in the business plan for a project this large."

The Container Prince let out a whistling sigh. "Real estate is a competitive business, and I didn't want it known that I was targeting the Human demographic or some of the established players might have rushed projects of their own, just to prevent my clan from gaining a toehold. But we were also concerned about unwanted publicity if things went wrong since it was our first project of this scale."

"What we saw while landing looked beautiful," Ellen said. "If John had told me we'd returned to Earth, I would have believed him."

"Thank you," the Dollnick said, "but it's just this one small continent where we've been working to duplicate your ecosystems, and it's been a learning experience for us all. It's difficult enough on a habitat or colony ship to make adjustments if nature gets out of balance on a single deck. Here?" He shrugged and gestured to his assistant. "Tell them about the beavers."

"Beavers?" John asked.

"We started with beavers because we were told they were natural engineers," Prume said. "That's another problem that arose from miscommunications with Human subcontractors on Earth. When the first thousand breeding pairs were delivered, we discovered that they were either intellectually or emotionally incapable of following our landscaping blueprints. Then we compounded our error by releasing them into the wild, and the number of dams those creatures built in less than eight decades is nothing short of astonishing."

"At one time I considered naming the world 'Millions of Beaver Ponds,'" the Container Prince added morosely.

"Then there were the mosquitoes to feed the fish and the frogs, the bats to eat the mosquitoes, raccoons to eat the bats, the list goes on and on. We learned the hard way that 'breeding like rabbits' wasn't just a Human expression, so we had to import foxes, snakes, owls, and raptors to regain control. Then the deer which were supposed to keep the vegetation from going wild proved to be quite wild themselves, so we brought in coyotes, wolves—you get the picture."

"We wondered about the coyotes and the wolves," Ellen said.

"I initially thought Humans might prefer a world without predators," the Container Prince said. "Space habitats and colony ships manage to maintain a balance of helpful species, like pollinating insects, and dairy herds, but adjustments are much easier to make on a single deck than on a continent. Ultimately we realized the best approach would be to duplicate the native habitats of Earth that matched various climate and elevation characteristics of this world. It's a work in progress that would benefit from the manpower supplied by Human immigrants."

"So you're not marketing Earth Two as a turnkey operation."

"I recently learned from Flower that the Stryx enforce real estate disclosure rules when it comes to selling planets to primitive species that are under their protection. It's not something that's come up in the last million years, so you can understand my surprise. I can offer financing on advantageous terms to responsible parties, but I'm done pouring cash into this place without any returns, and I'll have to insist on either a serious down payment or a co-signer."

"As it happens, I also received some new information just before leaving Flower," John said. "I've been authorized by my employers to open negotiations on behalf of a group of potential buyers who are willing to act in the interest of the nascent Human Empire, though we're talking about a payment plan that will stretch well into several lifespans."

"Our lifespans or your lifespans?" Prume asked.

"Human lifespans," John amended himself, and the Dollnicks relaxed visibly.

"I'll need to know who those buyers are if I'm going to start sharing proprietary data," the Container Prince said. "A non-disclosure agreement is only as good as the highest bidder."

"I don't see any problem with that. You'll be dealing with the owners of InstaSitter, who—"

"I know all about InstaSitter," Prume interrupted, jumping up. "We use them to watch the hatchlings whenever we visit a Stryx station. I teach a Dollnick university extension course on branding, and I've started using InstaSitter as an example of brilliance. A lesser entrepreneur may have gone for Five Second Sitter, but that would have left the door open to One Second Sitter. Milliseconds can be outdone by Microseconds, ad infinitum. But InstaSitter? It's game over!"

"So they've got good credit," the Container Prince said, waving impatiently at his assistant to sit. "Anybody else?"

"Aisha McAllister, the host of—"

"You really did line up the big guns. My great-grandchildren all watch 'Let's Make Friends' and I bought them the complete back episodes for Egg Day."

"My instructions are to request that we be given first right of refusal on any sale," John continued. "In exchange, I'm authorized to offer a refundable one million cred deposit, to be held by a mutually agreed-upon third party, such as the Tharks."

"The Tharks will do fine," the Container Prince said magnanimously, and then served himself a large chunk of the fruitcake. "I've been talking so much that I haven't had a chance to enjoy a snack, and then I look forward to showing you around and dispelling any negative impressions I may have put in your mind by complying with full disclosure. It is a very nice continent, and the rest of the planet could be brought up to spec in just a few lifetimes."

"Your lifetimes or our lifetimes?" Ellen asked.

"Touché," the Dollnick said, refilling his cup.

There was a sudden blast of wind as Semmi dropped out of the sky and braked to a halt right next to the picnic table. She folded her wings, took one of the open cider bottles in her beak, and chugged the remaining contents.

"Sorry about her manners," John said. "We only learned how to read the instruction manual recently."

The gryphon dropped the bottle, dipped into the leather flight pouch she'd taken to wearing, and brought out her cell phone.

"If you're wondering why you can't buy any streaming videos, it's because there's no coverage on this world," Ellen told her. "It's technology, not magic."

Semmi dropped the phone on the table, and sitting back on her haunches, drew a square in the air with her front paws.

"Oh, sorry," Ellen apologized, swiping the phone to life and bringing up the recent pictures. "Hey, look at these," she said, turning the phone so that John could see it too.

"Are those passenger pigeons?" he asked in astonishment. "They're extinct on Earth."

"There must be millions in that flock. And look at this," she said, flipping to the next picture where a shocked-looking eagle had just dropped a salmon mid-air and was wheeling about to flee. Semmi chortled and let out a fresh-fish burp.

"It looks like she's got the makings of a fine real estate agent," the Container Prince said.

"Wait, can you zoom in on that one?" John asked as Ellen thumbed past a picture of a pond. "That looked like a raft with people on it."

"I assure you that you're the first Humans to visit this world," Prume said, though his whistle seemed a little shaky.

"They are people, but there's something a little off about them," Ellen said. "Aren't their heads a bit too large?"

"Alts," John concluded, and glared at the Container Prince. "When were you going to tell me that they were here?"

"Since you already arranged to purchase the rights of first refusal, I didn't see the point," the Dollnick said complacently. "I wonder how your gryphon located them so quickly. I estimate at her top flying speed, she would have had to fly in practically a straight line to make it out to their location and back in the time since you landed."

"It seems she has a gift for locating sentient beings. We just found out that Tyrellian gryphons are telepaths and she's been ransacking my mind for passwords. It's a shame she can't project her thoughts the same way."

Semmi snorted, put her front paws on the table, and fixed the man with an intense stare. About ten seconds went by, and then he groaned.

"What is it?" Ellen asked. "Do you see anything?"

John nodded, pulled a treat out of his pocket, and tossed it to the gryphon. "I think we just graduated from click-training."

From the Author

My next release will continue the story of Semmi, John, Ellen, Larry, and Georgia, making it the third in what I'm now calling the **EarthCent Auxiliaries** series. If you're new to the EarthCent books, you can start back at the beginning with **Union Station 1, 2, 3**, a discounted three-book bundle, or if you're not that ambitious, with **Independent Living**, the first of four in the **EarthCent Universe** spinoff.

For notifications of new releases, sign up for the mailing list at www.ifitbreaks.com. I also post new releases to facebook.com/E.M.Foner/ and respond to all temperate e-mail sent to e_foner@yahoo.com

The first sixteen EarthCent books, also known as the Union Station series, are numbered in order. Following the sixteenth book, Last Night on Union Station, the timeline order is the same as the publication date order:

- Independent Living (EarthCent Universe 1)
- Soup Night on Union Station (Union Station 17)
- Assisted Living (EarthCent Universe 2)
- Freelance on the Galactic Tunnel Network (EarthCent Auxiliaries 1)
- Con Living (EarthCent Universe 3)
- Empire Night on Union Station (Union Station 18)
- Space Living (EarthCent Universe 4)
- Traders on the Galactic Tunnel Network (EarthCent Auxiliaries 2)

Made in the USA
Middletown, DE
04 February 2021